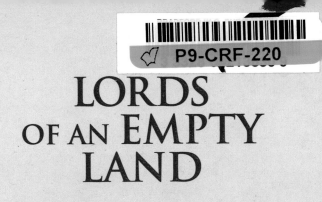

LORDS
OF AN EMPTY
LAND

LORDS
OF AN EMPTY
LAND

RANDY DENMON

PINNACLE BOOKS
Kensington Publishing Corp.
www.kensingtonbooks.com

PINNACLE BOOKS are published by

Kensington Publishing Corp.
119 West 40th Street
New York, NY 10018

Copyright © 2015 Randy Denmon

All Kensington titles, imprints, and distributed lines are available at special quantity discounts for bulk purchases for sales promotions, premiums, fund-raising, educational, or institutional use. Special book excerpts or customized printings can also be created to fit specific needs. For details, write or phone the office of the Kensington sales manager: Kensington Publishing Corp., 119 West 40th Street, New York, NY 10018, attn: Sales Department; phone 1-800-221-2647.

PINNACLE BOOKS and the Pinnacle logo are Reg. U.S. Pat. & TM Off.

ISBN-13: 978-0-7860-3536-6
ISBN-10: 0-7860-3536-6

First printing: April 2015

10 9 8 7 6 5 4 3 2 1

Printed in the United States of America

First electronic edition: April 2015

ISBN-13: 978-0-7860-3537-3
ISBN-10: 0-7860-3537-4

For Mom. We all miss her dearly.

Against them was to be pitted the wealth, the intelligence, the organizing skill, the pride, and the hate of a people whom it had taken four years to conquer in open fight when their enemies outnumbered them three to one.

—Albion Tourgée describing the small batch of men the Northern government sent to administer the South after the Civil War in his 1879 bestseller, *A Fool's Errand, by One of the Fools.*

PREFACE

Though this story and all its characters are fictitious, it does have some basis in historical events. I was in my office one day when a friend of mine and local politician, Mack Calhoun, dropped a dusty old manuscript on my desk. *Nightriders*, written in the 1950s by Richard Briley, told the story of the West and Kimbrell clans that terrorized the strip of land in north Louisiana between the Mississippi and Red Rivers in the years of Reconstruction just after the Civil War.

Further research into the story substantiated the events, and that this area served as a haven for many infamous outlaws of the time, including the James Gang, among others. It was also home to some of the most monstrous elements of white supremacy in the nation's history, the Knights of the White Camellia, Louisiana's early version of the Ku Klux Klan.

The treacherous deeds of the secret societies and guerrillas that ruled the north Louisiana nights still resonate and haunt the collective psyche of the people who populate the piney hills and cypress swamps along the Red River to this day.

Louisiana's contemporary image as a jovial amalgamation of religions, races, and cultures intertwined in a land of festivals and spicy cuisine where all classes congregate blissfully is a twentieth-century transformation born out of a brutal past. Much of this lore is derived from Louisiana's liberal social attitude, or that during the twentieth century's Civil Rights movement, when the violence in most of the South blazed across our black-and-white screens, little or nothing filtered out of the bayous.

Much of Louisiana's social strife had been settled decades earlier, before the advent of a far-reaching Federal government or the prying eyes of reporters from faraway places such as Chicago and New York. This Southern paradise was a very dangerous and bloody place well into the first half of the twentieth century, and especially in the years after the Civil War. It was the last state to have Federal occupation rescinded after Reconstruction, and was the focus of more military action by the Union Army during Reconstruction than any of the states that seceded.

Despite numerous, well-supported attempts by the Union Army, the Red River Valley in northwest Louisiana was never occupied or subjugated during the Civil War. Even the intrepid railroad did not conquer this area until more than a decade after the war. Oddly, it had a hundred-mile gap in North Louisiana, terminating from the east at Monroe, and recommencing its journey west at Shreveport, on the west bank of the Red River.

Hollywood's inflated version of the Old West pales in comparison to actual events that occurred here. Speaking of northwest Louisiana during Reconstruction, noted Civil War historian Ted Tunnell said: "It was probably the most violent place in America." This strip of land was also the setting for Harriet Beecher Stowe's *Uncle Tom's Cabin* and both the Coushatta and Colfax massacres, two of the most gruesome events in Civil War Reconstruction, the latter the nation's single bloodiest day in the postwar era.

1

Captain Douglas Owens stared up at the eerie white ring surrounding the moon. He looked down at the Red River, then across the fertile, flat plain to the gentle hills juxtaposed against the horizon a few miles distant. The miles of unpicked cotton in all directions almost turned night to day and looked like a fresh snow on the Ohio fields of Douglas's childhood. Overhead, the ageless thick pines cast slight shadows. From the forest came the incessant sounds of insects buzzing, bullfrogs belching, and an owl hooting.

Douglas turned to the river below, where it sliced through a tight gap in the two-hundred-foot-high hills. The moonlight flickered off the two smut-covered smokestacks and top deck of the small steamboat *Anna Bell,* now partially underwater. Its bow rested firmly on the river's bottom, but its two upper decks were still dry. He flashed his gaze to the two men beside him. One was Sergeant Red Simmons, his longtime subordinate. The second had just enlisted, a young private from Illinois named O'Neal.

"What time you think it is?" Sergeant Simmons whispered.

"Probably after midnight." Douglas wanted to remove his pocket watch and check the time, but doubted he could read it in the dark. The soldiers had been here maybe two hours. Just before dusk, Douglas had gotten word that the steamboat had sunk. The three soldiers had been in Natchitoches, a trading post twenty miles upriver, when the *Anna Bell*'s crew had arrived, having caught a ride back to Natchitoches on a passing northbound steamer.

Douglas immediately became suspicious. He knew that the *Anna Bell*'s valuable cargo would be a prize for the gangs and clans, the vigilantes who ruled this ungoverned area after dark. He had been trying to quell them for months. He and his two subordinates had galloped here without hesitation, half expecting to fight their way to the luckless vessel. Seeing the fifty or so cotton bales on the steamer's stern, Douglas wondered what loot lay unseen. There was certainly a strongbox somewhere holding the gold used to buy the bales along the river.

But Douglas and the army troopers weren't here to protect the ship's cargo. They were trying to set a trap, knowing word of the disabled vessel would travel fast. Maybe the steamer had even been sabotaged? Whatever the story, he could not pass up an opportunity to catch up with the cutthroats who roamed the north Louisiana nights. Their names and faces were unknown to all, even the rare, lucky souls who survived an encounter with these bandits. They all wore cloth masks while engaged in their dirty, deadly trade.

"Look," Sergeant Simmons whispered.

Douglas squinted at the steamer, forty feet below and a hundred paces away. Two distant images moved through the water to the steamer, maybe twenty yards from the riverbank. Shortly, the hazy figures, only a blur of movement in the shadows, emerged on the steamer's stern.

"Let's go get them," Sergeant Simmons said, pulling on Douglas's sleeve.

"No," Douglas answered. He took a minute to inspect his subordinates. All three men were dressed in their dark blue army frock coats adorned with insignia and gold buttons, but they had long quit the powder blue trousers on night escapes. "They haven't done anything yet. We'll wait a few minutes, then go down and catch them with the loot. Let's just move down to the riverbank, stay concealed. I want them alive. Bring that lantern."

Douglas looked back up the hill to where they had hobbled their horses. He stood and grabbed his shotgun, then motioned with a hand. As Sergeant Simmons slowly stepped into the darkness, Douglas followed, feeling his way through the trees as Private O'Neal followed. In less than a minute, the three men knelt behind some bushes at the river's edge.

The rippling water sloshed around the steamer,

now only twenty paces away. He reached down and checked the location of his pistol, a Colt .44, holstered on his hip. Slowly, he cocked the two hammers on his 16-gauge shotgun and checked to make sure the two shells' firing pins were aligned with the hammers. He made a quick inspection of the two other soldiers, armed similarly. Douglas had a fifteen-shot, lever-action .44 Henry slung to his horse, but it would probably be of little use now. Nothing dished out more devastation than a shotgun, especially in tight quarters or at night.

He turned again to Sergeant Simmons and Private O'Neal. They both understood not to do anything until he did. He looked back over his shoulder and scanned the thick hills. Were there other men out there somewhere? He cupped his ear with a hand and listened, but still only heard the natural sounds of the verdant land. The seconds passed slowly with Douglas's anxiety growing, his body perspiring. "Wonder where their horses are."

"Probably over that hill," Sergeant Simmons said. "Haven't heard or seen anything. Maybe they're alone."

Footsteps clomped on the steamer as the two men surfaced on the deck. One of the men carried a watermelon-sized box.

Heart racing, Douglas fought an urge to stand and draw his weapons. He put his hand on Sergeant Simmons's knee to restrain him.

The two men disembarked the steamer and waded to the bank.

Douglas slowly stood and put the butt of his

shotgun to his shoulder. "Fourth Cavalry, you're now in our custody."

The two men froze. Douglas shuffled forward a few paces, gripping his shotgun firmly.

"What do you want? We're unarmed!" one of the men yelled, very loudly.

Douglas looked down the double barrels. He still saw none of the men's characteristics. He stepped forward a few more paces, ten steps from the suspects. He saw the eye slits in the burlap masks and pointed his shotgun at one of the men. "Off with that mask."

The outlaw stood completely still, the evil slits in his disguise staring directly at Douglas.

Keeping his barrels leveled at the man, Douglas stepped forward, reached out, and jerked off his mask. A shot pierced the night.

Douglas flinched, swung his shotgun away from the man, and pointed it to the hills behind him. Three more shots rang out. He turned back to the unmasked man to get another look and recognized him, a provincial constable named Garrett he had met a few times in the bush towns. Douglas turned back to the hills, where he saw more orange blasts and the faint image of four horses coming down the hill in their direction at a full gallop.

Sergeant Simmons fired, sending a ball of buckshot toward the horses. The loud burst from Simmons's shotgun woke the night.

More shots blazed out. The two men on the riverbank scurried for cover as Douglas emptied both his barrels at the charging horses.

"Let's go!" Douglas shouted, plunging into the thick bushes.

As he disappeared into the pines, more shots erupted. Sergeant Simmons plummeted to the ground. The horses closed in. Douglas rushed up the hill with Private O'Neal. He dove over a little ridge, tasting the dirt as he landed on his stomach. Private O'Neal fell in beside him. Douglas pulled his pistol from his hip and crawled a few feet to peek over the ridge. A half-dozen more shots filled the dark night as Douglas hugged the ground.

Lungs heaving, vision foggy, Douglas lay silently for a few minutes. He had few options—two men against six. A few more shots erupted. A couple of screams sounded through the woods. The horses stampeded away. The night fell silent. Had the bushwhackers retreated? Exhaling, he turned to the private, the young man's eyes roving with terror. The two passed a few anxious minutes without hearing an unnatural sound.

Douglas let out a long breath and slowly stood. "Cover me—I'm going down there. See what I find. If I'm not back in five minutes, get out of here, best you can."

Douglas crept down to the riverbank. In the moonlight, the steamer rested peacefully on the river bottom. The water dribbled by. The sky sat plain over the now calm, ordinary night. Beneath his feet, Douglas saw the tracks of the fracas, horses and men. He also saw the distinctive trail where Sergeant Simmons's body had been dragged away.

He knelt and grabbed some of the sandy riverbank to let it filter through his hands and stared out into the peculiar land, listening. Did further danger lurk in the shadows? He heard only nature where a few minutes earlier he had seen the barrage of six-inch muzzle blasts, their echoing booms ringing in his ears. Now only darkness filled his vision. He dug into his brain trying to burn the image of the masked man into his mind. He would find him, somewhere. He exhaled a long breath, mixed emotions besieging him: frustration, bewilderment, and relief that he would probably survive this night.

He turned his voice back up the hill. "Private, go fetch our horses, and . . . be quick about it."

2

Douglas straightened his blue jacket and brushed the dirt off his trousers. He looked into the tall, thin mirror and adjusted his shoulder planks before combing his long brown hair. He then inspected his teeth, ensuring their cleanliness. He buttoned two of the gold breast buttons on his coat and donned his big-brimmed campaign hat, pulling it down firmly over his brow.

A week had passed since the shoot-out on the Red River. The bandits left him more befuddled than ever, with no clues to their origin other than the one face he had identified. Douglas had now been summoned to see the state provost in Shreveport.

He stepped outside the officers' barracks and onto the gravel sidewalk. Spotless Cotton Street was shaded with aged oaks and sided with gargantuan antebellum and Victorian homes, their thick grass and shrubs freshly cut. The ex-Confederate capital of Louisiana had not suffered so much as a scratch during the war. Here, the Southern way of life had hardly changed. It all seemed exotic, tropical, and foreign.

He headed for the large Fifth Military District's compound two blocks away, located in Shreveport's finest residential district. As he passed a timeless cemetery, he tipped his hat to two beautiful Southern debutantes, their long, wide skirts and perky, colorful bonnets bouncing with their graceful, aristocratic steps. Both women walked right by without even acknowledging his presence. This bothered but did not surprise Douglas. All things being commensurate, he should be one of the town's most eligible bachelors. He was twenty-six, healthy, handsome, from a good family of solid English stock, and educated at West Point. But Southern society and everything associated with it shunned him like a leper.

Douglas walked across the large parade ground at the army's headquarters, a onetime plantation house and grounds. A platoon of Negro soldiers drilled over the lawn. Freed slaves constituted most of the common ranks in the occupation army. Douglas didn't object to this in principle. He had on several occasions commanded colored platoons, but the sight of blacks in uniform still seemed a little queer. They made fine conscripts, tough as nails and accustomed to doing as ordered. He had no doubt about the fighting quality of these men. He had seen it in person, but still found himself not totally at ease with black ranks. Daily, he found himself somewhat ambivalent about the Federal government's current policy and the army's current role in the South: the protection of these freedmen's civil rights and their complete political and commercial incorporation into society. He had fought for the Union and believed in the war's goals. During his lonely hours over the years, he had read most of President Lincoln's speeches. Mr. Lincoln had sold the war to the public to save the Union, and later to eradicate slavery, both noble goals. But Congress's policy had recently evolved into much more. Mr. Lincoln had loathed the institution of slavery and thought Negroes had every right to fail and succeed as their abilities merited, but he had preached that Negroes couldn't and shouldn't ever assimilate into white society, and he had never promoted their full participation in the political system.

Unlike most of the Northern demagogues displaced from the realities on the ground, the army, and Douglas, were tasked with carrying out the government's new policy. Every day he moved through the foreign land trying to implement his orders. Douglas's emotions constantly ebbed from his stance as an advocate for the rights and protection of the Negroes to doubts about their viability as citizens, often even sympathizing with the South. Was he any different from the heathens he ruled? The thoughts perturbed him. Where and what would he be if he had been born five or six hundred miles to the south?

Douglas brushed aside the thoughts and looked at the impeccably clean and groomed lawn. The entire grounds exuded a sense of order, discipline, and control in complete contrast to everything outside town. The army complex, the shiny buildings, bright uniforms, and large flag hanging over the grounds beckoned Douglas's pride. He straightened his posture as he continued.

He had been in Louisiana since before the end of the war. Though many young officers zestfully volunteered for this occupation duty, Douglas considered it a dreadful, deadly, inglorious job filled with murky divisions where good and bad was not black and white, but decidedly gray. There were few amusements and little social society here, and the army's uniform mandates rarely provided space for local interpretation. Worse, his commanders and juniors spanned the gamut in their feelings about their current duties; some were fervent pursuers of President Grant's policies, others bordered on collaborating with the Southerners.

When Douglas finally stepped up on the porch of the provost's office, a huge brick abode fronted with a large porch and six forty-foot-tall Greek columns, he paused briefly, then knocked on the door. A feeling of pessimism fell over his soul. He had no idea why Colonel James wanted to see him. Most of their previous meetings had been a waste of time, standard military protocol or bureaucratic nonsense. The colonel had never shown any interest in Douglas's repeated requests for more men and matériel to tame Louisiana's hinterland.

"Come in."

As Douglas stepped over the threshold, he locked

his gaze on the overweight colonel, reclining in a fine leather chair behind his desk, the only fixture in the grandiose room. The room felt cool and damp. A subtle breeze funneled through the six large windows and brushed across the formidable wood walls.

Douglas paused, snapped to attention, and saluted. "Good morning, Colonel James."

"At ease, Captain," the provost said, casually returning the salute before brushing one of the long fingers of his mustache. "Have a seat. I read your report on the riverboat incident. No sign of Sergeant Simmons's body?"

"No. There never is any trace of the victims."

He was in his fifties and in impeccable uniform, though the colonel's black hair had started to gray, and his chubby, almost boyish face had already turned sweaty with the humid morning.

Douglas looked into the colonel's lazy eyes, trying to gauge his mood and the reason for the formal summons.

The colonel sat up straight. "I'm sure you've heard, but in case you haven't, we've got a new commander, General Mower. Things are going to change. President Grant is serious about policing this state. I didn't make that four-day trek from New Orleans through that godforsaken wilderness because I wanted to. I was ordered here. We've had two army pay-runners killed in this area in the last two months, now Sergeant Simmons. We can't tolerate that. We're going to instill some law and order around here. Civilize these hillbillies. They're going to be part of the Union, whether we want them or they like it."

"With all due respect, sir, I'm a little confused," Douglas uttered. "It's been like this for years. The army usually doesn't do anything about these clans and gangs that terrorize the Negroes and unionists, but you want me to go get this specific group of outlaws."

The colonel gritted his teeth. "Captain Owens, I hate an idealist. Our orders are the same: if you hear of anything that undermines peace and tranquility, the law, you are to investigate it. But we don't have the resources to police all the political infighting. The country's tired of war. What can you expect from these people? We've made them a minority in their own state. They're horrified by the thought of African rule. It's just human nature. Most of those clans don't pick scraps with the army. And none of that's been going on since last year's elections. It's not the army's job to get in the middle of local political bickering. It's not our Constitutional mandate to be a local police force. But we can't have pay-runners killed. It subverts our authority."

Douglas groaned to himself. When did hanging or beating blacks and white unionists become only political infighting? "I don't think you have any idea how bad it is. The general countryside is completely devoid of law, and this particular area is much worse. No one moves after dark. Tens, maybe hundreds of people have been murdered and robbed. I don't think they have a cause. Last year it was politically motivated, but now it's simply robbery. The story's almost always the same—the victims are almost always traveling through the country, then the bodies disappear. The local law and judges don't give a damn. Hell, they're probably vile highway-men themselves."

"We're going to change all of that. I'm sending a new judge to Natchitoches. That scalawag from New Orleans—the one who's got the niece you're so fond of—Solomon Butler." The colonel lit his pipe and took two long puffs. "And I've hired Basil Dubose to give you a hand rooting out these rogues."

"Basil Dubose?" Douglas let out a long, exasperated breath. "Wasn't he the one who gunned down five Union soldiers in cold blood? He's half-criminal himself, on his best day."

"*That* was during the war. All those deeds then have been pardoned. You know that. He knows what it takes to subdue those hills, and he's not afraid to get his hands dirty." Colonel James's face got tight and serious. "And he can be bought. You can't clean out these cutthroats with West Point recti-tude. It won't work here. You've been trying for months with dismal results. Besides, Dubose served down there during the Red River campaign. He knows the area. I've also heard he's fallen out with some of the same bunch that's probably causing some of the trouble. That gives him his own motiva-tions. We're going to use his skills for the good of the army, the republic."

Douglas spoke in his most diplomatic tone. He smoothed his hair in a nervous gesture. "Colonel, what good does it do to bring in these Confederate murderers, if we lower ourselves to their standards in the process? I thought we're supposed to be stewarding these people back into the Union, not giving a hired pistol man an unfettered rein to settle his scores with the backing of the army."

Colonel James blinked then let out a mouthful of air. "Damn it, Captain Owens, the war's *over.* We're the only sense of law for five hundred miles in any direction. Put all your romantic thoughts away. We've got a job to do, be it adverse or not. General Mower wants it done, whatever it takes. You and Dubose are going into that backcountry. An army runner should be able to ride through there without getting shot by an ex-Confederate war party. Our job is to make this state more civil than when we got here. Is that clear? And don't come back without heads. You've got a good future in the army, and the army looks highly on men that get things done, no matter the circumstances or methods." The colonel paused, but before he had a chance to continue, a knock came from the door.

Douglas turned to see a young private standing in the doorway.

"Mr. Dubose is here," the private said. "You want me to send him in, sir?"

"Yes," the colonel replied. "Right away."

Douglas stood silently. He knew Dubose and regarded him as a hired gunslinger with no scruples. He also knew the army. When orders were given, they were meant to be carried out, and without personal interpretations. His job was to follow orders, plain and simple. The colonel's tone hammered home the fact that this mandate was not to be shirked. But as the orders settled in, he began to decipher their magnitude. This was going to be dangerous, bloody sport, probably more so than any prior mission in his army career, even during the war. He would be forced to carry out these orders. Or die trying.

Boots clattered on the floor behind him. He looked over his shoulder at the man walking into the room. Basil Dubose wore all black, including his small Stetson. Gray trimmed his attire that matched his long blond locks and two-day beard. Silver jewelry hung from his neck and adorned his left pinky.

Basil had a smooth, handsome look. His frame was tall and lean with long, lazy strides, all giving the sinister feeling it could instantly transition into something deadly swift and hazardous. Basil's blue eyes were cold and dead serious, but somehow lifeless, and his flat, square, hard face seemed aged by the times.

"Mr. Dubose," the colonel said. "This is Captain Owens. You'll be serving under him. I've discussed all the details with him already. Your task is as we've agreed."

Basil turned to Douglas without speaking.

The colonel dug into his desk and removed a small leather pouch. He tossed it to Basil. "Five hundred in gold. As we contracted. The rest to be paid when we have a satisfactory number of these bushwhackers jailed or otherwise."

"And what about the locals?" Basil said in a deadpan voice. "They're not going to be too content that I've taken up the gun for you damned Yankee blue-bellies. What's to keep them from stringing me up, or putting me in front of a jury?"

Colonel James paused, and then slowly stood, sucking on his pipe. He smiled and picked up a piece of paper off his desk. "Somehow, I knew you might ask that." He handed the paper to Basil. "Here's a blank pardon from the governor with your name on it. It should get you out of anything you can't get yourself out of."

The army's newest servant wore a small grin as he looked over the official letterhead and seal.

"Any further questions?" Colonel James swelled his belly and looked at Basil before turning to Douglas. "You, Captain Owens?"

Douglas stuttered, "Will I get any additional troops?"

"Just that new private I sent you a few weeks back. We need the rest here." The colonel paused, chewing on his pipe for a few seconds. "You can have Huff if you want him."

"Huff Smith?"

"Yeah, he's in the stockade."

"What'd he do this time?"

"Beat the shit out of two white boys, almost to death. He's the meanest black bastard around. And can shoot the kernels off a cob at a hundred paces. We've got to do something with him. Flogging doesn't seem to dissuade him, and if we discharge him, the locals will hang him by week's end."

"I ain't riding with no *niggers*," Basil grunted.

The colonel turned to Basil. "You will if you want the rest of that bullion. I don't recall anything of that nature in the terms we agreed upon."

Douglas preferred everything around him to be rigid. He liked the army's structure and control. He didn't want a reckless soldier, much less a black one raging with animosity. He already had Basil. But he needed more men, fearless men, and Huff fit that bill. "Have him ready to ride first thing in the morning."

The colonel stared at the two men. "That's it, gentlemen. Get on with it. I'll be in New Orleans, hopefully by the end of the week, if you need anything."

3

Mid-morning the next day, Douglas mounted his fifteen-hand roan mare. He had packed and dressed lightly, donning brown cotton pants tucked into his knee-high leather riding boots and a white cotton shirt under a thin blue cotton coat, impersonating the army-issue version. Atop his head sat his blue, wide-brimmed campaign hat with his silver captain's rank pinned to its front. Douglas had long ago learned that the wool army field uniforms were completely unfit for the brutal Louisiana heat; the blazing sun and thick, muggy air as deadly as Confederate minié balls.

As he swung his boot over the mare and settled into the saddle, sweat beads were already forming on his face. Even after almost five years, he had not gotten used to the Louisiana weather. Cooked by the merciless summer sun, the temperature might stay above ninety until almost midnight. Even late into the night, just the simple exercise of walking

drenched one's body with sweat. A breeze of any
sort was rare. There never seemed to be a break
from the steamy, insect-infested air that instantly
turned the skin clammy and hovered over the land
like an endless opaque fog. He hated the chronic
rains and endless maze of green. He missed winter,
and the changing seasons of his home in Ohio.

Douglas gently pressed his spurs against his
mount's ribs and started down Commerce Street.
The muddy road cut through the immense cotton
warehouses and gins abutting the Red River, its
banks currently occupied with a half-dozen steam-
ers, some three hundred feet long with smokestacks
towering forty feet into the sky. The streets held a
mangled myriad of horses, buggies, stagecoaches,
and hundreds of bales of freshly picked cotton
stacked astride the road or rail line.

Half of Shreveport's five thousand residents were
Negro, and its citizens ranged from humble ex-
slaves working the docks or rail in sweat-stained
shirts to well-dressed Southern ladies or eastern
cotton brokers, all mixed together with the ambient smell of manure and sewage. The residents all
seemed to mimic the tumultuous, scorching climate. That they carried on with their lives in this
malaria- and yellow fever–infested oven often
amazed Douglas.

Shreveport was another world, as rough and
tough as any western outpost—a haven for all types
of outlaws and bandits. But it also had a sophisticated
side. Douglas rode on, past the streets all named

for Texas heroes: Crockett, Milam, and Travis. He looked down Texas Street at the department stores, banks, ladies' societies, lawyers' offices, and government buildings. The grand Planters Hotel and the Gaiety Theatre stood out, fit for any street in Boston. In the distance and above a canopy of tall trees stood the imposing Protestant churches, all constructed of thick stone. Farther afield sat the rows of shotgun houses for the middle-class whites. The poor whites and Negroes lived in shanties on the periphery of town.

Tension always charged the air here, even more than during the war. All the Southerners abhorred Negro equality and the carpetbaggers, wicked strangers as they called the latter, but most of all, they detested the scalawags. The impoverished whites struggled with the freed slaves for work, and most of the rich plantation class now found themselves downtrodden, willing to do almost anything to reclaim their social stature. Everyone in this land had a score to settle. Enmity and revenge permeated almost every breath, the kind of deep loathing that drives men, and even women, to commit treacherous acts without the slightest guilt. The illicit conduct seemed, if anything, to give the poor souls gratification. It all made for a desperate cauldron, a volcano ripe to erupt. In this environment, the army was charged with the almost impossible task of upholding law and order. In reality, it took the grandest effort just to manage the days, keep some impression of civility and structure in the major towns. Outside of Shreveport, little semblance of government or order prevailed.

At Shreveport's small university, Douglas turned down Fannin Street. He slowly rode past two brothels and arrived at the Red Devil, a two-story wood structure with a single glass window. As he tied his reins to a hitching post, he looked around again at the city. This cruel, uncouth, and deceitful land would be the last civilization they would see for a while.

Douglas had spent the previous night chewing on Colonel James's words, finally deciding Basil might be of use. The hired gun hand was an honest-to-God son of a bitch for sure. But he would use Basil as he saw fit. Douglas had learned that upholding the law was often objectionable work, often requiring one to act against his conscience. Certainly, he could channel Basil's nefarious skills into the outcome the army wanted, what he wanted: a better life for these people who now reviled his very presence. He would try to do this in the most law-abiding manner possible.

He opened the door to the Red Devil and strode inside. The little bar comprising the first floor stood empty, but the smells of sin almost overwhelmed him: liquor, cigars, and cheap perfume. Douglas slammed the door shut loudly, which brought a young, fair-skinned woman from the back to the bar. The prostitute sported a long, proper dress, but Douglas could not help but imagine what she had worn just a few hours earlier.

"I'm here to fetch Basil," Douglas said.

"Second floor, first door on the right," the girl said with a deep Southern accent.

"Can you go get him?"

"Basil? I'm not going to get him. You go get him if you want. He doesn't like to be disturbed."

Douglas ascended the stairs. Arriving at the door in question, he rapped on it firmly with his fist, twice.

"What do you want?" Basil yelled back, his words filtering through the door.

"Captain Owens here. Time to get moving. We'll be lucky to make Ringold if we leave now." Douglas slowly opened the door. Basil sat naked on the bed, his back against the headboard and his revolver in his hand. Beside him and under each arm lay two women, both without clothes.

Basil put his pistol back in its holster, hanging on the bedpost. "That's it, girls. Got to go to work." He playfully pinched both women on the bosom, and they giggled before he slowly stood and picked his pants off the floor.

One of the girls stood. She laughed and grabbed Basil's wrist, jerking him back to the bed. "One more time, we haven't earned all our keep yet."

Basil slapped the girl, sending her to the bed. The loud pop of bone reverberated through the room. Douglas cringed as if he had taken the blow himself. The speed and brutality of the strike scared him. He looked at the woman, now on the bed crying, her face beet red.

"No, bitch. I'll be back in a couple of weeks."

Basil, wearing a stern face, reached over and grabbed a small portion of the stack of money on the nightstand. He picked up the remnants of a bottle of whiskey and finished it. "You can have this then."

4

The bright orange sun blazed overhead the next afternoon when Douglas first saw the frontier village of Montgomery, a small river stop a hundred and twenty river miles south of Shreveport. From the deck of the steamer, the town spread out a mile or so to the east, where the plain collided with the hills. The town looked down on the rich Red River delta, the great river, and the fertile auburn soil and ivory cotton fields.

Douglas's feet hurt. It had been a long day on the steamer. The vessel's three decks overflowed with men and cargo, crowding onto almost every square foot of space. He had tried to rest, but the over-crowded planks and boat ride, as always, robbed his attention. He had spent hours on the bow unable to break away from the intoxicating scenery. The cool breeze on his face, the dense smell of the water, the natives waving from the shore, and the endless, un-tamed arcane landscape rolling by with its own sort of beauty were irresistible, almost romantic. The river served as the corridor to see this land, where almost all waters east met the ocean. There always seemed to be something to see: whitetail deer, exquisite sandbars, the captain working the boilers to run a rapid, a treacherous curve, or avoid a stump, or just the murky red water splashing in the paddlewheel. The craft itself never ceased to amaze Douglas, gliding over the water, a testament to mankind's ingenuity.

The steamer bumped into the bank, and Douglas felt its gentle careening stop. A half-dozen men on the craft's port caught ropes and promptly secured them to the boat's large iron trunnions. He turned to the pilot house. The captain studied the dock, maneuvering the bulky boat. The boilers howled, belching white steam from the stacks. Whistles and bells filled the air. The paddle dug in, turning the water to foam, and the deck vibrated. He reached up and brushed his mount's mane, the animal as uncomfortable on the shaky footing as he.

A woman on the deck, paying no attention to Douglas, jerked on a squalling toddler. "If you don't stop crying, the Yankees are going to get you."

Douglas chuckled and turned to Huff, standing beside him holding his horse's bridle. Everything about Huff's face was round: his chin, his accentuated cheekbones, even his nose. Private Smith wore his long, regal blue army frock coat, its gold buttons polished. Unlike Douglas, he showed off the uniform proudly with his single chevron affixed to his upper sleeves.

In his early fifties, Huff was over six-feet-two-inches tall, a sculptured statue as black as midnight and constructed of thick bone and muscle, bred and honed for heavy labor under the tropical sun.

Douglas searched for the right words. He knew this man well. Huff had genuine intentions, but also a short temper and a streak of incurable anger burning in his inner depths that had festered for a lifetime. This was a bad combination for someone backed by the authority and power of a uniform. His skin color made him a lightning rod, the onetime slave now the master.

Douglas extended his hand to Huff, gently poking his index finger into his chest. "Huff, you're going to do whatever I tell you. Is that clear? If you don't, there's not going to be any court-martial. I'm going to shoot you dead and leave you for the buzzards. That'll save me a lot of paperwork. It's going to be all we can do just to get through this with our hides."

"Yes, massa," Huff said, his tone deep. He smiled and exposed a large gap between his front teeth.

"That's yes, sir. This is the army. Act like a damned soldier." Douglas turned to Basil, asleep on the deck. He walked over and stood directly over him. The pistol slinger had spent most of the trip either in the steamer's small bar or in his current position. The local inhabitant had not found the scenery very interesting.

"Time to earn your pay," Douglas said.

Basil gradually opened his eyes and looked around quickly. "Reckon we should go see the sheriff," he mumbled.

"We won't make Winnfield today," Douglas said.

"Winnfield may be the parish seat," Basil countered, "but the sheriff spends most of his time in Atkins. Don't know why, the little hamlet is about the most miserable place in these hills. But we should make it before dark."

"It's a useless exercise," Douglas continued. "He won't help us a lick. Even if he did know something, he wouldn't tell us."

"Reckon so," Basil answered, slowly getting over his legs. "He may be the one we're hunting. Anyway, we need to let him know there's some new law in town. Law that doesn't answer to him."

Douglas handed Basil his reins just as one of the dockhands lowered the gangway from the steamer. As Douglas led his mare to firmer ground, the peaceful atmosphere of the river turned to pandemonium. This was the busy time of the year, the harvest, when the placid land came alive with fervid activity, day and night. Scores of men moved about the stacks of cargo and bales of cotton as taskmasters barked orders. Mules and horses hawed under relentless whips. A crew of freedmen readied a large pile of pine logs, stacked near the riverbank, to be loaded onto the steamer to feed its hungry boilers. Douglas stepped up into his saddle and looked down the muddy road leading to Montgomery, its edges blotted white with loose cotton bulbs.

Out in the fields, beside the road, the valuable cotton harvest was still picked as it had been for centuries. Though the Negroes had gained their freedom, they still toiled in the tall, seven-foot-high rows under the heavy burlap cotton sacks and stifling sun. They had not been freed from the drudgery, or their status at the absolute bottom of the social and economic order.

Though the war had been over for more than four years, here it loomed over the land and people's minds as if it still raged, its devastation abundant everywhere. The steamboat and telegraph broke down cultural and geographic barriers in much of the country, but deep in the Red River Valley, these modern advances affected little change.

"At a quick time," Basil grunted, trotting past. "We need to stretch our legs."

A five-minute trot found Douglas in Montgomery. From the saddle, he took a long look at the activity around him, a small sea of humanity on the dirt streets of town, maybe a hundred strong. He looked at the town's diminutive commercial district and all its smokestacks, now belching dark steam, then to a few houses, not extravagant but well built and fronted with trimmed azaleas and gardenias. Nearer the river, the houses were more run-down, most only a single room resting on piles. Around the squalid houses, pigs roamed around heaps of trash, discarded foodstuffs, excrement, and endless garments clipped to scores of clotheslines.

This was the crossroads of postwar Louisiana. To the foreign eye, it all looked simple, primitive, and peaceful. But Douglas understood the little bush towns and backwoods. The shock of occupation and defeat had now waned. Out there somewhere, the land harbored the clandestine leagues, the Knights of the White Camellia or white militia as they were sometimes called that ruled these streets after dark. He had spent most of the last year in a desperate but fruitless battle with these clans and gangs.

The previous year had brought the first free elections to Louisiana since the war: first the state elections in the spring, followed by the Federal canvassing in the fall. Louisiana was half black, and with the aid of a few carpetbaggers and Southern unionists, these outsiders had taken over the state government. The new governor hailed from Illinois; the lieutenant governor was colored. Neither had had any stake whatsoever in the state a few years earlier.

Indigenous white Louisianans, of almost every background, had become incensed by Northern and Negro rule. From the thick forest and dusty towns, the secret leagues materialized overnight. They terrorized the blacks and their corroborators, anybody with Northern interests. Just in Douglas's domain, a half-dozen political leaders, black and white, had been murdered, with scores more beaten, intimidated, or run out of the country. Anarchy ruled like he had never imagined. Anyone who got overzealous exploiting his post or promoting Republican rule became a candidate for mob justice. Schools, businesses, and plantations had been burned to the ground. Most of the rich whites publicly denounced these organizations and their dastardly deeds, but did little to deter their existence.

The trepidation among black voters had been such that statewide, the electorate had gone from majority Republican in the spring to being easily carried by the Democrats in the fall presidential race. To Douglas's consternation, the army and local officials had shown no stomach to oppose this.

The clans understood this, and having achieved their political desires and not wanting to invite further Federal meddling, had since settled down. The only exception was the current band of vigilantes that preyed on travelers. Though a horrendous lot, the scale of their atrocities paled in comparison to the organized terror. Douglas had no doubt these outlaws spawned from the Knights or some other group, having grown bored with peace and the toilsome chores of labor.

Looking at a few dirty, undernourished kids, Douglas wondered how he was to carry out his new orders. Out there in the woods were more than a thousand disbanded Confederate soldiers, organized, and with the silent support of the population. The government had trained him, educated him, manufactured him into a soldier and a symbol. This and his years in this war-torn land had turned him into the hard edge of the government, sent to the fringes of the country to uphold the republic's sanctimonious notions. These years in uniform, behind the firm arm of the army, had transformed him. He had lost his sense of self, becoming almost molded to the government's ideas, a willing instrument and upholder of its wishes, even if he didn't always agree with the mission's goals.

But here, there was no army, no bright proper uniforms, or impressive government buildings for support. To these people, those were only ideas they hadn't seen or felt for years. His daily grind was tedious, dangerous, nothing like the glorified stories of the Southern occupation that filled the Northern papers. He now chased shadows, at best, though he did have a lead—the man he had seen at the riverboat. Douglas groaned as he turned to Huff.

"You wouldn't really shoot me, now would you?" Huff replied and smiled.

"I don't know. I might." Douglas smiled back. "Probably leave that to Basil. He'd enjoy it. Let's go, so we can make Atkins before dark."

An hour and a half later, the three arrived at the sheriff's office. It sat on Atkins's main street, only a small, square wooden building with two glass windows. The town had only two major streets, bisected by four smaller roads, maybe eight blocks total, just a hamlet hidden in the hills that looked like so many others. On the streets, God's injustices stood visible in the meek faces and buildings. Basil dismounted without a word and stepped up on the porch.

"Stay here," Douglas instructed Huff before following Basil through the open door.

Inside, behind a wooden desk, sat a man, perhaps in his early forties and showing every day of it. Over his tan, leathery skin, the sheriff wore a nice white cotton shirt, freshly pressed, with a red bandanna around his neck. A black goatee covered his chin and a big scar stretched across his face under his left eye—probably a Union slug during the war. The heavy-boned man looked up with jaunty, steady brown eyes as Douglas watched Basil and the sheriff briefly study each other. Did they recognize one another from some event in the past?

"Sheriff Silas Thaxton. Can I help you boys?"

"Don't believe we've met . . . formally. Captain Douglas Owens, Fourth Cavalry." Douglas nonchalantly removed his hat as he continued to inspect the local lawman. He had the typical look of a frontier sheriff, straight out of a story in an Eastern paper. Douglas almost let out a smirk. Inside these worn, wooden walls so far from home, he now lived those stories every day. "This is—"

"Basil Dubose." The sheriff stood, putting his thumbs through his belt loops. "I've heard you're working for the damned bluecoats. Doesn't surprise me."

Douglas tried to take an informal tone. "Sheriff, we're on the same side, just want law and order."

Sheriff Thaxton grunted. "Well, damn General Banks and his bluecoats burned me out on his way out of here, for nothing more than sport. I saved for ten years and built my place myself. You're a smart lad. That should be easy enough to understand."

Footsteps rattled on the porch. Douglas turned as

two rough hands entered, both in their twenties with long stringy hair, slender builds, and shifty eyes. The two men had dirty, stained teeth, generally looking less well-read and refined than the sheriff.

"Sheriff Thaxton," Douglas continued, "we're looking for—"

"Let's cut through the bullshit," Basil snapped. He turned to stare down the two men who had entered the room briefly before returning his tempestuous eyes to the sheriff. "We're looking for Constable Garrett. He was seen at the killing of a Federal soldier, at the *Anne Bell* on the river a few weeks ago. We mean to bring him to justice."

The sheriff produced a fabricated smile, displaying his big, white teeth. He casually took a step forward, his face now only a foot from Basil's. He stiffened his stance and stared into Basil's harsh eyes. "Well, now, that's impossible. The night that shoot-out occurred on the river, Elisha Garrett was clear up in Winnfield with me and these two Dallon boys." The sheriff nodded to the two men standing just inside the doorway. "Ain't that right, boys?"

"Sure is, Sheriff," one of the two said.

"We'll let a judge and jury decide that," Douglas said.

The sheriff put on his big-brimmed straw hat and looked down at the insignia on Douglas's hat. "Everything is peaceful around here. The war's over. People just want everything to get back to normal. We don't need you boys or the army stirring up a bunch of trouble. No good can come from it." The sheriff turned back to Basil, giving him a patronizing appraisal. "And we don't need some two-bit, washed-up cutthroat administering frontier justice. I won't stand for it."

Basil's eyes filled with fury and the veins on his neck pulsed. He shuffled forward half a step, grunting and swearing.

Douglas put his hand on Basil's shoulder. "That will be all, Sheriff. Thank you for your time. We just wanted to give you the common courtesy of paying you a visit to inform you of our intentions. We'll be on our way."

Douglas grabbed Basil's arm, feeling his stiff muscles. With some effort, he turned him around, pushing him to the door.

"Now, you boys watch yourselves in the back-country," the sheriff said in a deep, earnest voice. He paused to achieve the maximum effect of his words. "I can't guarantee your safety there. I'd suggest doing most of your business around town."

Douglas continued out the door. The sheriff's words had an arrogant, almost threatening tone. Outside, he squinted as he felt the torrid Southern sun on his cheeks. "I told you we wouldn't get any help here."

"I already knew that," Basil replied. "We'll have to flush them out in the open. When they get flushed out, I want to make sure they know who's doing the flushing."

Douglas looked up at the setting sun and scratched his chin. He turned to a wooden church with dozens of horses and a few carriages tied up outside a few blocks down the street. "It's the Sabbath.

Going to step in for the sermon. It will be the last Godly thing I'll see for a while. Guess the sheriff's not religious."

"Probably just does the morning service." Basil grinned, grabbing his saddle pommel. He nodded across the street. "I'll be at the saloon."

"Fill our canteens," Douglas instructed Huff as he led his horse a hundred paces, where he tied the mare to a hitching post. He stepped up on the portico of the Montgomery Baptist Church, slowly opening the door.

The preacher's voice boomed down on the forty or so individuals bunched together on the pews. ". . . and the glory, for ever and ever. Amen."

Douglas's entry caused most of the congregation to crane their necks to look at the unfamiliar face. Two stands of candles surrounded the pulpit. The gold, flickering light and a maze of colors refracted through the stained-glass windows and fell on the reverend's gray hair and black robe. The cleric appeared sixty-ish, but had a strong, solid body and a graceful face.

As Douglas took a seat at the end of one of the pews, the reverend cast his aged, stern gaze on him briefly. The stare didn't seem holy, but more a harsh, condescending reprimand. An uneasy chill swept up his spine as he looked at the congregation, all now giving their loyal and undivided attention to the holy man.

The preacher raised the Bible high in his right hand. He cocked his head back and yelled in a fiery tone: "Hymn fifteen, 'Glory be the Father'!"

The congregation stood. The organ erupted. Douglas caught a few more quick, unreceptive stares from the flock. He didn't feel welcome, pious, or sanctified. He shouldn't have come to the service. He thought about leaving, but picked up the leather-bound hymnbook. Being an outsider, even here, gave him an uncomfortable and foreboding feeling as he began to sing. Could he trust anyone? Could he even trust his two soldiers outside? He felt more alone than ever.

5

The air hung still, filled with the rich aroma of yellow pine, when Douglas, Basil, and Huff rode out of the miserable little village of Calvin around noon the next day. The forgotten settlement consisted of only a disorganized collection of six wooden, ramshackle houses. In the heat of the day, they only saw an elderly woman, with no spare meat on her bones, sitting listlessly on a porch, and two barefoot boys playing on the settlement's only street.

It had been a long, hard morning in the saddle. They had traveled north by east, moving through the rolling pine. As always, the air in this other-worldly, verdant bit of earth hung moist and heavy, lathering horses and humans. The dust burned their eyes. The spiderwebs hung abundant, requiring the lead rider to hold up a stick, else the strands adhered to the body, adding to the misery. They had packed light, only the essentials. For some reason, Douglas's stomach wasn't turning with concern.

All this just appeared to be the standard, dull duty in the 4th.

Ahead lay an ocean of pine-covered and sun-beaten hills, a boundless forest. The hills took on a multitude of green colors, a thousand shades and shapes. Every few miles the range gave way to low-lying, peaceful-seeming hardwood bottoms, usually bisected with a brown stream that had to be forded. Abundant squirrels, turkeys, blackberries, sunflowers, butterflies, and birds singing charming melodies populated the serene hills. The valleys were more foreboding, rife with walnuts, cypresses awash with Spanish moss, and every ill known to mankind: snakes, turtles, wasps, mosquitoes, gnats, ticks, and occasionally alligators.

The army captain hated riding in this land, the lack of space it afforded. A day's ride rarely produced even a glimpse of the terrain. No beautiful vistas existed, only a continuous, ambiguous canopy of green, claustrophobic and frightful. An enemy could ride upon you with little effort—one never saw where he was going until he got there.

As the morning evaporated, Douglas found himself passing the time engrossed in idle conversation with Basil, more so in an attempt to get some sense of the man than articulate thoughts. Each passing burst of dialogue left him more perplexed as to the gunfighter's makeup, and more curious about his temperament. The gunman always kept a watchful eye, constantly giving the deathly still hills a casual inspection, only slightly distracted when required to duck under a pine limb or brush up against a trunk as the road weaved to and fro along the haphazard, rudimentary trail.

Huff had hardly muttered a word all morning, but the ex-slave and Basil exchanged several condescending stares, their disdain mutual, akin to two pit bulls eying each other.

Basil's horse was laden with matériel. Around his waist hung two polished chrome-colored pistols, Colt .44s, and in a scabbard on the right side of his horse hung a rifle with a long optical scope. The two sidearms seemed more a part of Basil, as opposed to accessories. Through the day, Basil's voice had carried little emotion, as if his body was almost dead inside, like he had no soul. This man had long been weaned from optimism; he who didn't fear anything, or at least didn't show fear. Douglas looked him over again. This man surely feared something, if nothing more than time. Time was not on his side. He had to fear the end, its ramifications, whenever it came.

They rode at a slow but deliberate pace. The group had talked to no one all morning. Basil nodded ahead where the trail moved along a high escarpment. "That constable you saw at the riverboat, Elisha Garrett, lives just up here, less than a mile. He's an ex-Confederate raider."

"White militia?" Douglas inquired.

Basil fashioned a devilish smile. "Who isn't?"

"You know him?" Douglas said.

"No, but remember those two pups back at the sheriff's office, the Dallons? I put a slug of lead in their old man, Dee Dallon. I hear he still has a slight limp. They run with the Garretts."

"What for?"

"You mean the slug," Basil uttered without interest, riding ahead. "Just a whore and a bottle of whiskey. What about your other man?"

"In Natchitoches. We'll catch up with him tomorrow. He's lucky. Doesn't know what he's gotten into." Douglas paused before continuing with a puzzled tone, "You've worked for Colonel James before? Why did he hire you for this?"

Basil scanned the green valley below, chewing on a piece of pine straw. "The men in these hills are professional killers. It takes a man like them to catch them, someone who can think like they do, act like they do."

Strangely it made sense, in some convoluted way. For sure, Douglas was no novice to bloodletting or the brutal business of the army. He had witnessed it at its worst, firsthand, in the war, where the sight of dead men, sometimes on a vast scale, occurred almost daily.

Basil slowly veered off the trail to the left, into a palmetto thicket. He lit a cigar, took two long puffs, then lifted his field glasses. "There, on that hill. That's where Garrett lives. We'll go see what he has to say. Then take our vittles." Basil put down his glasses and turned up a small bottle of whiskey. He took two oversized gulps and offered the alcohol to Douglas.

Douglas rebuffed the suggestion, having already made the mistake earlier in the day of tasting the rotgut rye. "How the hell can you drink that nasty sour mash in this heat?" Douglas wiped the perspiration off his forehead with his forearm and scoured the area with his glasses. He saw a small wooden house, a nice barn, and some stables up on the ridge. Behind the structures, a tall hill loomed over the shipshape little farm. To the west, the sun shone, golden, hanging over the horizon in the distance, the only sounds the squeaking of leather and horses' bridles rattling. A rabbit flushed from the bushes, causing Douglas to slightly flinch.

Basil sneered. "You worried about something, Captain?" He bumped his mount with his spurs. "Might as well get on with it."

Five minutes of silent riding found the three men in front of the little white plank-board house. A middle-aged woman walked out onto its porch, a curious look on her face. Basil lifted his hat and waved cordially, but continued to ride past the house.

Douglas glanced ahead to a corral, where a man was shoeing a horse. Behind the man, in the corral, two young foals played on the fresh dirt. Douglas immediately identified the face from that night on the riverbank. The hair on his neck rose a smidgen.

Basil checked his mount, bringing his horse to a stop adjacent to the corral's wood fence.

Douglas nodded to Basil, confirming the man's identity.

"You Elisha Garrett?" Basil said, his voice thick and direct.

The man looked up. "What's it to you?" The constable looked at Douglas, taking notice of his hat and its captain's bars and shiny gold cavalry insignia, two crossing sabers. He made a quick, patronizing appraisal of Huff and the lone chevron proudly displayed on his arm. He then looked down at Huff's army-issue Henry rifle sheathed on his horse. The constable, maybe forty, brawny, and red-skinned, today wore no shirt or hat.

Mr. Garrett bowed back over to continue his work.

"Captain Owens here says he saw you down on the river a few weeks ago, looting the *Anna Bell.*" Basil increased his tone. "Army had a man killed there. That makes it our business. We got to take you in."

The constable lowered the horse's foot and turned to face Basil, indignation in his movements. "Is that so? I've got four witnesses and the sheriff who can claim I was all the way up in Winnfield that night. Ain't no judge or jury anywhere round here that would take the word of a damned Yank scamp over that. You boys get on down the trail. Stir up some trouble somewhere else."

A slight jingle came from Basil. Douglas turned to look. He saw the pistol rise. A loud shot punctured the air, booming through the hills. Douglas jerked back, twitching as the constable spun around, dark blood jetting from his chest. A second shot sent the crooked lawman to the worn turf.

Douglas reined in his mount, who had reared. He sat dumbstruck, catching his breath. "What the *hell* you doing? Nobody told you to do that."

Basil slowly returned his smoking gun to his hip and turned to ride off.

"You don't go shooting anybody until I tell you to, or we get shot at. You understand?" Irritated, Douglas dug his heels into his mount and pulled abreast of Basil. "We're going to give these outlaws justice, in a courtroom. Not vigilante justice or anything else."

"Can't you hear," Basil replied, brushing off the rebuke. "He told you, you'd never convict him."

The woman from the house ran toward the corral, screaming at the three men, her light red cotton skirt bobbing around her in a tangle. Douglas turned back to the corral. The horses stood around the dead man like nothing had happened. "Now we're back to chasing phantoms."

"Not at all," Basil retorted. "Kill one out in the open, boldly, that'll flush 'em out for a fight. You won't have to look for them. They'll come find us. Be less bloody and a mite easier in the end."

Douglas sucked in a long breath, his current situation coldly setting in, the only sound the constable's wife's footsteps. He closed his eyes, replaying the shoot-out. Almost in slow motion, he saw the glinting gun barrel rise, lightning quick. Basil had not fired from the hip, like an amateur, but instead waited until the steady barrel, its bead, covered the wretched soul before efficiently pulling the trigger at the exact instant required. The gun coughing, rocking in his hand, had a sick beauty, symmetry.

"Let's have those vittles," Basil said. "Over there in the shade."

6

The streets of Natchitoches were crowded. Maybe a hundred of.the town's thousand residents mingled on Front Street. Late the next day the three soldiers rode into the only major settlement in the area that sat on the safer side of the Red River in the heart of the cotton kingdom. Despite worries of a hostile posse in pursuit, they had seen little on their day's ride back out of the bush.

Douglas still felt a little dazed by the shooting the day before. Basil had gunned down a man, be it an outlaw, like an animal. That was completely at odds with all he had been trained and taught. His initial inclination had been to arrest Basil, but that wouldn't have gone far up the ladder. Like many things in the army, begrudgingly, he had to swallow it.

The muddy Natchitoches street rested on the top bank of the Cane River, the town's buildings fronting the water. An early afternoon shower had saturated the ground. Where the sky met the land, heat waves danced against a beautiful rainbow. A few of the town's residents carefully stepped around the abundant mud holes or gathered on the wood walkways fronting the buildings along the road. Douglas passed a congenial nod to several onlookers. Everyone in town knew him, one of only two soldiers in residence here, and the only officer.

Many of the natives remained belligerent to the uniform. But as many or more had decided, reluctantly, the time had come to move on, get back to being Americans and enjoying the fruits of it, ready to heel to the loathed Yanks if it meant things could get back to normal, or at least Douglas thought. But the lines between these cliques were as murky as the waters of the Red River.

Though the populace despised Northerners, they reserved their most visceral hate for the scalawags, the locals who aided the pro-suffrage forces, most for personal gain, or at least according to local lore. This internal strife struck a vehement chord that transcended everything. The blue coat, what it stood for, was also utterly abhorred, but being a soldier provided Douglas a small reprieve from the scorn. He just carried out orders handed down from somewhere else. The Southern society revered its veterans above all else, and Douglas's uniform provided him a little more respect than his fellow carpetbaggers.

"Might could get some cooperation around here," Basil cracked, "if you bastards hadn't've burned the town during your retreat . . . especially after we kicked your ass."

The hasty buildings were mostly new or being repaired, their white studs a sign of renewal. Hammers banged away as carpenters worked on the new courthouse across the street. The army had burnt much of Natchitoches after its defeat at Mansfield, as it beat a retreat south. Scattered about town, a half-dozen chimneys poked up, bare, above the remnants of their old support structures. Around him stood the other vestiges of the war: a legless young man hobbling along on crutches and another poor individual with only a stub left for his right arm.

"Think they'll come after us?" Douglas finally asked, pulling back on his reins.

"Yeah, but not in town."

"Think I'll get a shave." Douglas pointed to the barbershop across the road.

Basil wheeled his horse around. "Fixin' to head over to the Cotton Palace. That's where I'll be if you need me. You know it?"

"Yeah." Douglas stepped down from his saddle. He removed his pocket watch from his shirt and opened it. "Huff, post is just down the street. You board there. There's a Mr. Jones just across the street. Turn our horses over to him and get settled. I want to have a word with you and Private O'Neal at five."

As Basil rode off, Douglas stepped onto the barber's porch, stomping his feet a few times on the planks in an attempt to extract the mud caked to his boots. Inside, only a single customer occupied one of three chairs, but three elderly men sat against the wall yapping on about everyday things.

When Douglas entered, the conversation paused.

"Did I startle you boys?" Douglas said with an amiable tone and small smile. He took a seat in one of the chairs.

"No, no," one of the old silver-haired barbers said, lifting a large white apron and shaking loose a handful of hair from it. He laid the apron on Douglas's shoulders and fastened it around the captain's neck.

Adhering to his common custom when sitting in confined quarters, Douglas removed his pistol from its holster and set it in his lap, ensuring its visibility to all. "Just a shave, Joe."

The barber stirred his little cup of cream with a wood spoon. "Paper says you murdered Constable Garrett yesterday in cold blood."

The room got quieter, all eyes on him and the old, sunbaked barber. "Word travels faster than me. What else the paper say?"

"That the army has hired that damned ruthless Basil Dubose to harass the people."

Douglas put his fist to his mouth and cleared his throat. "Surely you boys don't believe everything in that Democratic daily. I was going to bring in Garrett for killing Sergeant Simmons. I wanted to try him." Douglas paused a second. "When Garrett threw down on us, Basil shot him dead . . .

self-defense." Douglas squirmed a bit at the lie, but he was very familiar with the rhetoric and propaganda of the anti-Northern papers, all that existed in the area. They daily slanted the army and the Republican government's work as nothing short of the devil's deeds and exploitation of the trampled Southern people. He lifted his head as the barber worked the brush around his chin, the cool, wet cream refreshing.

"Paper also says we got a new judge coming in," the barber continued, his words quick and jittery. "John Butler's brother, damn turncoat."

Douglas looked at the other five men in the shop. "All coming down from the new general. Going to bring all the ex-Confederate criminals hampering commerce around here to justice. Be good for business, for everybody. Then maybe I can go back home where you all want me to go. And I want to go. Done had two army runners and a sergeant killed. You boys know that can't be tolerated. Not in any army. Bobby Lee wouldn't put up with that. Nor would anybody else."

Despite his gaze falling on each of the men individually, Douglas's lecture drew no response. Almost regretfully, he continued to prod the old-timers with a jolly tone. "Clean me up good. The vile Yankees are having a big fiesta tonight. I don't want to disappoint. There'll be some young ladies there. A sight more talkative and interesting than you old hags. I've been on the dusty trail for three days, and I can't even prod you to heckle me. I thought you Rebs were a feisty bunch. I'm going to have to find a new barber just to have somebody to quibble with."

The sun had just set. Maybe thirty minutes of twilight remained. Overhead, the Spanish moss, elegant oaks, and cypresses began to blend in with the graying sky. Ahead, on the banks of the Cane River, lay what remained of Natchitoches, Louisiana's oldest town, its gaslights reflecting off the water in a wonderful golden waltz. Along the river's high bank, the architecture stood admirable, French and Spanish. The buildings were mostly square and fronted with second-story balconies cased with wrought-iron rails looking over majestic courtyards. The city still had an antique, tasteful veneer. Most of the landed gentry in the delta maintained homes here before the war, the rich gathering here for their opulent balls or the annual meet held at the local horse-racing track. As opposed to the strictly Protestant churches in the wilderness, Natchitoches also hosted Catholic houses of worship.

The Cane River itself was a reminder of the turbulent land. Only thirty years prior, this had been the Red River before it had moved a few miles away, its wandering path cutting off the picturesque city from the world. Still, the region's wealth, or what remained of it, displayed itself here.

Outfitted in his freshly cleaned dress uniform

and immaculately polished boots, Douglas rode on toward downtown and the four-story Natchitoches Hotel, his gold waist sash bobbing with his mount's strides. A tad of bliss oozed from his soul as he looked ahead to the small crowd congregating outside the hotel. This was somewhere he should feel a little more at home, accepted, not shunned by unfriendly eyes. The earth beneath his horse's feet appeared so beautiful, serene, but this was a lonely land, especially for Northerners.

Douglas had few friends. Worse yet, his profession courted solitude. He rarely fraternized with the ranks and only a few officers lived within two days' ride. There were Northerners around, and Southern sympathizers. They would be in attendance at tonight's gala. But he didn't care for their company. Most were opportunists, here to plunder in the wake of war.

He had been here so long he had grown numb, hardened to the world and the privation, suffering, and death in this repository of misery. Even his nightmares of the Rebellion and terrifying memories of exploding shells, excruciating screams from the field hospitals, piles of decaying flesh, faceless men hanging from a rope along an unknown trail, or just the daily sight of starving children had started to wane. Almost in a dehumanizing way, his stomach now rarely got nauseated at the sight of blood. He had even lost his sense of home; his images of the placid Ohio fields and charming towns had become only decaying memories.

Douglas tied up his horse and entered the opulent hotel. In the foyer, the white marble floor sparkled marvelously. Around him, the hand-carved mahogany and fine leather furniture announced affluence. The band in the ballroom played a popular eastern tune. He strode toward the music.

Several hundred people stood in the giant room, the region's tight society of unionists, all dressed in their finest attire. A waiter offered Douglas a glass of champagne from a tray covered with fine, polished silver. He accepted the drink and studied the crowd, catching bits of several conversations over the background hiss of merry patrons, busy babbling away, reinforcing each other's social status. The party had the ambiance of frontier gaiety.

But Douglas was here to see only one person, Hannah Butler. He sipped the champagne and scanned the room until he saw her beside her uncle, alluring, radiating. She was superior to any woman he had seen in rural Louisiana, a perfect example of Southern beauty, grace, and sophistication.

After a few seconds, she flashed her gleaming, penetrating blue eyes at him. Douglas formally and dramatically took off his hat, pressing it against his chest, and bowed as he continued to stare at Hannah's long, light-red hair, gorgeous pale skin, and tall, delicate frame silhouetted with her plentiful curves, covered with a long blue dress that matched her eyes. He then approached.

"Uncle, you remember Captain Owens?" Hannah said with a confident, spunky smile.

In his late fifties, Hannah's uncle had gray hair and a flat, serious face, with firm, square angles. Extremely robust for his age, he wore a suit stitched of fine wool and maintained a dignified, stately bearng.

Douglas extended a hand to the man, presenting a firm handshake and steady glance. "Good to see you, Judge Butler. Glad you've been sent here. This place needs some justice."

"I will do my best." The judge nodded in a proper fashion before walking off. "I'll leave you two alone for a few minutes."

"It's been a few days since I've seen you," Douglas said. "I'm delighted your uncle is here. You, your sister, and mother now have some family in town. Is he staying with you on your father's plantation?"

"Yes."

"Excellent, that will make my courting less of a chore. I'll be able to drop in on official business."

Hannah giggled, crinkling her nose. "Captain Owens, I do enjoy your company. Educated gentlemen are rare around here since the war, but you should learn to be a little more subtle. You tried to kiss me in broad daylight one day. Despite your unsympathetic government's attempts to tear down our social order, I *am* a Southern lady. And the army *did* burn down most of the town. What would people think of me kissing you?"

"Are my intentions regarded unfavorably?"

Douglas smiled. "It's been rumored that I'm quite a gentleman. I thought you told me you were putting the past behind, and that you felt everyone else needed to also."

Hannah laughed again. "You could be useful." She stared into his eyes with sincerity, her long lashes fluttering up and down. "It is true that I have enjoyed our walks and picnics. I stay cooped up too much. It's boring. Any entertainment beckons me. But there are proper ways to court a Southern lady."

Douglas turned to look at the well-heeled crowd, the fine room and fixtures, all a world away from the deadly trail he traipsed every day just across the river. He looked back at Hannah, feminine splendor at its finest. "Would you like to dance?"

"No, I'm not here to celebrate, and most of these people are not my friends. I only came because my uncle asked me to accompany him. I'd like to go home."

"Well, you shouldn't ride home alone, after dark. Why not let a young, healthy cavalry officer escort you? That would be squarely within my professional duties."

"I hardly think it's necessary, but if you insist. It will make my uncle happy and allow him to stay a while. But you'll have to go when we get to the house. You know how my sister feels about Yankee soldiers."

"Terrific, let us go then." Douglas extended his elbow to Hannah.

"As you wish." Hannah placed her hand on his

forearm. "I will let Uncle know you will escort me home."

The sounds of night filled the air: insects incessantly popping and buzzing, crickets chirping. Douglas rode along, Hannah beside him on a tall bay gelding, her long dress covering her saddle. The two had already traveled more than half the six miles to the Butler Plantation. The thirty minutes had passed delightfully as they conversed.

Under the full moon and tall oaks, Douglas felt at ease, like he was no longer a soldier in a strange land. His only home for years had been the flag and the regimented schedule he kept daily. His tough duties and standard daily routine had all but forced him to quit living and only exist. He yearned for real company, friendship. And his days around an army of harsh, tough men had solidified his want for the soft touch of a woman, making the excursion a wonderful escape.

Douglas looked into the eyes of the town's most desirable debutante, a woman sought by many of its most eligible young men. Hannah was the daughter of one of the region's most prominent plantation owners and war heroes, Colonel John Butler, an ardent secessionist killed by an artillery shell at Chancellorsville. A year earlier, she had returned home to help her mother and sister's attempts to salvage the family's plantation from the creditors and teach at a new children's school built by the

Reconstruction Act. During the last six months, Douglas had talked to her at least a dozen times, sometimes to her apparent unease, but with time and the displaying of his most charming attributes, he had noticed her resistance to his attention fading.

Hannah stood in the stirrups to readjust her saddle. "Before the war, we had a nice carriage to transport the Butlers back and forth to town."

"Do you and your mother and sister live alone?"

"Mr. Jones lives with us, in the old overseers' house. He was one of our overseers before the war. I wish we could hire some more help, but since the end of the war we've had to mortgage the farm. Between the new taxes and the payments, we have little money. Sister is planning to rent over a larger portion of the farm this year in forty-acre tracts to some of the Negroes on a shared basis. We get a portion of their crop sales. Despite my independent leanings, running a large farm is difficult without a man in the house."

"The party must have been strange for you. Your father was a Confederate colonel, and your uncle is a unionist."

"As you say, Captain Owens, we must move on. What my father and uncle do has no bearing on me. It's true that I'm not as spirited as Mother and Sister. I'm the most progressive thinking. I guess it's my Eastern education. And you, why are you still in the army? The war's over. Why haven't you gone home?"

"I don't know. Sometimes I wish I had. I stay in

the army for my father. I'm all that's left of the family. My mother died years ago and my brother was killed at Cold Harbor. It was the proudest day of Father's life when I graduated from the military academy. He still loves to tell everybody what I'm doing. That, and I don't have a profession or job waiting on me back home. In Ohio, there are still thousands of veterans needing work. But I'm doing some good here. I'm trying to catch these discontents that are killing all these innocent people."

"If you do catch them, many people will be happy, though I doubt they'll ever tell you that. . . . You think you can catch them?"

Douglas wheeled his horse a little closer to Hannah. "Maybe; convicting them is what's hard, but since they've now attacked the army, I can use all the resources of the Federal government. Because of that, I may be able to also get some of the men who have killed many of the Negroes and Northerners in this area."

Hannah pulled back on her reins, slowing her horse and looking at Douglas. "Their methods are regrettable, even worthy of punishment. I'm for social justice, and I hated slavery. Slavery turned us into worse people, lazy, but surely you do not think we should be ruled by ignorant Negroes and Northern miscreants. Learned men, vested in the community, should hold political power, in any society."

Douglas sat silent for a few seconds, trying to find

a polite rebuttal. "Louisiana just passed the Fifteenth Amendment, and it says everybody can vote."

Hannah looked off toward the house, and Douglas stared down a long line of trees abutting a side road, almost regretting his statement.

"It's not far from here. I can make it the rest of the way on my own." Hannah pointed. "That's the new schoolhouse where I teach. We did get the Republicans to buy a piece of land from us for it. I just have to walk over there every day."

Douglas looked at the schoolhouse and then to the Butler house, a quarter mile down the road. A few sprinkles of light shone through the night. He stepped down from his horse and extended a hand to Hannah. "Let me say a proper Southern goodnight."

"As you wish," Hannah said, taking his hand and hopping down. "I enjoyed our ride. It passed quickly. You're certainly more talkative than Uncle."

Douglas looked again at the Butler residence.

"The house was one of the few along Cane River General Banks didn't burn. That was because Mother and Sister stood up to the soldiers, showed them some real courage. They told the Yankee officer they would not leave the house, and he would have to burn it down with them in it. Finally, some officer with some sense and passion decided it could be used to garrison Federal troops." Hannah put a finger to her lips. "Captain Owens, you are a handsome and entertaining gentleman, even if you are dressed in the wrong colors."

Douglas stared deep into Hannah's intelligent

and amused eyes. He sensed she was in no hurry to get home. He had also begun to notice over the months that the more isolated they were, the more receptive she was to his flirting. He bent his head down and quickly kissed Hannah on the cheek.

"Don't," Hannah said, slightly recoiling. "We shouldn't."

Douglas grabbed her hips firmly and put his mouth to her ear, kissing it lightly. "Nobody's around. Nobody's watching," he whispered.

Hannah moaned and let out a deep breath. "We mustn't."

Douglas continued to whisper. "No matter my views on the South, personal or professional, don't you Southern ladies prefer strong men of honor, men who believe in something? That's more important than what they actually believe." He slowly thrust his lips onto Hannah. She resisted briefly before he delighted in the feel of her moist, warm tongue reciprocating.

Hannah finally pulled away, exhaling a deep breath. "That was better than your first attempt. You may eventually learn how it's done." She turned and looked to her house. "I better go. Caroline and Mother are leaving tomorrow for a trip to New Orleans. I need to help them get ready."

"I need to go, also," Douglas said, letting go of Hannah. "I've got to be in Coushatta Chute tomorrow for a trial."

"I'll see you soon." Hannah saddled up and promptly rode off.

Douglas watched her silhouette slowly disappear. Could this even be? Hannah was something forbidden for him. The gorgeous Southern belle, the daughter of one of the region's heroes, possibly beginning a tryst with him—nothing could inflame the Southern psyche more. Just their walks around town drew suspicious glances and whispers. His heart pounded rapidly. His mind raced with excitement and apprehension. Could it be?

7

At mid-afternoon, Douglas looked out the open window of the small, sultry courtroom. Across the street, the Baptist church, the biggest structure in town, shone wonderfully through the grove of pecan trees. Its tall spire, painted shiny white, reached for the heavens and sat in complete contrast to three rough, unpainted shacks beside it. Douglas had gotten up early this morning and made the two-hour steamer trip to Coushatta Chute, a riverfront community in the heart of cotton country where the piney hills fell off onto the rich red soil.

He pulled out his pocket watch and checked the time. The court proceedings had commenced at one, and the prosecution planned to hear his testimony sometime this afternoon. After the opening remarks, the defense had spent the last hour going on and on about the injustices of the current government, the general state of lawlessness in the area, and how over the last few years, the good citizens of the area had been forced to arm themselves and fight just to protect their lives and property.

The defense attorney, in his late fifties and named Jenkins, was dressed slickly in a nice pressed white cotton suit. He spoke fast and lacked the lazy Southern drawl and pace that typically reduced conversation to a crawl. The nine-man jury looked to be a good representation of the populace, minus the blacks. Five looked rough and tumble, probably sharecroppers, poor farmers, or laborers of some sort, but the other four men appeared to be of some means. They were all freshly bathed and attired in clean clothes. Two or three of the latter probably had some formal education and owned property or some type of business.

Mr. Jenkins continued his tirade about the injustices of the government, hypnotizing the jury. He was good. The ears and faces in the deliberation box followed the orator's movements and gestures, taking in his words. The attorney raised or lowered his voice to emphasize the points he wanted to convey, and the jurors nodded several times.

Behind Douglas, every seat in the small courtroom was full, and thirty more men stood along the walls. Four or five newspapermen jotted feverishly on their little pads, and Mr. Jenkins, ever aware of their presence, paused a few times to allow the reporters to catch up. To this point, the defense had carried the proceedings; each man in the jury box seemed completely convinced of his general dissatisfaction with things at large.

The trial revolved around a highly publicized event four months earlier in the neighboring parish of Bossier, just north of Natchitoches. For reasons still unknown, a small skirmish had occurred between two groups of opposing races in which two blacks and two whites had been shot and killed. After the incident, rumors spread that armed blacks had killed two whites, and gangs of blacks were currently on the hunt for more innocent, upstanding citizens. Several posses had been raised in the Shreveport area, and before order could be restored, more than a dozen more freedmen had been killed, their bodies thrown into the Red River.

Douglas was familiar with the often-used proclamation of a Negro revolt or uprising where colored men were planning to go on a spree of murder and rape. Though he'd seen some violence in the colored communities, the Negroes were generally more docile and peaceable than the whites. But the fear of this, especially the claim of Negroes rampaging and raping white women, stirred even the moderates and was used as a catalyst to make what would normally be atrocious, unacceptable crimes completely acceptable behavior by the general public.

Hearing the reports of unrest, Douglas had sped to the location of the killings. His men arrived too late to prevent the massacre, but he witnessed one of the killings and promptly arrested the man responsible, a farmer named Hank Johnson. Under normal circumstances, Douglas doubted they could get a conviction. It came down to his word against that of the accused, and the case would be tried in a local court. For years Douglas had hauled culpable criminals into the local courts, but had rarely gotten anybody convicted by a local jury, the citizens unreceptive to Northern laws and edicts. Most of the time, the judge, whether friendly or not, would look at the evidence and dismiss the case without trial. It took more than the word of an honest Yankee or Yankees against the word of a dishonest local to convince a full jury of anyone's guilt.

This case did have a sympathetic judge and prosecutor appointed by the Republican governor, which gave him a chance. Due to the hyperbole the crimes had evoked, the prosecutor had gotten the trial moved to another parish. During the trial, the prosecutor would likely win more battles over legal haggling. But could he convince a jury of white Southerners that the government was right and one of their own was guilty?

The odds of conviction would surely be higher if the case were prosecuted in a Federal court, but even the pro-suffrage and liberal Grant administration considered local crimes out of the realm of Federal jurisdiction. Only if the army or some other Federal entity was directly involved in the action could the full power and resources of the Federal government be used to prosecute the guilty. This was why Douglas thought he might have a chance of convicting the bushwhackers and why he currently put all his energy to that course.

The defense attorney finally finished his speech,

and the prosecution called Douglas to the stand. He stood and straightened his uniform. In the crowded courtroom, he stuck out like a blooming rose in winter in his full army blues. He had pondered what to wear. His uniform represented everything that most of these people hated, but he also knew the high esteem in which the population held soldiers, especially when it came to truth and honor. He had finally decided that the uniform might add a little credence to his words. Douglas stepped forward, placed his hand on the Bible, and made his brief pledge of allegiance and to tell the whole truth.

"Please take a seat," the judge said, looking down at Douglas and lifting his glasses off his round face hidden by a big gray beard and mustache.

"State your name and occupation," the court reporter, a small, wiry man, said loudly.

"Captain Douglas Owens, Company D, Fourth United States Cavalry, Fifth Military District."

"And how long have you been at this post?"

"About two years."

The prosecuting attorney stood and walked to the witness stand. A tall, thin man, with a long, deliberating face, he looked every bit the intellectual equal of his adversary, but without the charisma and gift for animation. "Captain Owens, can you please tell the jury where you were on June four of this year, and what events you saw?"

Douglas cleared his throat. "About two hours before noon, I had ridden onto the Tall Oaks plantation. The night before I had heard the rumors of disorder there, so I led a patrol of four soldiers to the plantation. In front of the farm's storage house, I saw two dead black men. The blood spilling from their wounds was still fresh, so I sent my men in different directions looking for the perpetrators. I took off alone toward the river. About twenty minutes later, I heard some screaming and raced in the direction of the voices. I shortly came into a little field. I saw two men bickering. I then heard two quick shots. I raced forward and found Mr. Johnson standing over a dead man, a freedman. I placed Mr. Johnson in my custody, securing his hands behind his back with a piece of rope. I now know this dead man was Jeriamh Taylor."

"Can you identify the man you arrested that day?" the prosecutor asked.

Douglas pointed to a man sitting at a table in the front of the room. The accused was a slight man with long stringy red hair flowing down to a nice black suit. Douglas's actions resulted in no change in the man's trouble-free expression.

"Have the record note that Captain Owens has identified Hank Johnson," the prosecutor said. "Did you have any correspondence with Mr. Johnson during his detainment?"

"Yes, I asked him what he was doing. He told me he had killed the man in self-defense. That the man had taken a shot at him and he was defending himself. I believe he said something to the extent of: 'the damned black dog tried to kill me. The sum' bitch is just a dead nigger now.'"

The courtroom came to life with a few snickers,

*uhh*s, and *ohh*s, and the judge pounded his gavel. "Order."

"And did you investigate the accused's claims?"

"I did. I searched the dead man for weapons, but found none. I then searched the accused and his horse for weapons. I found a rifle still sheathed on his horse and his pistol in his belt. The rifle had not been fired, but the barrel of the pistol was still warm. I checked it over well and found that two of its cartridges had been fired."

"What type of pistol was this?"

"It was a Colt, Navy Revolver. Model 1860 or 1861, I believe."

"Is this the revolver you took from Mr. Johnson?" The prosecutor raised a pistol and showed it to the jury. He then handed it to Douglas.

"That appears to be it," Douglas answered.

"Did you notice anything else at the scene that might be of aid in determining the perpetrator of this crime?"

"Nothing much else, other than Mr. Johnson appeared to be drunk. I could smell the whiskey on his breath."

"Objection!" the defense attorney stood and yelled. "We're only interested in the facts, not any of the captain's assumptions or dreamy ideals. We already know what he thinks: that we're all drunks and murderers."

"Sustained," the judge said, turning to the jury. "Please strike the comment from the record."

The prosecutor turned to the defense. "No further questions for now. Your witness."

The defense attorney rose and turned to the jury at an angle that put his back to Douglas. "So tell me, Captain Owens, in the two years since you've been in your current post, how many white men have you arrested?"

"Probably about twenty."

"And how many of these honest men that you have arrested have juries from all over your dominion convicted?"

"Two."

"It is my understanding that in both of those cases, the charges you brought were dropped, and the men pleaded to lesser crimes that did not result in incarceration."

Douglas sat silent for a few seconds, trapped. Was the attorney about to trick him into saying something that could be misconstrued by the jury?

With his back still to Douglas, the defense attorney continued, "Captain Douglas, the jury and the good people of this parish would like to hear your answer. Is this true or false?"

"Yes, that is correct," Douglas mumbled, as he felt his forehead burning and sweat building on his back.

"And during this same time period, how many freedmen has your command arrested?"

"I'm not sure."

"I am. Over this time period when you have hauled twenty-one good citizens off to jail, none of whom were guilty of the crimes charged, you have arrested exactly two freedmen, both of whom were found guilty by a jury." The defense attorney finally turned to face Douglas. "It does seem, Captain Owens, that you spend the badly needed tax dollars of our republic trying to throw the good citizens of this state in jail. Worse, you seem to be only interested in putting white people in jail. The war has been over for more than four years. I ask you, hasn't the army killed enough people around here? When will we have equal justice?"

The defense attorney returned his attention to the jury, leaning on the rail surrounding the jury box and looking over each man for a few seconds. "Mr. Johnson has given written testimony that he acted only in self-defense. It is a tragedy that Jeriamh Taylor is dead. I will concede that. Captain Owens, I have been to the spot where he died. There is open farmland around that spot for a hundred yards in all directions. You have stated yourself, under oath, that when you entered the opening of the field you saw Mr. Johnson shoot Jeriamh Taylor. I know you Yankee soldiers think you're superior to us, and you may well be, but I would be amazed if you could see the details of a scuffle from that distance. Look out that window. I have paced it off myself. It is only fifty yards to the church across the street. A hundred yards is a long way. That in itself should create the reasonable doubt beyond what the law requires to convict any man."

The defense attorney paused, continuing to stare at the jury. He now had all nine men's complete attention.

"Further, you are the only witness. You have demonstrated your disdain for the local population.

Mysteriously, despite the fact you commanded almost thirty men on the day of this crime, you are the only one who claims Mr. Johnson acted unlawfully. I cannot say what happened on the tragic day of Jeriamh Taylor's death, but I can say that I myself live in terror that I might be shot down on any day by Union soldiers. It has also been proven that whites were killed in the area by blacks the day before. The army was clearly unable to protect all the citizens of Bossier Parish, black or white. Everyone in this area knows that if they are not prepared to defend themselves, no one else will do it. As awful as it is, these are the simple facts: Mr. Johnson was in a place where rampant murder was taking place, and he acted like any citizen would. When his life was in jeopardy, he defended himself. Mr. Hank Johnson has lived in Bossier Parish all his life, and I have found not a single incident where he acted outside the law and have heard nothing here today to suggest anything otherwise except your testimony, which should be taken in the context of your documented record."

The defense attorney paused and walked over to his desk, where he grabbed a stack of papers and raised it above his head. "Over a dozen men, all of lengthy good standing in his community, have testified in writing to this jury that Mr. Johnson is a hardworking, peaceful citizen. The fact that he should even be brought before this court is a travesty."

The defense attorney turned and faced the judge,

raising both his hands in the air. "I have no further questions for this witness."

Douglas stood, looking at the jurors as he stepped down from the witness box. Staring into their eyes, he knew there'd be no conviction. A few of the jurors might have some doubts about the defense's reasoning, but in their eyes, he saw nothing that would likely lead to the unanimous consent required to convict Mr. Johnson. Constable Garrett's words before he'd been gunned down by Basil rang in his ears: "You'll never convict me."

His anger rose. He only felt an urge to get back to Natchitoches and pursue the night riders. There, he would have all the government's resources. And there, he could do something to make a difference.

8

The air in the dark room was thick and pungent with the sweet smell of opium and hemp. Candles flickered, sending a strange yellow light through the hazy air. The aroma lingered in Douglas's nose, slightly dizzying his senses as he looked over at Basil, sitting at a table in a back room of the Cotton Palace, a rough hotel, brothel, saloon, and gambling house a few miles outside of Natchitoches at a small river port named Grand Ecore, where a ferry spanned the Red River.

Basil's eyes were bloodshot and foggy. Standing above him, a beautiful blonde, probably in her late twenties, had her silky ivory arms draped around the gunfighter's neck. She looked at Douglas with eyes as wasted as Basil's.

"What time did you get back last night?" Basil said.

"The steamer got back here about ten," Douglas replied.

"This is Nancy," Basil mumbled. He turned to the

fair-skinned and dainty woman. "Go on upstairs. I've got business."

The whore stood up straight and looked at Douglas, blinking her deep brown eyes in an almost irresistible fashion. The slight daze induced from the drugs floating through the room accentuated her lustful stare. "Mister, I have someone here who can remove you from your uncompromising mood." The courtesan kissed Basil on top of the head. "I'll be upstairs when you're through."

Douglas sat down as the girl started to walk out of the room. "It's going to be hard for you to earn your money, whoring and wallowing in opium all the time."

Basil lit a thin cigar and offered one to Douglas.

"It's never agreed with me," Douglas said.

"I'm working now." Basil took a long puff and stared at the red glow on the cigar's tip. "This place is a trove of information. My first two nights here were quite a learning experience."

"Don't think the army's going to pay for your run of the house."

"Don't need the house. I'll just take up with Nancy. She's more than enough woman for me."

Douglas sat up straight, resting his elbows on the table. "Share all your new knowledge."

Basil reclined in the chair, bumping the cigar in an ashtray. "Nobody knows who these masked raiders are, maybe white militia. They call them the night riders. What I do know is that when something valuable, or somebody carrying something valuable, moves from here to Natchez, or the other way around, word gets passed to the highwaymen, probably from here or Natchez or one of the ferries. Then the unfortunate souls are never seen again. These are just thieves who kill to cover their trails. A lot of the community is scared silly. Been going on for years, but it's gotten much worse lately."

Douglas let the words sink in, not sure what they meant, or if they even helped. He already knew most of this. "Well, let's go," he said and stood. "We've got some things we need to take care of before we go back across the river. You can come back here and continue your snooping after hours, on your own time." Douglas took a few steps to the door that led to the saloon and then back outside. He opened it and waited on Basil. As he led the gun hand through the door, the late-morning light filtering through the windows lit the vast barroom, its twenty or so tables and two roulette wheels empty. At the bar stood two men partaking from a bottle of whiskey and conversing with the lone barkeep, an elderly man dressed in a black suit.

One of the men twisted to look at Douglas. It was Sheriff Thaxton. The man beside him turned up a shot glass, downing his whiskey. He threw the glass on the floor, shattering it and pointing his finger at Basil. "You gunned down my brother in cold blood, you son of a bitch."

Douglas stopped in his tracks, a queasy feeling gripping his belly. He again spied the big, almost vacant room. Not a sound echoed off its wood walls. The short burly brute packed a six-shooter on his hip. The man had a bald, shiny scalp, slightly pockmarked face, and roving, intense turquoise eyes, like none Douglas had ever seen before. He appeared wound tight, moving with a quick, aggressive nature, his denim pants adhering tightly to his legs.

"I told you boys not to go stirring up any trouble," the sheriff said as he squared his shoulders to Basil and Douglas. "Moses Garrett is not at all happy about what happened to his little brother. He just wants the man responsible to get what's coming to him."

"Constable Garrett should have come in with us instead of resisting arrest," Douglas said. "And I don't believe either of you have any jurisdiction over the actions of the Fourth Cavalry. Surely, you're not picking a fight with the army."

Moses Garrett jerked his pistol from his holster, pointing it at Basil. "We'll end all this right now!"

Douglas pulled his own pistol, but before he ever got Moses in his sights, Basil had drawn a steady bead on the man.

"Do it!" Basil screamed, his words echoing loudly off the walls. "You'll be in hell in less than a minute."

Feet rapidly shuffled on the wood floor. The saloon's swinging doors squeaked. Slowly, Douglas glanced left. The two Dallon boys whom he had met at the sheriff's office came to sliding stops just inside the bar, their hands dangling over the pistols on their hips. Basil calmly readjusted his stance, squaring his shoulders between the men so he could easily eye all four.

The squeaking doors opened again. Huff stood in the doorway, his broad shoulders almost spanning the opening and holding his Henry in front of his chest with both hands. Douglas heard his own heavy breath, his heart pattering fast. He wiped the wet palm of his free hand on his trousers. He stole a glance at the bartender, his jaw hanging open with disbelief as he waited for the earsplitting eruption of flying lead.

Sheriff Thaxton slowly lifted a hand, placing it on Moses's extended arm. "Let's all settle down," he said softly, pulling the arm down.

Douglas slowly lowered his pistol and nodded to Basil to do the same, but his partner kept his steady weapon locked on the constable's brother's chest.

"*Lower* the pistol," Douglas said, irritated with Basil. Basil did not react, and Douglas followed the sheriff's lead and reached over himself and pulled down Basil's arm.

"I'll see you again, soon," Garrett said to Basil, turning for the door. He stopped and pointed at Douglas. "You too. We're going to run you and your godless soldiers out of this country, once and for all. Damn bloodthirsty swines. I'm hoping you come after me. We have ways of making these problems go away around here."

Garrett marched toward the door, the sheriff and the two Dallon boys behind him.

"If you break the laws of the republic," Douglas yelled, "I'm going to haul you in, to stand in front of a Federal jury!"

"I suspect we won't have to worry about you, one way or the other, before long," Garrett said as he walked out of the room.

* * *

The morning had all but ended. The searing sun now commanded the day. Douglas walked down the street, chewing on that morning's melee with Moses Garrett as he went through his stash of mail that he had just retrieved from the post office. He looked ahead to his office. Over the door, the weathered wooden sign read: Freedmen's Bureau and US Army Post, 4th Cavalry Regiment, Troop A. Above the building, on a long wooden pole, the Stars and Stripes, weathered and frayed, hung flat in the dead air. To Douglas's knowledge, it was the only American flag in the parish.

The Freedmen's Bureau had been closed for almost a year, and he had a new sign made, but had yet to get around to installing it. Uneven, unpainted boards covered the spacious building. Though only he, Huff, and Basil currently resided here, the building contained his office, a mess room, quarters capable of housing a squad of cavalry, and a small detention cell constructed of iron bars. Local businesses catered to almost all of his and his men's needs. Most of the citizens would have preferred not to pitch in, but the army paid cash, Federal script, a rare commodity that few refused.

The building's appearance didn't please Douglas. He wanted it to look more like his vision of a post he commanded. It needed a fresh coat of paint and some carpentry work. He reminded himself of the repairs he planned to initiate after the harvest when labor would be plentiful.

He unfolded the letter he had scribbled out this morning and planned to send by telegram this afternoon, reading again.

To: Assistant Adjutant General
Headquarters, District of Louisiana
New Orleans, La.

Colonel M. J. James:

In discharging my duties as given me by you on September 7, 1869, I am forwarding the following. My initial inquiries into matters as instructed indicate that on the subject of general violence in the area of the upper Red River parishes, and the recent murder of several men under my command, I can expect no help from the local authorities, state or local. Additionally, recent investigations indicate that these stated elements may in fact be aiding the perpetrators, if not directly involved. Threats to me and the authority that I represent have in recent days been made directly to my person. Based on my professional judgment, I deem it essential that additional troops, two squads of cavalry, be placed under my immediate command. Considering the size and organization of the parties hostile to the army, these forces will be sufficient to achieve the goal of stated orders, calm elements of society, protect the rights of all citizens, and promote general peace that will benefit all parties.

I am, very respectfully, your willing and obedient servant,

Captain Douglas Owens,
Commander, Company D, 4th United States Cavalry

When Douglas entered his office, a large room with a desk, several chairs, and a mess table, he found Hannah, her left hand toting a small picnic basket. Judge Butler stood beside her, and Private O'Neal sat at the table.

"Private O'Neal," Douglas said in a loud, professional tone.

The eighteen-year-old freckle-faced and redheaded Irishman jumped up and turned to face the officer, his long hair waving as he snapped his stance stiff.

Douglas made a quick inspection of the private's uniform, covering his short, stocky frame. "Run over to the corral and fetch Basil and Huff."

"Yes, sir," the private said and quickly departed.

"Good morning," Hannah said, putting the basket on the table. She opened it and began to place its contents on the wooden table. "Uncle John and I brought you and your men some lunch."

Douglas stepped forward to inspect the grilled beef, string beans, bread, and blackberry pie.

"You look tired," the judge said to Douglas. "Have you been out on any more nighttime missions to escort citizens home safely?"

Douglas quickly glanced at Hannah trying not to be noticed, then turned back to the judge. "How I spend my nights is the least of my worries. It's not even noon, and I already damn near got in a shoot-out with Sheriff Thaxton and that psychopath, Moses Garrett . . . down at the Cotton Palace."

The door rattled open as Private O'Neal led Huff and Basil inside.

"You men eat up," Hannah said, continuing to arrange the food.

As the four soldiers sat at the table, Judge Butler turned to his niece. "Hannah, can you excuse us? I need to discuss some things in private with Captain Owens and his men."

"But, Uncle," Hannah said, "can't it wait until after lunch? I'd like to visit also. I'm not domestic help."

"Go along," the judge insisted. "You can visit later. You know how politics stimulates your free spirit. It gave your poor father endless hours of grief. There's nothing more worrisome than that from a young, respectable lady."

Douglas looked at Hannah and then the judge. "Judge Butler, I hear you're a very fair man. How can it be acceptable for your niece to ride home late at night with a stranger, but not have a mind of her own?"

The judge flashed his focused eyes at Douglas, crinkling his forehead as he moved over a few feet to make room for Hannah at the table. Douglas spent a few seconds relishing Hannah's complimentary gaze.

"I'll say grace," Hannah said, and everyone bowed their heads in silence.

"Captain Owens," the judge said in a sincere voice when Hannah finished the quick prayer. He put his hands on the table and quickly glanced at the other three men. "I am a little disturbed about the shooting of Constable Garrett. Not that he didn't deserve what he got, but we have to bring these outlaws in front of a jury. We can't just gun them down. That will do no good. We have to demonstrate to the population that there is law and order around here, and that we're above this violence, that we follow the rules. This is the only way to subjugate the masses. Shoot-outs might get rid of the immediate problem, but only the rule of law can keep the peace."

Douglas's throat went dry as he searched for a response. He tore off a piece of bread and drank some coffee. He turned to Huff and Basil, both continuing to eat. "Judge, I understand your concerns. And they are accurate. But it is a lawless jungle outside of town. We have made and will continue to make every effort to bring these men to your courtroom, as much as it does not unduly endanger us."

"If it *does* endanger you," the judge continued, "so be it. The law is not up for interpretation. And it is the only thing that will work."

Basil set down his fork and leaned back from the table. "There's a family of five with two loaded wagons in town. Hear they're headed east, to

Winnfield and then to the railhead at Monroe. Been in town a few days. Hear they're headed out in the morning. We could trail them. Might catch somebody preying on them."

Douglas took in the statement as the entire table got silent. Even the sounds of eating paused.

After the awkward silence, the judge spoke up. "I wouldn't recommend using innocent civilians as bait, much less women and children."

Basil continued to eat. "I wouldn't consider them innocents. If these people run into those highwaymen, the only thing they'll be meeting is their maker."

Douglas didn't like the idea of it, but Basil was right. All they could do was help, and they might catch somebody alive, somebody they could try and interrogate. He turned to Basil, then Huff. Neither were interested in the judge's idea of justice. One had a poisoned heart, his current state forced on him by a pitiless world, the other had gotten there by choice, but both seethed with a desire for their own form of justice.

Douglas picked up his fork. "We could never follow them out of town, or even cross the ferry a few hours later. That would arouse too much suspicion. We'd need to cross the river to the north and catch up with them on the trail. . . . Basil, check around today, discreetly, confirm this, and see when they're leaving. Basil's right, they're already bait, whether they want to be or not. All we can do is help. We'll take the Sparta Road, cut through the woods, and be able to catch up with them by dark. Be there in case there's any potential problems. Be much safer for them that way, and it will satisfy our needs."

Douglas looked at his men, then the judge. "Let's be ready to ride in the morning. Get ready today and tonight. We'll need a sharp eye; this may take us a few days, and nights."

9

In the distance, a few lights glowed. Douglas looked up at the belt of stars stretching across the sky, then to Hannah as he leaned back on a blanket spread on the bank of a small bayou on the Butler plantation. Her fresh scent and fair skin, glowing in the starlight, induced his manly cravings. Douglas had experienced women before, knowing the benefits of their soothing touch. He had in fact been engaged once, while at West Point, but his fiancée had succumbed to typhoid. He had also patronized a few of the brothels in New Orleans.

He finally handed Hannah the almost empty bottle of champagne.

"Where did you get this?" Hannah said, her speech slightly slurred. "And how did you end up at the Butler house just after dark?"

"I stole it at the Yankee ball the other night. I'm quick. I did it within eyesight of you and everybody else. And I thought I'd ride out here and check on you. Your sister and mother are gone, and I knew the judge would be in town until late. This is strictly a call within my current duties."

"And you happened to bring the champagne on this routine trip?"

"Kind of like that." Douglas laughed. He rolled over on his side and stared at Hannah and the big ball of light crimson hair pinned up above her ears. He leaned forward and gave Hannah a quick peck on the lips. "It's probably after ten."

Hannah grinned. "This was terrific . . . my father's probably rolling over in his grave, bless him. Let's stay here a while. It's a magnificent night. If Uncle drinks too much, he may not even come home tonight."

"What about Mr. Jones?"

"He's sound asleep. He doesn't worry about my passing fancies, generally never gets out at night unless there's some type of ruckus, and Uncle would love the thought of a captain calling on me. I think he likes you. He'll forgive me for almost any transgression. . . . You look a little more worried than normal. What's the matter?"

Douglas stammered over his words. "It's just the shooting of Constable Garrett the other day was rather traumatic, ugly. It just didn't go like I wanted it to. The meeting with your uncle today reminded me of it. Now, I'm heading back into the back-country, for no telling how long." He passed a few quiet seconds before speaking. "Tell me about your uncle. How much credibility does he have with the local people?"

"He spent the Rebellion in New Orleans, aiding the Republican government. Never made much of himself prior to that. Had a small law practice in Shreveport, but it failed. He has no real family, never married."

"You mean he fits the current definition of scalawag perfectly."

"Some might say that just because he's returned home a man of authority. Maybe he just never profited from our past sins. I do know he's very honest and intent on doing what's right. He believes in a New South."

"How's your sister taking all this? I mean the judge staying with you three?"

Hannah rolled her eyes. "Caroline will be fine. She'll eventually come around to the fact the world has changed. She needs to find a man to help her get over the loss of her dear husband in the war."

Douglas looked at the bayou. "Are there alligators in there?"

"Not around here. Mr. Jones shoots them."

With his feet, Douglas slipped off both of his boots, then stood and bent over and grabbed Hannah. "I'm burning up. These Louisiana nights are steamier than August afternoons in Ohio. Let's go for a swim."

"No!" Hannah said as Douglas cradled her in his arms. "These are my favorite pants."

"Just a short dip." Douglas staggered to the bank,

then threw Hannah into the water and jumped in behind her.

"Captain Owens!" Hannah said, wiping the water from her face. "You *are* a feisty gentleman. Maybe drinking doesn't agree with you." Hannah walked by Douglas, splashing him with several handfuls of water before climbing out of the bayou and walking back to the blanket.

Douglas stumbled out of the bayou and over to his horse, where he grabbed a dry towel and clean cotton shirt from his saddlebag. He then flopped down beside Hannah, wiping her face with the towel.

"I'm all wet," Hannah said.

"It feels great." Douglas put his hand behind Hannah's head, pulling her close. He then bestowed a long kiss on her, lingering on her lips. "Here, put this on."

Hannah looked at Douglas for a few awkward seconds, her eyes big with bewilderment.

"Let me help. I won't look." Douglas reached over and grabbed the bottom of Hannah's shirt, feeling the bare flesh of her stomach. The soft, cool skin aroused him. Hannah leaned back, hesitating, her breath getting deep. He looked into her eyes. He wanted more. It had been years since he had experienced any real intimacy, and Hannah exploded his suppressed desires, displacing him from his indifferent military disposition and this wretched land so far from God.

Douglas closed his eyes, and lifted the wet shirt over her head. He stole a quick peek and then kissed Hannah's ear, before moving his lips down her neck.

Hannah took a few more deep breaths, before retreating. "We can't. I don't know if this can ever be."

Douglas craned back, opening his eyes and inspecting her bare breasts and strong, youthful body. "Don't you like me? It's only natural."

Hannah exhaled. "Yes, I do. I'm just confused."

Douglas studied Hannah. Her face told him she longed for more, the same wants and desires as he and any woman of her age—the natural yearning for the company and care of the opposite sex. And similar to him, few ideal suitors existed for her around town. She had to be more friendless than he. At least he had the army to worry with. He caressed her cheek, grabbed her firmly, and pulled her close. "Hannah, I can't help it. I don't care about the situation, or what people think. I think I love you."

Hannah grabbed her wet shirt, pulled it over her head, and wiggled her midsection to aid in sliding it back down to her waist. "These things take time. You can call on me again. I promise I'll try not to think about what everybody thinks, or our backgrounds, but our first cherished encounter, when and if it ever happens, *will not* be on the bank of a bayou."

Douglas lay down on the blanket, resting his head on his propped-up hand. "I would like that. The country has changed, rejoined. You've told me you think Louisiana should be back in the Union. These things will become normal, like they were twenty years ago."

"I hope so." Hannah stood and put a hand to Douglas's ear, softly fondling it. "I am terribly lonely."

Douglas stood and sighed. Tomorrow, he would be back at his bloody business. He hated the hastiness of this. He didn't want it to end so soon. He gave Hannah another long kiss, delighting in the feel of her full, soft lips. "Come on, let's go before somebody finds out about our scandal."

10

The next morning found Douglas inspecting the five sturdy steeds they would take into the piney hills in an attempt to shadow the two wagons and family of five. All the mounts had the distinctive US brands on their front shoulders. The sky transmuted from light ginger to cobalt. The morning had a refreshing nip, but the day promised to be hot. Satisfied with his inspection, he walked back into his office. His men had all their rifles spread out on the table. The room carried the pungent smell of oil. Basil and Private O'Neal were cleaning and lubricating each of the weapons.

"How come these folks won't act right?" Private O'Neal asked, wiping down his gun barrel.

Douglas grabbed a biscuit off his desk as Huff handed him a cup of coffee. "You have to understand this place, how these people have been trampled on. There's nothing like it anywhere, not even in the postwar South. The War here was much crueler than back east. The first Union commander here,

General Butler—the locals called him the Beast because of his savagery. The Beast was even too much for Lincoln, who eventually replaced him. This is the same President Lincoln who let Sherman burn Atlanta and march to the sea. General Banks was a little better, but he still pursued Butler's scorched-earth policies. Burned everything when he retreated, which was often. Hell, the Rebs got to where they would burn the towns beforehand because they knew General Banks would do it and thus they'd prevent him from any loot. And worse, when the war was over, the Confederates hadn't lost. They just read in the papers it was over. There weren't any honorable surrenders like back east where the armies saluted each other or had big formal parades written about in the papers. There was just a desolate land with no Federal government or army to keep the people from starving, or uphold law and order. Violence is all these people know, rich or poor, black or white."

The heavy aroma of the coffee awakened Douglas's senses. He reached over to his desk and grabbed a large envelope, a week of reports he needed to send to headquarters. He then picked up a map, only a rough hand drawing. It was all that existed of the interior backcountry. The map documented the main roads, rivers, fords, a few towns and distances, but outside of the sparse roads and towns the map lacked ink. As he studied it, he continued to respond to Private O'Neal's inquiry. "This rich delta soil and hot, wet climate makes the best environment for crops God made anywhere in the world. Louisiana produced almost a third of the country's cotton, almost all its sugarcane. The biggest slave-trading houses for the entire country were in New Orleans. The Northern government has decimated this place, at least in their eyes. This is what happens when civilization and society are destroyed."

Basil continued to wipe his rifle with a rag, but looked over at Douglas. "That sounds like typical Yankee rhetoric from some crackpot idealist. Y'all think this is just random violence. It's not. These are hard men, with local concerns. Most of the general trouble is very organized terror with political goals: to rid the state of carpetbaggers, and keep their Negro pawns from voting, by any means necessary."

Douglas turned to Huff. "Get on down to the baker and get our bread. Mail these logs I spent all day yesterday writing. We'll depart in twenty minutes. If we hustle, we might make the ferry at Campti by noon. It will be much easier to cover the ground in the morning. We should be able to cut over to the Winnfield road a few hours before dark. I'm going to take a quick dip. Might be a while before I get another chance."

Douglas walked out the back door of the office to a large iron bathing tub. He quickly slipped off his clothes and eased into the cool water. He plunged his head into the tub and quickly worked his body over with a bar of soap. As he continued to lather up, he turned to the office's back door when he heard some feet on the porch. There, Hannah stood, smiling and looking down at him.

"Why, Hannah, what on earth are you *doing* here?"

Hannah continued to grin and raised a small package. "I had to come to town this morning before school to drop off some papers for Uncle anyway. I thought I would bring you some fresh jerky for your trip . . . but I didn't expect to see you in such a compromising position."

Douglas smiled. Hannah had the quality of making one feel she never rehearsed her words. "Well, turn your head. A lady's not supposed to see me like this, not in broad daylight. And no peeking." Douglas stood, shook his body like a dog, and stepped into his pants before sliding on his boots and hastily pulling a shirt over his shoulders.

"Can I open my eyes now?"

"Certainly." Douglas stepped up on the porch, catching a whiff of her scent, making his knees weak. "You're just in time. We're leaving right now."

Douglas led Hannah over to the lawn behind the office where O'Neal and Basil had just saddled up. He climbed up on his mount, rested his elbows on his saddle horn, and looked down at Hannah.

She handed the jerky up to Douglas. "Now you be sure and come back, and . . . don't do anything stupid."

"Tell your uncle we're planning to bring him some customers. Maybe then, you'll let me take you for a public outing, maybe the theater."

"But no more swimming."

"We may be gone awhile. Who knows when we'll be back?"

Douglas's stomach danced as he stared at the smiling Hannah, on her tiptoes and waving her

hand in the air. With some pomp, he reared up
his horse, then wheeled the mare around, pressing his legs against her ribs and riding off at a
smart trot.

His face and clothes foamy with sweat, body exhausted, exposed skin parched fresh red and caked
with dust, Douglas looked at the late-day sun hanging over the pines. He smelled the rank odor from
his clothes.

A big black crow perched in a tree above cawed
loudly, the call resonating through the hills. From
the saddle, he looked ahead. The sun at his back ra-
diated the image of a man on horseback. Through
the dancing heat waves, the man traversed a high
ridge on the trail ahead, maybe a quarter-mile distant.

It had been a fitful day. The four men had
crossed the Red River fifteen miles north of Natchitoches on a little-used ferry. The route cut the distance to the Winnfield Road considerably, but
entailed the negotiating of almost twenty miles of
virgin country on little-used trails that bisected two
vast swamps.

Somewhere in these marshy bottoms, they had
gotten off course, slogging along for hours through
the uninhabited land, unsure of their location or
way. The primitive trails were a garbled mass of disorder. Some started east, but went north. Many
didn't begin anywhere, but went everywhere, split-
ting into four, five, or six trails, perhaps more.

Mired in confusion and by compass only, they had trudged on, trying to keep an eastern track while weaving through and around the horrendous, patchwork terrain, a mosaic of thick green hills, wide bayous, and mushy turf, all populated with swarming insects and chiggers. The plentiful bayous were the worst, a perplexing enigma, an endless maze almost impossible to traverse. Teeming with insects, alligators, logs, cypress knees, and thick black water, their banks a mass of mangled vegetation, the bayous appeared to have neither inlets nor outlets. They slashed through the land, sometimes almost a mile wide, other times as narrow as a mountain brook, making navigation an almost hopeless chore.

"That's Huff," Private O'Neal said, still staring through his field glasses. The private was new to this land, and his pale skin had not only turned dark red, but had already started to bubble up with blisters that matched his flaking lips. "Maybe he found the Winnfield Road."

Around him, Douglas saw nothing but the intense glare of the sun and green everywhere. How did people live here? He fought off an urge to moan about the heat. Not wanting to complain in front of his men, he looked at his long shadow and felt the sun on his back as he removed his canteen and guzzled its contents, letting the water spill over his mouth onto his shirt. He removed his hat and poured several mouthfuls over his head, the refreshing water washing his salty perspiration into his eyes. He rode off the trail under a large pine, stepped down from his saddle, and sat on the ground, leaning back against a tree trunk. His once polished black cavalry boots were now coated in dust. "Let's take a break. Wait here on Huff."

Under the shade of the pine, the three waited ten minutes for Huff to arrive. The harsh climate, coupled with the long day, didn't seem to wear on the elderly ex-slave as it did on the three feeble white men cowering in the shade. Huff's blood, his lifetime of toiling in this heartless land, made him much more suited for the brutal climate. He sat horseback, as nimble and fresh as ever. Douglas was reminded, as he often was, that the grit and sweat of men like Huff had carved up and conquered this bountiful land so unsympathetic to the fair-skinned creatures of the world.

"Road to Winnfield is less than a mile ahead," Huff said, wiping his brow with his forearm.

"Not as bad as I figured," Douglas replied, relieved. "Why do you look so worried?"

"We's much farther south than we expected," Huff said. "Probably only ten miles east of the river. Maybe netted fifteen miles today, total. They's two sets of wagon tracks in the road. I'm guessing they's five, maybe six hours old."

"Six *hours*," Douglas moaned, his head hanging between his knees. "If they push on till dark, it'll be damn near midnight before we catch up to them, if at all." He looked to the east, to a half-moon already rising. "We'll have some moon, probably till midnight."

"Not all bad news," Basil said. "At least we found

the road. We'd have no chance if we had to wander around in this jungle at night."

The four rode on through the night, down the well-beaten road, just wide enough for two wagons to pass. The degree of vision constantly deviated from a few hundred feet under the trees to maybe a quarter mile when the topography afforded. They had been riding, slowly, for three hours in the darkness. Douglas wanted to stop. The horses were nearly spent. On the ground below the horses' hooves, the tracks of the two wagons rambled on. By Douglas's calculation, they should be nearing the wagons soon, assuming they had stopped at dark. If viable, he wanted to camp with the travelers in case the bandits raided.

As Huff led the patrol down a steep incline, the air turned dark, a black void impenetrable to the eye. Down they went, maybe fifty vertical feet to a little stream.

"We've got to stop. Take a break for a while," Basil said in a grumpy, downbeat tone. "Let the horses water and graze a spell."

Douglas didn't even have to pull back on his reins, but only remove his spurs from his mare's ribs to bring her to a stop. He slowly stepped down to the ground, his saddle-sore bones aching. Where were they and where were they headed? This all appeared to be another useless, comical escapade. In the darkness, he heard the horses' long gulps from the little creek. "What do you think?" he said to

Huff, who was splashing some creek water over his face. "Don't let the horses drink too much, they'll founder."

"They can't be far, less than a mile," Huff replied, the groggy whites of his eyes roving against his black face and the night.

Two quick pops drifted through the thick foliage. Douglas's heart raced as he jumped back on his horse. The other three men hustled to their mounts. He whipped his reins and kicked his heels. "Leave the packhorse. We may get lucky and catch somebody!"

From his saddle, Douglas saw only the rush of trees through the darkness. The rumble of hooves below filled his ears. He had to duck under or around several branches to keep from being unsaddled.

Five minutes of riding put the soldiers at the top of a small hill where Douglas jerked back on his reins. In a small valley down below he saw the orange glow of a fire. Without words and over his heavy breath, he removed his Colt from his holster and held it high. Lunging onward in his saddle, he forced his horse down the hill.

As the glowing embers of the fire got bigger, two wagons came into view. Beside them, six men appeared out of the night. All donned masks over their heads, cut-up cloth or cotton sacks with slits sliced in them for seeing and breathing. More gunfire awakened the night. Muzzles blasted. Behind him, his comrades opened fire. In the darkness and from a horse, getting a sight on a silhouette was almost impossible. Two of the highwaymen, conveniently beside horses, saddled up and charged off, disappearing. Another of the outlaws dashed for his horse, saddled up, and grabbed one more of the bushwhackers, pulling him on his horse and also disappearing into the night. But two of the outlaws scattered into the woods, quickly absorbed by the shadows.

Douglas stormed on toward the men, his horse trampling over one of the night riders who had drawn his pistol. The man ducked to the side, managing to stay on his feet. Douglas pointed his Colt at the man's back and cocked the hammer. "Drop the gun or you're dead."

The man slowly dropped his pistol and turned to face Douglas.

Two more shots erupted. Douglas turned.

Behind him, Basil fired from his saddle at a man on his stomach who crawled for the cover of some bushes.

"Quit shooting!" Douglas yelled. "We want 'em alive."

Basil fired a final shot.

Douglas heard it smash into flesh as the hazy figure on the ground stopped moving.

"I left you one to try," Basil said, looking over his shoulder.

Douglas turned back to the cloaked man standing in front of his horse. "Private O'Neal, tie this man up."

Almost as quickly as it had started, the night suddenly got quiet. O'Neal jumped to the ground as

Huff rode forward and pointed his pistol at the lone masked man still alive. Douglas slowly got off his horse. He walked to the ghostlike figure and waited for Private O'Neal to finish lashing his hands behind his back. With a quick hand, Douglas jerked off the mask.

He didn't recognize the sturdy, middle-aged face. He slowly turned and walked to the wagons. But before he got more than a few steps, he saw the two bloody corpses sprawled out on the ground and three more already loaded in the wagons. He saw the teenage boy first, then two young girls, just toddlers. All had been shot in the head and thrown in the wagon. On the ground, the parents lay flat where they had been executed, their bodies perforated with bullet holes, the anxiety and fear still on their faces and almost making their grisly wounds unnoticeable.

Douglas struggled to get some air. He poured water from his canteen down his throat then turned to look at Private O'Neal, now pale white. The private bent over and vomited. Douglas felt his skin go cold. His mind went dizzy. He had never seen anything like this, civilians murdered for the few valuables in the wagon, maybe a few hundred dollars in gold. Despite all the death he'd seen during the war, he'd never seen civilians, much less women and children, simply murdered.

He looked to Basil, standing over the man he had shot. Basil held the murderer's burlap mask in his hand.

"It's one of those Dallon boys we saw at the sheriff's office the other day," Basil said.

Douglas turned to the captive. Where earlier he saw only a man, an outlaw, an opponent, now he saw utter evil. He walked over, stopping a few paces short of him, fighting off an urge to pistol-whip the man across his head. "You're going to trial. What's your name?"

The captive just gritted his teeth in silence, his muscles tensing up as he worked them against the coarse rope tied tightly around his wrists.

"We've got bigger problems," Basil said, approaching. "The others may be back. It's still six hours till daylight." He stopped walking and struck a match to light his cigar. The night hung so quiet, the scratch of the match on his leather belt drifted over the land.

Douglas looked around, thinking and calculating. It appeared that the outlaws had been hitching up the horse teams to the wagons and loading the slain when the army patrol arrived.

To the west, the moon crept below the trees. Even so, he easily saw the ridges of the surrounding hills, none further than a quarter-mile away. "We sleep here. Secure the prisoner's legs and gag his mouth. Let's put out the fire and post a guard." He turned to Basil. "How far to Winnfield from here?"

"If we leave at dawn, we can make it by noon," Basil replied, mincing off a piece of jerky with his knife. He offered a chunk to Douglas.

Douglas declined, his stomach still jumping and thoughts racing. He looked around again, sharpening his gaze. The Louisiana nights were always alive, filled with all sorts of critters moving and flying that made it impossible to tell if anything else was wayward. Was there anyone out there? He feared nothing more than squatting here at night for six hours. "We'll tidy up the dead in the morning. Let's cut the horses loose for grazing. I'll take the first watch."

11

The land was calm. The red dust dangled in the damp air. It was very hot under the midday sun. Douglas led the patrol into the outskirts of Winnfield past a large chicken coop. Only a half-mile ahead, down the dirt road, sat the town's center, twenty or so wood structures around the tree-dotted parish square. On the edge of town, most of the houses were unpainted and surrounded by small gardens. In the road, a few un-penned cows mingled around a water trough and salt lick.

Behind Douglas rode the outlaw, his hands bound at his lap, his horse tethered to Douglas's saddle. Basil rode behind the outlaw holding Douglas's shotgun, its butt resting on his thigh, as he whistled "The Bonnie Blue Flag."

Behind Basil, the lifeless Dallon boy lay sprawled crossways, belly-down over a saddled horse, a rope securing him to the saddle and his arms and legs hanging from each side of the horse. The bright rays of the sun clearly illuminated the dark bloodstains and open wounds on the dead man's body. Farther back, Private O'Neal and Huff drove the wagons leading the spare horses. The murdered family, stowed in the wagons, had been covered so as to conceal their bodies.

As the small cavalcade moved farther into town, the residents all stopped whatever they were doing to watch. Odd among the buildings, horses, carriages, and bystanders, all stood quiet, so quiet he heard the horses' footsteps. The curious, strange eyes of the townsfolk moved between the dead Dallon boy and the soldiers' eyes, shaded by the big brims of their hats. The citizens, about thirty, didn't look shocked, interested, mad, or happy, just entranced. All wore dumb stares.

His tired horse walked slowly. Douglas nodded ahead to the Parish Square and a large single-storied wood structure. "The courthouse. The sheriff's office is across the square, just around the corner. Be a good day for you, Mr. Dubose. Looks like you'll make all the papers tomorrow. You'll like that."

Basil gave a slight smirk as Douglas pulled up on his reins in front of the sheriff's office. Under an awning in front of the office stood a tall, slender man with long blond hair and clad in brown trousers and a blue cotton shirt. Douglas looked at the shiny badge pinned on the man's chest.

"Sheriff Thaxton here?" Douglas asked.

"No," the man replied flatly. "Down in Montgomery, I 'spec."

Douglas grabbed his pommel and swung a foot over the saddle, easing to the ground. "What's your name?"

"Weaver."

"Deputy Weaver," Douglas continued, "we've got a man in custody. And we've got jurisdiction to hold him in your jail." As Douglas stepped up on the pine planks, he turned to look at Basil, who was getting down from his horse and instructing the outlaw in custody to do likewise. "You know this man?"

The deputy nodded to the man whom Basil led to the jail. "Francis Garrett."

Douglas turned to the short, wiry man with simple gray eyes and a steely, square face. "Any relation to Moses and Elisha?"

"Their youngest brother," the deputy said.

"Since you've hired me," Basil commented, pointing the shotgun at Garrett to instruct him to walk over to the sheriff's office, "we've 'bout put the Garretts out of business." Basil removed a big chew of tobacco from his mouth and threw it into Garrett's face.

Douglas stepped down off the porch and grabbed a handful of the dead outlaw's hair. He lifted his head to inspect the man, his skin now gray, his lips and eyes turning ebony.

"I'm sure you know this one," Basil uttered to the deputy.

Douglas walked inside the sheriff's office. He commandeered a set of keys hanging against the wall and walked over to the single cell in the little office. Placing the key in the iron door's lock, he opened the cell and waited and watched as Garrett was escorted into the holding pen. Douglas slammed the door shut, generating a loud clank, and turned to the deputy, now wearing an anxious and disgruntled face. "You can have the murderer, the abomination, draped over the horse outside. Do with him what you want."

Deputy Weaver walked out of the office, bumping into Huff and Private O'Neal as they entered. Douglas reached into his pocket and retrieved three gold coins. "Huff, take the family and find the undertaker. Make sure they get a proper grave. O'Neal, find somebody to tend to the horses, get a few hours' rest, then I want you to go to Natchitoches and get Judge Butler. Bring him here. We're going to try Garrett here. I'll send him a telegraph this afternoon."

"Here in *Winnfield*?" Basil said. "You think that's a good idea?"

"Yes, I do," Douglas replied, walking out of the office.

As Basil followed him outside, Douglas nodded to the courthouse across the square, partially visible through the lofty oaks. Unlike many in Louisiana, it wasn't an epic structure carved of stone towering above its surroundings. It was built solidly with white walls fronted by big, conical windows and topped with a rough cupola.

"There, I want to try him where the entire parish can witness the law taking hold, see the consequences of outlawery up close and personal. . . . Basil, after we get settled in, I want to cut that bandit horse loose, the one we brought with us from last night. Want you to follow him this afternoon. See where he goes."

Above the wood roofs lay the emerald hills. Across the square, a few people standing in front of the blacksmith's and shoemaker's shops still looked at the jail and the strangers in town. This area was at complete odds with the delta. It had in fact been the only parish in Louisiana that had voted against secession—due to the fact that the yeomen here didn't care to spill blood for the benefit of the wealthy plantation owners. That said, these people didn't care for Yankee rule any more than the rest of the state. When the men in these hills had been called to task, they had been some of the ablest soldiers in the Southern cause, among the few that had never been defeated.

Douglas still held the vivid memories of the 28th Louisiana Regiment, raised here, and their spectacular attack at Mansfield. The brave boys from these cotton fields and tall trees had breached the bluecoats' formidable lines and sent the Northerners and their army not only in retreat, but completely out of this area, all despite being outnumbered almost three to one and supposedly fighting with scant supplies.

This area now harbored hundreds of ex-Confederate soldiers, mostly French and Scotch-Irish. Douglas was now in the belly of the beast, as isolated from the world as possible. A telegraph line stretched to Winnfield but could easily be cut. Douglas took in a deep breath. To the west, above the Louisiana horizon, the sky flashed in an uncanny mix of dark indigo, white, and crimson as some beautiful but ominous heat lightning danced over the hills.

The air hung thick in the little jail. Only two large candles lit the room, their flames completely vertical and casting a small, steady halo of light. Outside the window, darkness prevailed. Douglas stretched his weary arms, then unfurled his bedroll on the hardwood floor as he looked at the prisoner, sound asleep in the cell. Basil lay on his back on the floor, snoring loudly. He looked at his watch, ten minutes short of midnight. He bumped Huff, also dozing on the floor, with his boot.

"Your watch. Wake Basil up in three hours. He can take it to daylight," Douglas said, sitting on the floor and removing his boots.

"Did you get a telegraph back from the judge?" Huff asked, wiping the sleep out of his eyes.

"Yes, he's departing early in the morning. Probably be here by late afternoon tomorrow."

"What's about that bandit horse?" Huff continued, yawning. "Where'd he go?"

"Right to Moses Garrett's place."

"Well, that confirms that." Huff chuckled and slowly stood. He pulled on his boots and grabbed his rifle before walking over to sit at the office's small desk.

"It's good to know, but following a horse won't hardly stand up to a jury." Douglas scratched his chin with a forefinger. "We need dead bodies and witnesses, and we've got both. It'd be better if we had some witnesses not on the army payroll. But we've got a sympathetic judge. Should be enough to get a conviction of some sort. . . . That damn Basil's not so smooth when he's sleeping. He's rattling the rafters in this place."

Douglas leaned back on the hardwood floor, balling his blanket under his head. As he did, he looked over at Basil, his earsplitting breaths almost vibrating the floor. The pistol fighter, in his all-consuming vanity, didn't look that intrepid now as he placed his hat over his head, covering his face. He closed his eyes and began to think blissfully about the only thing that got his mind off his daily routine: Hannah. He almost couldn't wait to get back to Natchitoches and feel her touch. He thought of her zeal, her wit, her optimism and compassion, all of her that he cherished. They were the perfect match, her fair, delicate urbane appearance beside his rigorous, tan athletic figure dressed in his bold, gallant uniform. In her arms, he lost all of his worries. The thoughts seemed to comfort his aching, tired bones.

In only an instant, his eyes having barely closed, he felt Huff over him, shaking him and imploring him to get up off the floor. In his sleepy haze, he couldn't understand Huff's broken, heavily accented slang. Disoriented, Douglas shook his head, gradually opening his eyes. He grabbed his watch, and turned it so the glare of one of the candles brightened its hands, indicating two in the morning. "What is it?" he grumbled.

"Come look, a fire."

Douglas jumped to his feet. He looked out the window. Outside, he heard a few desperate voices, chaotic, busy movement. He grabbed his rifle and rushed out the door, Huff behind him. From the porch, he saw the orange flames licking at the sky. The courthouse across the square was now a raging inferno. There was no saving the structure. The local pine contained thick layers of sap, a fuel rarely extinguished even with ample men and material. The amazing, gigantic blaze now reached the cupola and grew exponentially by the second. He felt the pulses of heat as the flickering red glow illuminated the tall trees in the courtyard.

"What you's thinking?" Huff said.

"Don't know. Doesn't look like we'll be having a trial here day after tomorrow. . . . Doubt this is an accident. Good thing the courthouse is surrounded by a square. It won't get any other buildings. That's pretty bold, and desperate, much more so than I ever imagined. They're taking the gloves off, as the Irish would say. We've sure's hell got a war on our hands now." Douglas paused, thinking for almost a minute. He looked again at his watch and sighed deeply. "That fire will be out in an hour. It'll take another hour or so for everything to settle down and the town to go back to sleep. I want to get out of here well before daylight. I don't want us riding out of town tomorrow in front of everybody. We'll look like we've been defeated, run out. We leave here at 4:30, with the prisoner. We'll catch up with the judge and O'Neal on the road to Natchitoches. Turn them around and have the trial there. We'll look like we've outwitted these malcontent hoodlums. Let's just lay low until then."

12

Douglas stood dumbfounded, almost dizzy. Around him, the day was still. His comrades uttered not a sound. He looked up at the hanging body, lifeless, limp, dangling from a rope tethered to a tree on the side of the trail, its head cocked slightly sideways. He grabbed the thigh of the man and twisted him around to look at his face. Even before he got his first glimpse of the dead man's face, he knew who it was. A sick feeling engulfed his gut as he looked up at the now colorless face of Judge Butler.

"Damn it," Douglas muttered, looking down the trail.

The army patrol had managed to discreetly depart Winnfield an hour and a half before daylight, the fresh smell of the fire's embers still in their noses. Out of town, they paused to rest and wait for daylight before traversing the gauntlet back to Natchitoches. They had now been on the trail five hours, about half the trip, when they came upon the gruesome scene.

Douglas turned to look at Francis Garrett, sitting on one of the horses, his hands and mouth gagged. The outlaw wore apathy on his face. "Let's cut him down. We'll bury him in Natchitoches, proper. I shouldn't have sent that telegraph. I'm sure they've got a source in the office. I won't make that mistake again." Douglas paused and looked to Basil. "Where's Private O'Neal?"

"Don't know," Basil said. "Gone, probably at the bottom of the Red River or some other bayou, wherever they dispose of the dead."

The words rang true, Douglas knew it. The bandits, as brazen as they were, wouldn't leave a Federal soldier hanging by the road. That would rile up too much unease in their communities. He would just be someone who mysteriously disappeared, maybe he deserted—nobody would ever know the truth. But a Southerner, a full-fledged scalawag, who had gotten in bed with the Yanks, few would mourn his passing, no matter how unjust. The judge wasn't the first Republican official murdered openly in this area. And probably wouldn't be the last.

"Who *are* these people?" Douglas said, turning to Basil, lament and anguish in his voice. "I know these people are backwards, but there's plenty of good people here, too, educated types. I can't believe they would tolerate this. This is too much."

Basil slowly climbed down from his saddle, looking up at the army captain. "This is white trash of the lowest form. A lot of people, including the well-to-do, overlook the deeds of the Knights as they're called because they approve of their goals, and because it appeases the lowly whites. These groups, their killing of the freed slaves, their general violent manner, allows them to stay a notch above the niggers. It makes them feel like they still have the power that your President Lincoln took. It reestablishes white supremacy. And that, in turn, allows the plantation class to do what they've always done—exploit the poor whites and slaves for their own riches."

Douglas knew this, or at least he thought he understood it in some way, but nobody had ever said it so clearly, bluntly. He started to speak up, but Basil continued.

"But this is what I figured all along. This is a bunch of rogue white militia. It's likely the clans and gentry would like to get rid of them, quietly. The clans have strict rules, especially during nonpolitical times like now: they don't do anything that might warrant more Federal troops in the area, or arouse national attention, especially picking a fight with the army. This killing innocents is a tad too much for anybody. I'd say most of these outlaws used to be patty rollers or slave drivers, out of work now that there's no slaves to catch or drive. Most of the people in the community wouldn't mind if this bunch went away. That's the only reason I signed on to this job. Only a fool in my position would try to take on the entire political apparatus."

Douglas looked at Huff, still on horseback but studying all the hoofprints in the road.

"Captain," Huff said, "I believe these tracks in the road are real fresh, less than an hour old."

Douglas reached out and put a firm hand on the judge's midsection. "This body's still warm."

"They took off yonder way." Huff pointed down the trail in the direction of Natchitoches.

Douglas wanted to catch the perpetrators of this crime, desperately, but he had a prisoner and now a body he needed to get off the road before it became a spectacle.

"No need to hurry," Basil said. "I say we just follow their trail, see where it goes." He paused, turned, and smiled at Francis Garrett. "They're probably figuring we'll pick up their trail. They don't want Garrett here to make it to trial, one way or the other. If they'll kill a judge and burn the courthouse, they're probably planning to keep him off the witness stand, even if they have to shoot him. They knew when we'd be passing here." Basil looked down at the road and studied the tracks for thirty seconds. "Doesn't look like they made any attempt to cover their trail. I agree. These tracks are very fresh, maybe thirty minutes old. Looks like six horses. There's a small creek just up the road. If they don't use it to cover their trail, they're expecting us." Basil then chuckled loudly and turned back to the captive. "Garrett, looks like you'll get your justice in a day or so, either way."

Francis Garrett stared at Basil as he gritted his teeth.

"Okay," Douglas said. He smelled trouble, but tried to maintain a calm façade, his insides at odds with his mind. He had feared this when he had met with the colonel a few weeks earlier, his little band against the odds and in the middle of nowhere. At any second, the peaceful land might erupt. When it came, it would be quick, and it wouldn't be a glorious death on a battlefield, a soldier's death. It was doubtful anyone would ever know how and where he died, or if he were even dead. Douglas feared this more than anything. As a professional soldier, this possible mysterious undoing haunted him. It would trample his reputation, even cast doubts about his service. What a terrible way to go after all he'd sacrificed.

He removed his pistol from its holster on his hip, spinning the cylinder and checking the hammer to ensure its readiness. "Let's cut down the body and bring it with us. Huff, I want you to ride out front, a hundred paces, nice and slow. Keep your eyes and ears peeled."

Twenty minutes later, Huff paused on the trail, turning to look at Douglas as he crossed a small wooden bridge that spanned a little creek, all but dry this time of year. He then wheeled his horse around and quietly trotted back to Douglas.

"What's up?" Douglas whispered.

"The tracks play out around that bridge," Huff replied. "On both sides of the road."

Douglas studied the small hills and thick vegetation surrounding the small bottom. He turned and looked into the thick wall of timber and willows rising around them. Though the sun scorched down through a cloudless sky above, beneath the dense canopy of trees, the day resembled twilight. This was the night riders' element, not his. The outlaws had spent their lives traversing these hills and bottoms. If they attacked here, he faced slim odds. It would be at least six on three and the bandits had the high ground.

Douglas strained his eyes and ears, looking and listening for something, maybe movement or a twig cracking. Did he see something? He removed his pistol from his holster and held it up, barrel toward the sky. Then he saw the red flash fifty steps up the hill, even before he heard the gun's report. "Into that ditch!" he yelled.

As the roar of gunfire exploded, Douglas wheeled his horse around and raced thirty paces to the deep ditch's bank, the other horses behind him. He pulled back on his reins and jumped from his horse, landing on his stomach in the ditch. The air now full of deafening muzzle blasts, he lurched up the steep bank, peeking his head slightly out of the ditch as he raised his pistol and returned fire.

Basil and Huff did likewise. The gunfire came from both sides of the road, the bullets splashing into the turf and trees around them. Douglas tried to gather his senses. Visibility was terrible in all directions. Fretfully, he saw nothing to get a good aim at. The angry bullets landed everywhere, almost randomly. The bandits had as little to shoot at as they did. They'd be lucky to hit Douglas's party from where they were.

Huff and Basil both scattered along the ditch, twenty feet away. Basil fired two pistols, one in each hand. Unlike Douglas, the gunfighter didn't fire haphazardly into the trees, but waited until he saw a flicker before shooting, each pistol firing in sequence and carefully aimed. Douglas looked for the horses, now scattered off the road. "Where's Garrett?"

"Don't know," Basil replied, firing two quick shots into the trees.

"What do you mean, you don't know?" Douglas yelled back as he slid down into the cover of the ditch to reload his pistol.

"I took just about as much notice of him as you did when the lead started flying."

In the bottom of the ditch, Douglas hunched low and scurried to Basil. He shuffled up the ditch bank beside him to look around. Thirty yards away, Huff still recklessly fired his rifle into the woods. "When we unassed, Garrett must of made for the woods instead of the ditch." Douglas fired three more shots up the hill, more in anger than anything else. "Hell, we've lost him, for good."

"It's not all bad," Basil said. "The firing is easing

off. We might get out of here with our hides. Maybe we even got lucky and got one."

Douglas squatted in the ditch. Around him, the zinging bullets died off. How could this be? Just yesterday, he thought he had a leg up on the bandits.

"No sense in scheming," Basil said, still studying the trees. "Ain't nothing we can do about it now. They're hightailing. I hear their horses running."

"We're going after them," Douglas replied.

"No way, seven on three, at least," Basil said. "Now's not the time."

"I don't care."

Basil squinted and frowned. "I'm sure they're headed back the way we came. If we hurry along, we can get to Lookout before they cross Gum Creek. We can get a shot at them there, but it'll be a long shot, a quarter mile. But we'll have the sun at our back."

Douglas stood. "Huff, fetch the horses, fast. Dump the judge in the bushes. We'll pick him up when we pass back through here. Let's go."

Fifteen minutes later, the three soldiers lay prone on their stomachs, staring down at a wide valley. His elbows resting on his saddle, removed from his horse, Douglas looked through his field glasses into the impregnable forest. At two places, three hundred feet below and almost a quarter-mile distant, the trail sliced through the trees, just an orange thread cutting through the jade background. From atop the prominent hill, he saw ten miles in all directions, a peaceful green blanket of rolling hills and ridges. The sun, still high, brightened the wonderful venue like a portrait, one of the few lovely, serene sights he had ever seen in this area. A small, intermittent breeze slid over the hill, poking up in the sky, cooling his sweaty body.

Beside him, Basil and Huff also scanned the valley. Douglas handed his glasses to Basil. "We'll probably only have a few seconds before they break for cover." He moved his rifle up onto the saddle and aimed it at the trail. "From here, the bullets will land around them before they ever hear the shots."

Basil handed the glasses to Huff, and now adjusted the sights on his rifle's long scope.

Douglas had never seen a rifle like it. It had foreign words, probably French, carved on the barrel, and loaded a single paper cartridge via a bolt. "We're going to see if you're worth all that gold we paid you." He chuckled. "We'll scare the hell out of them if nothing else. Let them know that we're here to stay."

"We may do more than scare them," Basil replied, resting his cheek on the rifle's stock and adjusting his saddle to ensure he had a solid stand. He put his eye to the scope. "Wish that breeze would settle down. You boys need to aim at least a couple of horse lengths high."

Douglas picked up his glasses, studying the area where the road came out from under the trees. With the sun over his shoulder, he might get a glimpse, a reflection off some shiny metal. A few minutes passed. Then Douglas's heart skipped a beat. Two horses emerged on the road, then five more. "Has to be them," he mumbled, staring through his glasses. From this distance he saw only hats and horses, no details.

"When they move into that next opening," Basil said softly, "I shoot first, then you two open up."

Heart racing, Douglas looked down the barrel of his Henry. The horses reappeared—a second's pause before Basil's single shot cut through the pristine air on the hill. He thought he saw a horse fall as he opened fire, he and Huff sending three rounds each into the tiny opening in the trees, rapidly working their levers between shots.

Basil fired a second shot, but as Douglas turned back to the valley, he saw nothing, the only movement a horse lying in the road.

"Think we got anybody?" Douglas asked.

"Doubt it," Basil replied. "Just scared the shit out of whoever was riding that horse I shot."

Douglas shook his head. They had no one to bring in. Though they had killed the one Dallon boy two nights earlier, a family, one of his soldiers, and the judge had all been murdered. He had few leads or ideas, and the bandits had sent a stern message by burning the courthouse.

He didn't know what to do. He finally reckoned he needed to get back to the safety of town and regroup. Maybe he could come up with some new ideas, a plan that would work? He exhaled a long breath. What he really needed was more troops to have any real chance of subduing the clans. He pondered the letter he'd written Colonel James.

Maybe he'd get a couple of squads in a few weeks. "We'll wait here a couple hours, then go down and take a look before we go. Then see if we got anybody back at the bridge. No sense getting in a hurry. I don't want to get back to Natchitoches before dark. I'm sure the papers published the news we killed one of the Dallons and brought Francis Garrett into Winnfield. Word's probably also gotten back about the courthouse burning. We don't want to ride into town without Francis Garrett and with a dead judge. We'll look incompetent, at best."

13

At the end of a two-acre pecan orchard, the stately priest said a few words from his leather-bound bible as the small congregation, almost twenty people all dressed in black, stood around the wooden coffin. To the west, the late-day sun burned down through a cloudless, clear Louisiana sky. Ten tombstones filled the little Butler cemetery. Behind it, the Butler mansion, two stories of red brick fronted with a porch and tall, cylindrical columns, stood grand, but worn. Off in the distance, behind the house a few hundred yards, stood the now abandoned slave cabins. At the other end of the small grove, a flock of blackbirds, thousands in number, darted between the trees squawking all kinds of frenzied calls. The unruly racket hovering over the funeral seemed to mimic what lay out of sight.

A bereaved Hannah sat adjacent to the coffin, in a chair, crying into a lace handkerchief. She had said a few words that constituted a eulogy. Her mother and sister, in New Orleans, had probably not even gotten word of the recent events. The judge had few friends or family in town. A dozen of the town's influential citizens stood in attendance, about half Northerners, and three leaders from the black community. The judge was lucky; at least he had a funeral. Private O'Neal would never be afforded as much, his body likely never to reappear.

Two days had passed since the army patrol had made it back to Natchitoches. Despite lengthy investigations at both sites where Douglas and his party had engaged the bandits, they had found not even a trace of blood. Back in town, Douglas had tried to disguise the judge's death as natural, but the local papers had gotten a whiff of the real events, probably from the bandits, and ran a story that suggested someone had killed the judge, likely in self-defense as he had tried to administer some personal justice. The news had traumatized the residents, leaving Douglas unsure of how they felt. Most were simply awestruck at the series of events. In town, he only got reticent stares.

Douglas smelled the fresh dirt of the grave as the preacher consummated the service with a psalm. "Surely goodness and love will follow me all the days of my life, and I will dwell in the house of the Lord forever."

Those in attendance reverently walked by the casket, passing condolences to Hannah. Douglas turned away, still shaken and completely at a loss for his subsequent course of action. In the last week he had lost considerable ground to his foes. He felt a soft touch on his shoulder and turned to see Cyrus Carter, the Freedmen's Bureau's onetime agent in the parish.

The Indianan and decorated ex-Union officer now owned a hardware store in town, selling goods to the freed slaves and other sharecroppers. His business had been so successful, he had recently brought his brother down and purchased an abandoned plantation. He planned to bring the rest of his family down the following spring. In his late forties, his hair had now grayed over his aging face. He carried a tired charisma and honest blue eyes to go with his slim, lanky frame. Notwithstanding his appearance to the contrary, Cyrus was a warrior, every ounce of his body and soul dedicated to espousing Northern doctrine. He was one of the few in the area who fought and pursued the region's forces of darkness, often at gunpoint. It was no secret that these same elements had him on a short list of people to root out of Louisiana, one way or the other.

"You have to do something about this," Cyrus said. "We can't just let these ex-Confederates hold sway over everyone."

"I plan to," Douglas replied. "But not until I'm ready. I sent a telegraph to headquarters today. The army won't be pleased with all of this. I'll likely get some more troops, but we have to do this right. I may finally get the army on our side. I've been thinking this over. For the first time, some of the guerrillas have crossed the line. If we're smart, we can use this to get some of our other enemies, the political bosses, the ones we've been chasing for years. We need to catch a few alive, put them on trial. We might get them to turn on each other. If nothing else, get their deeds out in the open. That will send a powerful message, make them fear more occupation, especially under the new Grant administration. There's plenty of people who benefit from Northern rule, they're just too scared to come out in the open in support of it. We've got to let them know the current situation will not be tolerated, and we'll not just win the battle, but the war."

"I've got an uneasy feeling in my gut," Cyrus said. "That all sounds hypothetical. A sword for a sword is all that I've ever seen work here, all they heel to, but I'll ride with you. You know that. These bastards don't scare me." Cyrus's voice got somber and serious. He put a hand to his chin and deliberated for a few seconds. "There's a planter, across the river in the delta, Hiram Vaughn. Why don't you go see him? I hear he may be sympathetic to your cause."

Douglas thought over the proposition briefly. He didn't like it. "I'm not sure that's a good idea. Until I get it sorted out, I don't trust anybody around here."

"I want you to go see Senator Dunn, tomorrow evening. See if he can help. I've already arranged it, six in the evening. I've told him you'll be there."

Late that night Douglas lay in Hannah's bed, eyes wide open and unable to sleep. In her state of grieving, she had completely given herself to him, completely abandoning her concerns for place, protocol, and setting. The two had made passionate love for almost an hour. Their first intimate experience had been more intoxicating, more soothing than he had ever imagined, relaxing his tense psyche into something more like a young boy's, but he had been unable to sleep, the recent events reinitiating his gruesome nightmares from the war that besieged his nights. Combining everything, his mood raced up and down, from bliss to torment.

He looked at Hannah, asleep on her side beside him, her soft frame slowly rising and falling with her long breaths. He looked up at the tall ceilings, at least twelve feet high. Like most of the affluent houses, it was wonderfully airy. If Hannah's father hadn't rolled over in his grave yet, he surely now reeled as the Yankee soldier lay unclothed, unwed, with his daughter in his house. He hoped the killing of Judge Butler had put Hannah firmly and openly in his camp.

Douglas's worries refused to free his mind, allow him to slip into peaceful sleep. Above all the murders, the guilty going free, he feared failure the most. He had rarely failed at anything he put his heart into, but failures in the army were the worst kind, public failures, known by all: his superiors, his subordinates, often even made public through a demotion or transfer, or leaked to the newspapers.

In the last few weeks he had killed two of the clan, but two of his men had also died. Those may have been acceptable losses in the war, but not here where his enemies outnumbered him thirty, possibly fifty to one, if not more. Worse, his domain had gotten more lawless and dangerous in these past few weeks. His authority and control over the masses would not survive much more of this.

He lifted the mosquito netting hanging over the large double bed and walked into the house's living room. On the wall, a painting of Colonel Butler, in his dress grays and cased by a wood frame, looked down on him. Outside, through a window, the insects droned around the century-old estate. He looked down the long line of tall oaks and magnolias abutting the house's gravel drive, fantastically lit by the half-moon and starlight. From the window, he saw the impressive buildings of the plantation: blacksmith's shop, barn and corral, scales, and large mess hall, now all but dormant. He felt lonely, he and Hannah alone within these aged pine walls, and he walked back into the bedroom.

"Come back to bed," Hannah whispered.

Douglas turned to see the sheets stirring, Hannah leaning up. He walked back to her and sat on the bed. Just her waking caused the room to come alive with her radiance. The starlight, filtering through the window, lit her firm, white anatomy. "I figured you were too exhausted to wake."

Hannah grabbed his hand. "You look so troubled. I'm here for you now."

"What are your sister and mother doing in New Orleans?"

"Business." Hannah sat up in bed, leaning against the headboard. "They've found someone to buy half the plantation. Enough to pay off the debts. The sharecropping hasn't earned anything the last two years. Since the war, we've had nothing but floods, droughts, an endless invasion of caterpillars, cholera, and yellow fever . . . this land's cursed. The price of cotton is sky high, but there's nobody to loan money, only a line of Northern capitalists buying in cheap. It's terrible."

Douglas felt Hannah's hand as she reached over and touched his chest. He got the feeling that she had a hunger for affection, a soul mate, someone to confide in, a hunger that matched his own needs.

"Sister and Mother are also having a meeting with a man, someone who knows farming, an ex-planter. They're going to hire him to run the half of the farm we keep. My sister and mother are dreadful at it, and negotiating with the freedmen. Supposedly, this man has gotten several other fallow farms profitable since the war. Now, what's got you so worried?"

"Everything. I haven't done much to bring these animals to justice. They could storm in here right now and kill both of us. Ride off into the night. Nothing would ever come of it. There wouldn't even be a trial. They'd throw us in the Cane River and be done with us."

"Doubtful they would storm the house of a Confederate hero like my father. And you might shoot back. If word got out, it wouldn't be good for them."

"That's it, only a dead man's honor is protecting me."

"What are you going to do?"

"I got a warrant issued for Francis Garrett. He'll be on a poster on every Federal building for two hundred miles. I've also asked for more troops. Don't know if I'll get them. If I do, it will probably be several weeks before they arrive."

Hannah sat up straight and some color returned to her face. "What do you mean, you don't know if you'll get them? They killed a Federal judge and a soldier, not to mention they burned down the court-house."

"We don't know that they burned the court-house. And nobody knows who killed the judge. In a practical matter, there aren't that many troops in the state, barely enough to police the cities. This isn't the only place where transgressions occur. There's less than a thousand Union soldiers in Louisiana, down from almost ten thousand the year after the war."

"Didn't President Grant get elected supporting the Republican Reconstruction platform? He knows the problems here. Phil Sheridan was the military general of Louisiana just a few years ago."

Douglas sighed a long breath. "There's no new troops coming south, not large numbers or new divisions. The country's tired of war, sending its treasure and sons to sort out this vile land, and so is Congress. Even the Northern press is tired of barking the same old tune. The call now is to re-unite the Union and move on. They've all but decided to just let all this be handled locally, by the states, without Federal intervention. It's sad, but true. The North thinks they've done enough. Even so, I may get some additional troops, probably from New Orleans. General Mower's not going to tolerate the shooting of a judge, under any circumstances. Probably get a new judge, too. We'll see. I've sent for some more resources, money. We will sort this out, subjugate these outlaws, I have no doubt, but we have to do it with fortitude, resilience, and the resources we have now."

"How's your pistol man, Basil, working out?"

"All right. Does pretty much what I tell him and is very competent at gun work, though he shoots the hell out of everything and asks questions later. He's really strange in a way. Doesn't seem to care for anything, just what he's paid for. Very empty inside. Spends his time sinning. Wrong or right doesn't matter to him. He's almost like a ghost. I've tried to understand him, but maybe there's nothing to understand."

Hannah massaged Douglas's shoulders. "And your black soldier?"

"Similar in a way. Good soldier. But just the opposite within. Brewing with a disgust at the old order and keen to right it." Douglas paused. "Maybe I can initiate some infighting, turn the bandits against themselves. It would help if I could get the local papers on my side." Douglas brushed the back of his hand across Hannah's cheek and smiled. "That young man that owns the local paper is one of your admirers who can't stand your fondness for me." Douglas put his arms around Hannah, pulling her close in a warm embrace.

Hannah smiled playfully. "You didn't expect

courting a good woman such as I would be without sacrifice, did you?"

Douglas lay down on his side. He cleared his throat. "Is it true that you have a brother and sister by two of your father's slave girls?"

"Yes," Hannah said, remaining still and not looking at Douglas. "My family has plenty of its own sins. This land wasn't as tranquil and heavenly as many believe."

"What happened to them?"

"Father sent them all away, mothers and children. Nobody knows where. Mother made sure of that."

"Ever wonder about them—want to meet them?"

"I wondered where they went at the time, but no, I don't want them back." Hannah's voice carried no emotion. "My family has suffered enough. It would bring disgrace on us. I know some Northerners would look down on that, but I can't help it. It's the way I feel. Doesn't really matter. It would be almost impossible to find them. Who knows if they even survived the war? Maybe they'll show up here one day."

Douglas turned onto his back. The grand estate around him made him feel small and out of place. Certainly, it once brimmed with life and activity. How much Hannah had lost. Her once pampered and lavish lifestyle of society balls had vanished forever. She hadn't created the world around her. She had only been born into it. He realized that unlike his family, the Northerners, she had lost much, much more than they had. The war had not been a transient interlude, but a permanent ordeal. He stroked her hair a few times. "You know a man named Hiram Vaughn?"

"Yes, a large planter. One of the few back on his feet. He's done very well since the war. Why?"

"Cyrus Carter recommended I go see him. He might be able to help me quell these gangs."

"Maybe. Some say he survived the war by secretly selling provisions to the Federal Army. If that's so, it might make him more helpful. On the other hand, it may make him more adversarial. Hating the Yank to cover his sins. I always thought him an opportunist, but nobody around here has more to lose if the current order gets tilted."

"Cyrus says he wants to ride with me, help hunt the judge's killers. Not sure that's what I want, but I don't have any choice. He'll storm in there and shoot everybody and everything up. He's also arranged a meeting between me and Senator Dunn tomorrow at six in the evening. You want to go with me? Aren't you a favorite of the senator's?"

"Yes, I'll go. It's a lovely ride out to his place. I don't like Cyrus. His ways aren't effective. He stirs up too many people." Hannah paused before continuing, changing her tone to a more serious nature. "The judge was right. You can't just kill these bandits. You'll have to subdue them through legal means. If you just murder them, more will materialize. I know these people. If you show them disobedience of the law will not be tolerated, that there's a government here that upholds the law, they will change. Just killing them will only quell the short-term problem. With that method, it will take fifty years for civility to take hold here."

Douglas pulled Hannah closer to him. He slid one of his legs between hers. She was right, but these details made his job that much more cumbersome. He closed his eyes, trying to fall asleep, and put these thoughts off until tomorrow.

14

The heir to a long line of cotton planters, State Senator Marshall Dunn owned the largest estate in the region. It had been in his family for more than a century. Before the war, he had operated the leading and most successful plantation in Winn Parish, worked by several hundred slaves. His large farming and ginning complex sat on a bend in the Red River, on nearly three thousand acres, some of Louisiana's richest soil.

At the end of hostilities, he had been one of the first of the planter class in the region to "swallow the dog," as the locals said, and swear his allegiance to the Union. He had even taken up the Republican cause and been elected to the State Senate, primarily with the support of black voters.

Hannah and Douglas had been riding for almost an hour when they topped a one-hundred-foot ridge to see the vast Dunn Plantation, resting like a portrait in the alluvial valley below, the Red River in the distance. The scene stood wonderful, the fields lying over the land like a checkerboard, the straight ditch lines and roads bisecting them. A half-mile ahead along the ridge, above the annual high water, the plantation headquarters glistened in the late-day sun.

Douglas had stopped to point out a panther lying in the grass below and a hundred yards away, his six-foot-long, golden body visible in the grass only from above. "We better get going," he whispered to Hannah.

"He's so beautiful," Hannah said, handing Douglas his field glasses.

"We're going to be late," Douglas said, exhorting his horse along. "What do you know about Senator Dunn?"

"I've known him since I was a kid. He only recently took over the Dunn plantation. His parents both fled during the war. Took their money and moved somewhere up North, Philadelphia I think. You know Mr. Dunn keeps a common-law Negro wife—a son by her, too." Hannah pulled abreast of Douglas.

"I've heard. Only met the man twice, in town." The two rode under a brick arch that led down a short road to a large residence. The Dunn house, though large, wasn't gaudy. Single-storied, it had plain wood siding and a small porch, giving it a more practical, mundane, and working appearance as opposed to many of the more grandiose residences in the area. Unlike many of the plantation homes, only the stables and carriage house stood near the manse, but the vast farm enveloping the headquarters' grounds added to the magnificence. The two rode past a noisy chicken pen and an elderly black man standing beside the drive, sucking on a mouthful of snuff.

Douglas pulled back on his reins at a hitching post in front of the house. On the porch stood three men: Cyrus Carter, Senator Dunn, and Juba Sampson, the latter the black commander of a local colored regiment of the Louisiana State Militia.

Douglas tipped his hat. "Good evening, gentlemen. I'm assuming all three of you know Miss Butler."

Hannah tipped her own hat, grabbed Douglas's hand, and got off her horse. As she did, Douglas inspected the three men again. They couldn't have been more different. Cyrus was a Northerner, educated, well dressed, and more a trained soldier than anything else. Marshall Dunn, in his mid-forties, was disgustingly overweight, almost bald, and walked with a severe limp that required a cane and had prevented him from serving in the Confederate Army. The third man, Captain Juba Sampson, today wore his uniform, almost identical to Union Army standard issues. He was a literate ex-slave, and Douglas regarded him as nothing more than a hired gunslinger in the mold of Basil.

The Louisiana State Militia wasn't a real army or police force. It had been formed by the Northern governor, Henry Clay Warmoth, not to fight, but to protect freedmen and unionists, most notably during elections or exercises in the democratic process. It was there to prop up and protect the foreign Republican government. The black regiments were forbidden from drilling in public and conducting any exercises at all unless ordered by the governor. Juba's regiment of seventy or so men represented the militia's only presence in the four-parish area.

Douglas knew that Juba interpreted his orders rather liberally. In fact, the militia captain often employed clan tactics, riding during the night with his government-sanctioned posse administering his own form of justice. He also knew none of these men had a chance of surviving a brawl with the locals. It meant certain annihilation. Even where troops were abundant, it took the army and all its resources just to keep the bandits at bay. But Juba was unrepentant. Like many blacks, he distrusted most whites, and Douglas thought he was reckless and his ambition exceeded his brains. The Negro commander had become hypnotized by his new power over his former masters. Douglas identified with the danger of this. During the war, he had seen many Federal officers, most good men, become spellbound with their newfound power. In the end, this intoxication led to an infallible self-righteousness that oftentimes resulted in merciless and unjust deeds, the officers becoming callous to death and never wanting to give up the struggle, or relinquish their authority.

Senator Dunn asked, "When's General Grant and

the army going to send us some more troops to keep the peace?"

"Don't know," Douglas replied, tying his reins. He turned to Cyrus and Juba. "Wasn't expecting the entire government contingent here."

"Let's go inside," the senator said. "Have some tea and talk politics."

Juba stepped forward. He looked at Douglas, then Hannah before speaking in a deep, domineering voice. "No offense, but not sure I want to talk about anything in front of the daughter of a Confederate colonel."

"If you're going to talk to *me*, you're going to talk to *her*," Douglas responded.

"The death of Hannah's uncle is a tragedy," Senator Dunn continued, chaperoning the four into his spacious kitchen. "But there's no need for us to do anything rash or uncalled for. We should find and punish the perpetrators, lawfully. There's no need for us to do any more. I've always maintained we should stay above that. Time is the only thing that will mend this area, make it conform to the new conventions of the world, and time will do it without bloodshed. It's the only thing that will work."

"That time may be after we're dead," Cyrus snapped. "The way things are going, that time for us may not be much more than the judge's. I'm not going to wait around to be slaughtered."

"Me either," Juba said.

Senator Dunn sat down at the large wooden table

in the kitchen, gesturing for everyone else to do likewise. "You can't fight these people, collectively. These men are warriors, born in battle. The army never defeated them. They're more proficient, organized, and motivated than the worst Apaches or Comanches Captain Owens's army is sparring with out west. And more numerous. They've got iron nerves, and aren't going anywhere. You can't run them off. You'd have to exterminate them . . . an impractical task."

"You've got a higher assessment of these no-account bastards than objective analysis merits," Cyrus said, continuing to stand. His voice rose. "We can't continue to let them run roughshod over us!"

An elderly black woman entered the room and set a tray with a pitcher and five glasses on the table. Not getting any instructions from the senator, she turned and left the kitchen.

"These mysterious masked men have visited me a few times," the senator said. "Told me to leave, go somewhere else, threatened me. They don't scare me."

"You may be able to be a little more brash than me," Cyrus said. "You employ or provide for fifteen percent of the parish, in some form. It's a little harder to get rid of you than me."

Douglas sat down and motioned for Hannah to join him at the table. He looked at the large kitchen, the dozens of pots hanging over the wood-stove. "I've requested more troops, will probably get some. I'm going after these outlaws with everything I can muster, going to catch them and try them in a Federal court. Anybody who wants to ride with me can be deputized and join the hunt. But we're going to do this all under army regs. I'm here to ask for your help. To see if you know of any men who might join me, or if you can get the governor to send up some more state militia, that would be helpful." Douglas paused. He turned to Juba. "I don't want your militia unless it's been ordered to help. No offense, but I don't want any black troops unless they're enlisted soldiers in the army or ordered here by the governor."

Douglas hadn't wanted to make this last statement. He had thought about it for a while, and how to say it. Weeks before he had determined it. Negro troops incited the local population. Negro troops enlisted in the army and sent here by someone far away was one thing, but raising a local army of local Negro men was an entirely different matter, not likely to be well received by anybody. It would only make his job harder. He continued to look at Juba. "I'm just trying to get a job done properly, the only way I think I can get it done."

"You can swear me in now," Cyrus said.

"I'll have it telegraphed off tomorrow," Douglas added.

"I'll ask around," Senator Dunn said, "see if anybody wants to help. I should be able to find a few good men to ride with you."

Juba slowly, meticulously put on his hat. "I can see

my trip over here was a waste of time. I don't give a shit whether you want me. I've got plenty of the Lord's work to do already. I won't be staying for tea." The captain turned on his heels and made for the door.

15

The next afternoon, Douglas sat in his office looking down at the telegraph he had carefully drafted that morning, reading over it silently.

To: Assistant Adjutant General
Headquarters, Western District of Louisiana
New Orleans, La.

Colonel M. J. James:

In reference to the events I recently reported to you by a brief telegraph regarding the death of Judge Butler, and knowing that correspondence was hurriedly transcribed due to the nature of events hereabouts, I now realize I did not properly paint a picture of events here. Based on this, I am forwarding the following request. It should be assumed that forces opposed to the army and its goals in this area read all correspondence transmitted to and from this district.

It is likely that the forces responsible for Judge Butler's unfortunate demise are allied with the white political elements that have, in recent years, demonstrated a propensity for violence in an attempt to influence the electoral process. Stating the previous, and knowing what elements of our government Judge Butler represents, it is imperative that all resources at our disposal be sent here with all possible haste. In an earlier telegraph, I requested two squads of cavalry. Though I still maintain that request, additional troops may be required to reestablish civil authority in the Red River parishes. It is my opinion that if larger units of infantry and cavalry can be mustered here, not from New Orleans, but from other places in the country, and openly directed here by the highest authorities in Washington, a firm message will be conveyed to all citizens, without regard to political loyalty, that peace and stability will be achieved at all cost. Such an action would no doubt forestall further bloodshed and go a long way to achieving the army and government's larger goals in the state. I look forward to your response at the earliest possible date.

I am, very respectfully, your obedient servant,

Captain Douglas Owens,
Commander, Company D, 4th United States Cavalry

Douglas folded up the paper and looked through a stack of newspapers that had arrived that morning by steamer. He skimmed over a few headlines, reading them aloud to Huff, sitting beside him. "They are calling it Black Friday in New York. Nothing to do with Negroes. Jay Gould, a very rich man, and his partner have tried to buy all the gold in the United States. They say it may cause an economic collapse."

"Any news I should care about?" Huff said.

Douglas scanned the headlines. "Yeah, President Grant appointed the first Negro ambassador in American history to Haiti, that's a country in the sea off Florida that's mostly colored. And the first train arrived in San Francisco. The Transcontinental Railroad is complete. A man can now cross the whole country from sea to sea in six days."

Huff picked up the paper and looked at a hand-drawn image of the train.

"Huff, why don't you go see that lady who's teaching the Negro kids to read. I can have the army pay for it. I'll just get the cost lost in the shuffle somewhere."

"I's too old to learn all that stuff in 'em books."

Basil walked in the room and fumbled through the mail until he found the New Orleans paper. He sat down, propped his boots on the table, and opened the daily. "Now the damn women want the right to vote, they've formed a suffrage association. Give these niggers the right to vote and the whole system gets turned upside down. God damn, won't be long before I have to go to Mexico to have a good time."

Huff looked at Basil, then slowly stood and walked off.

Douglas flashed his gaze at Huff and then Basil, lowering the paper. "Florida's passed the Fifteenth Amendment. That's enough with the Yankee states. Everybody will be able to vote soon, like it or not."

"Yeah, I know, and Grant's about to let Virginia back in the Union too." Basil coughed hard a few times and looked over his paper at Douglas. "I don't know why you read that Yankee paper. It's got no relevance down here. Like reading a paper from France."

"That cough's getting bad. I want you to go see the doctor. I may need you."

"What you been up to all morning?"

"Just gathering forces, trying to formulate my plan. I'm waiting on a telegraph from Shreveport today that may help my cause, and then I want to go over it with you. . . . I got a tip that the local Tax-payers' League is meeting in secret tonight, out on a farm near Alligator Bayou. Get some rest this afternoon. We're going out there tonight and see what transpires at those meetings. There's a special election here in a few weeks to replace a local Republican State Representative, an elderly Negro preacher, who died a month or so ago. The Democrats are probably gearing up for the election."

Basil lit a cigarette. "Who killed him?"

"Nobody, died of natural causes. We investigated it. He just fell over dead at the dinner table one night."

"Any sign of Francis Garrett?"

Douglas lifted a piece of paper off the table and handed it to Basil. "None. Got a Federal warrant for him."

"He's gone to Texas, I suppose."

"You hear anything lately?"

"Not much, other than the whore I've taken up with is Sheriff Thaxton's favorite. Don't suspect he's too pleased with the fact she's now with me."

"Any news in that Reb paper?"

"Yeah, looks like the army and Republicans got Bob Lee over in East Texas. This Major Chaffee and his local posse of unionists must be a lot of mean, determined sons-a-bitches. I ran with some of those boys back in the war. They're as tough as nails, and fine Southern gentlemen, though apparently not conforming to the new ways of the world."

Douglas set down his paper. "What's with you, Basil? You used to do the Rebs' bidding, and now you're working for us. I hear you've been up in Arkansas working for Governor Powell."

"He's a sorry lot. I work for whoever can pay me. Used to be the Rebs, but now you're the only ones with money. But the radicals up in Arkansas have pert' near licked the clans. They got a firmer hand on the situation. They're better organized, got better government men."

Douglas frowned at Basil and rolled his eyes. "Whipping a bunch of hillbillies is a tad easier than whipping these Louisiana boys."

"You city boys don't have the stomach for this fight, any of it in the long haul."

"Bullshit," Douglas said. "That's what you all

said during the war. General Grant's no President Johnson. He's got the stomach for it. He licked the Confederate armies." Douglas raised the paper. "He's decided to do something about the troubles in South Carolina. He'll put those bushwhackers where they belong, in a jail somewhere."

"Yeah, yeah. It's not General Grant. It's the Northern people. This isn't the war when they were fighting to save the Union. They're not prepared to spend a bunch of blood and treasure for the sake of these niggers and you know it. Y'all are no different than us, just far enough away to lecture us. You don't know this because the Northern papers never say it, but the Northern business bosses, the bankers, shipping houses, and mills need this cotton. It's still the country's biggest export. These people down here ain't no dummies. The slaves and land constituted most of their wealth. You've taken one and are buying up the other. This is a fight for survival and self-preservation as they see it. They are not going to allow themselves to be a political minority, no matter what Congress and the Constitution says. You may win this battle, but y'all will lose this struggle. You ain't got the grit for the fight. The war's been won; you prepared to die for the political and social equality of the freedman?"

Douglas pondered the question briefly, his heart pattering faster, his forehead getting hot. He leaned back in his chair and let out a long breath. "Well, you still haven't answered my original question."

Basil set down the paper, lowering his feet. "Professionally, I don't have an opinion. I go to the highest bidder. But personally, I'm an Old South man. There, everybody knew their place. Before the war I was a patty-roller, a damn good one too. Now, I'm just like the cotton baron and whore, a slave to the dollar, but all this ruckus is good for business." Basil coughed again and lit a cigar. "What you got planned for the afternoon?"

"Going to take Hannah for a walk."

"You better step light with that. These boys down here don't take much to the thought of you dipping your wick in that. You're going to make this personal instead of just a job." Basil chuckled. "That must be some good stuff she's slappin' on you."

"You don't need to talk about that, or make those types of remarks."

"I know all about these Southern belles. Back in the day, word was that these pretty, dressed-up plantation gals were the best when unleashed from all their social controls. Maybe your General Grant did do us a favor getting rid of most of those standards of womanhood."

"You don't know any such thing."

"Frankly, sir, I'm only speaking from personal experience, not hearsay."

Douglas stood and walked off. "Go see the doctor. I mean it."

Lying prone, Douglas peeked through the thick brush, down to a barn, only a wood roof supported by six columns. The night was black, the moon not up, and only a sprinkling of starlight filtering through the thick pines. The gold flickering of several torches in the barn danced through the thick, balmy air.

Douglas cupped his right ear, listening attentively to the muffled sounds of casual conversation trickling from under the roof. He focused his gaze, but from his vantage point, all the barn's occupants, twenty or thirty he figured, were hidden from view under the roof. All he had seen thus far was an occasional figure step to the edge of the barn to relieve himself. Four of the locals' deadly needle guns leaned on one of the columns, reminding Douglas of what might be in store if he were discovered.

The Northwest Louisiana Chapter of the Taxpayers' League was a political club, officially advocating anti-suffrage and almost anything anti-Northern, or as Douglas believed, the political wing of the local clans. The club's meetings were often held in secret, but Cyrus had tipped him off about this meeting at a farmhouse a few miles out of town.

Cyrus had said the meeting would start at ten, but Douglas had now been hiding in the thicket for what seemed like thirty minutes. So far, the meeting looked to be nothing more than a social gathering.

As Douglas scouted the area for a better observation point, the collective babbling finally waned, and a loud, coarse voice ripped through the night. "The hour of redemption is at hand. We will never submit to Negro rule, or this tyrannical punishment by the radicals while they line their pockets off our backs. The rule of the Republicans, and the ignorant and vengeful Negro, will end. We will reassert the natural course, reestablish the difference in the races created by God, peacefully if we can, but forcibly if we must. I say white rule now and forever. I've had enough of this lunacy, educating the darkies. White rule for Louisiana today, forever. We will never submit."

The fire-eating man's voice rose to a crescendo, paused briefly, and continued. "We will purge this state of the thieves and plunderers, dreamers and idealists, and put Mr. Nigger, who helps them, in his rightful place."

"Down with the scheming radicals," someone yelled. "Let's get rid of these rabble-raising Northern schemers for good."

Another deep voice shouted, "By God, I want to whip Cyrus Carter, and that uppity Juba Sampson. I mean I want to whip 'em, like a young insolent nigger buck. Feel the whip tear into them until my arm cramps. Hear their cowardly screams. I want to do it. God damn I want it." The man grunted. "I'm getting dizzy with joy just visualizing it."

"Settle down, Junior," the first voice said. "You'll get your chance in due time. We're here tonight to talk about this upcoming election. How we win it. It's our instinctive urge for self-preservation that will lead us to victory. It's our God-given right and duty, and we owe it to our heritage. We will not scruple about the means, and we will end these outrages forever. The proper order set down by Providence will prevail."

Douglas felt his heart patter wildly. His stomach tumbled with a nervous twinge, and two beads of sweat ran down his cheek. He took a deep breath and looked over his shoulder. If the clans wanted to get him, finding him here, like this, would exceed their grandest desires.

He exhaled a long breath, reminding himself that Basil was just down the hill, guarding his rear with the horses ready. He fought off an urge to slide back down the hill and hightail it back to the safety of town. Gathering his composure, he refocused his senses on the spectacle.

Another man now spoke, this one with a more educated, polished voice. His accent was distinctive, not the deep, long Southern drawl, but the quick, high cadence common to New Orleans, its European tone unique, and easily discernible. "We're going to give you all the support, the resources you need to win the election. It's only a small rural district, but it's the only state election in October. What happens here will carry weight. Winning it will send a message that we can again carry the state, that we haven't lost the will or grit that brought us victory in the Federal elections last fall."

Douglas moved some leaves to the side as he saw the bodies of a few men standing at the edge of the barn. He strained his hearing. Thus far, he had heard no voices he recognized, but he was certain many of the men in attendance were familiar foes. Again, a sense of anxiety raced over his body as he continued to listen.

"We will carry this election, but we need to remember not to do anything to arouse Federal attention, draw press, or give the reckless adventurers a reason to request more soldiers. We have to be smart. We need to be diligent, making sure we attend all the Republican meetings, always armed, and eyeing the scalawags and lazy, bad niggers who are stirring mischief. Yes, in this country, it is still legal to arm ourselves for protection. This show of force will frighten the feeble Negro. We will not let the white man be excluded from the political process."

A few yells came from the crowd.

The speaker continued. "We do not want violence, and it is not our purpose to harm or harass the radicals or Negroes; the latter can be our ally. Our goal is to obtain an electoral majority. If our most effective tactics are required, it is very, very important that they not be employed until a few days before the election, when it will be too late to call in Federal troops from New Orleans or Shreveport. When the time is right, we need to focus on the bad apples, those obstructing progress. Cut the head off the snake, and the majority of the uneducated niggers will become docile."

"I can do that," a voice yelled.

The speaker continued. "As much as we lament violence, it may be necessary. When the army leaves, we have won forever. This is very important. Remember it. Any force needs to have a pretense of self-defense, or a personal feud, never giving an inclination that we are an organized political entity. It's always best to avoid violence and intimidation in public or in daylight. There will be time for the just punishment of the radical."

Tiring of the rhetoric, Douglas finally relieved his

worrying heart, and carefully slid back into the bushes and down the hill. He crawled a hundred paces, before standing.

"Psst. Over here," Basil whispered.

Douglas came to his feet, feeling his way through the underbrush until Basil's silhouette came into view. "You see anybody back here?"

"Not even a possum. Been real quiet. How about you? You learn anything?"

"No, I was hoping to get some details, a tip, or something, particulars about some planned nefarious deeds, but it's just the standard political stuff. Nothing that would stand up to a jury, even up North. I know it's not any worry of yours, but it sounds like they're planning to make a real push in this election. They've got all their old tricks and trades planned."

Basil let out a muted chuckle. "Why shouldn't they? It's a free country." He raised his hand to muffle a cough.

Douglas flashed his eyes at Basil, his figure finally forming out of the black haze. "Figured that'd be your point of view. I want you to go to the doctor, first thing in the morning. I mean it."

"Well, I didn't sign on for politics. I made that clear to the colonel. I vote the Democratic ticket, when I vote. And I'm damn proud of it, too. . . .You ready to go?"

"Ain't hardly worth risking my hide like this just to hear the standard Democratic discourse I can read in the papers daily. There's some political bosses over there from New Orleans. These boys probably aren't too apt to discuss any details while they're here, but we're out of options. Let's just squat in the bush here. Maybe those bosses will get on back to town before long, and then I may ease back up there and do some more investigating. We might not get another chance like this for a while. At the very least, I may be able to catalog some faces when they break up. "

16

Mid-afternoon the next day, Douglas sat at his desk trying to finish his monthly paperwork. The most tedious task was reconciling the garrison's bills. The army quartermaster in Shreveport, an annoying little man with thick glasses, was a stickler for details. Douglas needed to get all the corrected paperwork on the next day's steamer so the government paymaster would keep his little outfit supplied and the local merchants content. As he re-added a long list of numbers on a bill of lading from the town's largest general store, a knock on his door broke his concentration.

"Come in."

Cyrus entered the office. "You called. . . . Find anything out at the Taxpayers' League meeting last night?"

Douglas motioned to one of the two chairs in front of his desk. He paused a second, putting a hand to his chin. "Yeah, those boys have got it in for you."

"That's news." Cyrus rolled his eyes.

"I'm serious." Douglas's tone got flat and direct as he focused his eyes at Cyrus. "I've heard them talk about you." He paused a few seconds. "Why don't you lay low for this election? Maybe go back up North. I'm sure you have some business that needs tending to. Go see your family."

Cyrus's voice rose. "You mean just give the election to the Democrats?" He pointed his finger at Douglas, his face tightening. "Now's not the time to capitulate. What we need is more help from the Federal government. I've written the governor three letters to explain our situation in the last month alone. I don't know why he can't do more. Why he isn't more determined with President Grant. Doesn't the Constitution guarantee equal protection under the law to all Americans? Can nothing be done?" Cyrus's voice grew more urgent. "Is there no protection available for us? Are we to be butchered? This is open rebellion against a freely elected government. Daily, we Republicans are being killed or drummed out of the state. There is no rule of law. Is the government powerless to protect us? Killing Negroes and unionists is not even a crime here. There hasn't been a single conviction, and the general public doesn't have the slightest inkling of remorse. To the contrary, the press openly calls for our murder. I can not fathom why we are left to fend for ourselves."

"I almost daily make requests for more troops."

"That's not enough." Cyrus stood. "This is not

what you or I fought four years for. I know you probably don't care if these Negroes vote, but what is a country that doesn't protect its citizens? I don't understand you, Douglas. You seem too apathetic. Maybe you've just been in the army too long. Death and injustice are routine. The war is over. You seem to only want to catch these outlaws, these vermin, because they're your enemy, and you have orders to bring them to justice. Don't you care for the bigger picture, the cause we fought for? These people's only crime is their color. Admittedly, they are ignorant and uneducated, but they can vote as intelligently as the poor whites. Should they be returned to a condition of slavery? Where is your righteous indignation? They have nothing to fight with. Why can't they be full citizens? I beg you to do more. Only the nation and the army can protect these people."

Douglas groaned, exhaling a long breath, the words and accusations ripping open the scars to his deep, internal differences and conflicting emotions. "It doesn't matter what I think. You know that. I can't make policy. I represent the collective will of the president and Congress. I'm doing all I can with the resources I have. You know the details. This all seems abstract to the Northern public. For every report of atrocities by the army, the Democrats flood Congress with reports that everything here is peaceful, that this is all overblown, sensationalism, only for the purpose of a Republican electoral majority for decades."

"Bullshit," Cyrus grunted.

"I'm a pragmatist. I have to be. This is a violent place." Douglas narrowed his eyes on Cyrus. "And that's not going to change anytime soon. Whether you like it or not, at some point, you and the Negroes will have to stand on your own, wean yourselves off the Federal government's protection. The president has to suspend the writ of habeas corpus for the army to simply make arrests. The Congress, the army, and the democracy will not allow that to go on indefinitely. You better sit down and come to grips with that reality."

Douglas stood and walked out from behind his desk. "Now I've got work to do, and plenty of problems myself." He put a hand on Cyrus's shoulder. "I'm going to do something, soon, some things that will make a difference. And I'm going to catch these outlaws, but I need you with me. Now, I've got to go. I will come by in a few days to go over some of my plans."

Thirty minutes later, Douglas looked down at Basil, lying in his bed at the Cotton Palace. In his underwear, he leaned back against the headboard. The room smelled of sweat, stale food, and tobacco. Beside the bed on the little nightstand sat two almost empty bottles of whiskey, a couple of newspapers, and one of Basil's pistols.

The doctor, an elderly fat man dressed in a gray suit, reached over and felt Basil's sweaty forehead with his palm. He then bent over and looked into the gunfighter's bloodshot eyes before putting his stethoscope on Basil's chest in several places, listening for a few seconds.

"Is he going to live?" Douglas inquired, turning to the doctor, his hands on his hips.

"Reckon," the doctor replied.

"What's wrong with him?"

"I get these spells every now and then." Basil coughed from the bed. "I'll be back on my feet in a few days."

"Probably consumption." The doctor turned to Douglas. "But he won't be back on his feet for a few days. 'Spec he's had it for years. These flare-ups occur periodically." The doctor turned back to Basil and picked up his little black leather bag. "A few days' rest. Drink plenty of water. Take a bath twice a day. Keep taking two of those calomel pills everyday. I'll be back to check on you in the morning. If you're not better in a few days, we'll bleed you."

Douglas walked the doctor to the door of the hotel room.

"On your way out, tell the barkeep to send me up another bottle of whiskey," Basil yelled grumpily from the bed. "Have Nancy bring it up."

"Thank you, Doctor," Douglas said, closing the door after the physician exited the room. Douglas put his ear to the door and eavesdropped to ensure the man had walked away. By now, he didn't trust anyone he didn't know. He turned to Basil with a slight smile. "You're lucky the Dallons and Garretts haven't stormed in here and shot you dead, laid up lame like this." He handed Basil a cup of coffee.

Basil grabbed one of the bottles beside the bed and poured some liquor into the coffee.

Douglas retrieved the bottle from Basil and turned it up, taking a large gulp. The brown alcohol slid down his throat, and a relaxing sensation draped over his body.

"Didn't think you was a drinking man."

"This place will turn anybody into a drinking man." Douglas finished the bottle with another big swig. He looked out the window briefly to the Red River, rumbling along, wide and deep, and then into the mysterious hills beyond. Little activity bustled on the street, only two elderly black men pushing a wheelbarrow loaded with fruit toward town. "How do you know Nancy's not Sheriff Thaxton's whore, and he's sent her to you on his behalf?"

Basil scoffed. "That old worn-out sheriff? Women adore pistol men, one of the benefits of the trade. And gunslingers know how to please women, make them obedient. I'm the best at all aspects."

Clearing his throat, Douglas turned back to Basil. "I've got seven hundred dollars in gold coming in two days, from Monroe. May use the money to put out some rewards, deputize a couple of US marshals. There's people around here, plenty of them, who want these highwaymen gone, even if they hate the army."

"I'd be careful. You may be paying your enemies. . . . Just hang around. They'll come after you to settle the score, sooner or later."

"Since you've got the undivided attention of the sheriff's whore, why don't you pass on this information? Have her let the good sheriff know there's seven hundred dollars in army gold headed here in two days. I'm sure somebody will want the loot, just to have it *and* to keep it out of my hands."

Basil coughed violently a couple of times and then wiped his perspiring forehead. "You're signing the death warrant of the carrier."

"I've ordered two men to bring the gold. I'm planning to meet up with them halfway here. I'll have Huff and Cyrus Carter with me. That'll give us five well-armed men. Maybe we can lure them into a gunfight. Of course, you shouldn't pass that latter information on."

"A shoot-out . . . I thought you wanted to bring these outlaws in front of a jury?"

"I do, and I will. You can rest assured of it, one way or the other. But we've only seen three commit a crime. You shot two of those, and the third got away. We won't shoot them all. Might catch another live one."

A soft knock on the door interrupted Douglas, and he turned to see Nancy entering with the bottle of whiskey. She walked to the bed, her heels clattering on the floor, then sat down and gave Basil a kiss on the forehead.

Basil grabbed the bottle before wrapping an arm around the girl and pulling her close, roughly, but playfully. He laughed loudly. "I was just telling the captain here how fond I am of you. He seems to think there may be others that you serve." He reached over and patted her on her rear and then took an oversized swig from the bottle. "We'll have some fun in a few minutes."

Nancy rolled over on her side, stretching out on the bed, exposing her long, shapely legs covered with black fishnet stockings. She put a hand on Basil's bare chest and began to massage it as her big eyes locked on him, her body completely subservient to him.

Basil was right, about the woman anyway. Douglas didn't understand it. Maybe she feared him, or the danger excited her. He didn't like the thought of heading out into the backcountry without Basil; the man was certainly an asset. Somehow, he now found himself needing, wanting the assistance of this man whose lifestyle he abhorred. A few weeks earlier he had been in complete opposition to his employment by the army. His current requirement for a gunslinger didn't seem right, totally against what he stood for, but it had now become practical, almost compulsory. "Okay, I'm going to do it."

"Do what?" Nancy said.

Basil set the bottle down, kissed Nancy on the lips, and pulled her to him, rolling over on the bed. The two laughed. "I'll tell you after I've had my fill."

17

Three days later, a few hours before dusk, Douglas slowly cantered over a tall, narrow wooden bridge on the rudimentary, solitary road west of Winnfield. He looked down. The magnificent wood trusses spanned a quaint little stream, fifty feet below, its muddy water trickling along slowly. The bridge and the impressive modern truss stood as a testament to man's engineering and resourcefulness in the middle of nowhere.

Behind Douglas, Huff rode with his Henry resting across his lap. Out in front, two young sturdy sergeants, hardened veterans, weaved along the road on their imposing geldings, each giving the woods a prudent inspection. Douglas turned in the saddle. Behind him, Cyrus followed the column. Earlier that morning, he, Cyrus, and Huff had rendezvoused with the two soldiers north of Winnfield. After the rendezvous, Douglas had only let one of the men ride through town. He and the other three had branched off on a side road that missed the town in hopes the town folks would take heed of the lone soldier riding the road.

Strangely, Douglas had enjoyed the trip thus far. They had seen little, only a possum, two whitetail deer, and a few often-used campsites along the road where the endless stream of travelers making their way to Texas or farther west had bivouacked for decades. The camps' fires were now just black ash. He looked out through the thick trees and over the endless sheet of rust-colored pine needles and combs covering the land. Though the pines grew thick, the space below the limbs, high above, and the ground remained relatively open, only blotted by the rows of the tall, thin, perfectly straight trunks, affording some view for almost a quarter mile. The day was splendid, a flawless blue sky. The country had a tranquil quietness.

Though deficient of beauty, this dreary, bleak, isolated land could at times have an enchanting serenity. Unlike the vast expanse of the West or more mountainous terrain, the confining, almost unpopulated, and unspoiled forest gave one the sentiment he loomed far from any of man's doings. The air was clean and clear and in complete contrast to the foul manufacturing holes of the Northeast.

Resting on his pommel, Douglas looked down at his map, and then at a few high ridges, trying to find a valley that correlated with a vast stream. He loved picking his way through the rugged, quiet, virgin territory with only his map, compass, and knowledge of their pace. Something about it afforded a pleasure, a sense of using his skills, far from the civility of town. In this country, on the twisting trails, getting any sense of direction at all required his full attention.

As the monotonous time passed, minute by minute, Douglas reflected on the last few weeks. Was this all worth it? His lengthy conversations with Hannah and her uncle and his hopes of catching one of the outlaws alive weighed on his mind. He and the army had been trained to defeat the country's enemies in an open scuffle. They were good at that, but that meant killing on a vast scale and taking willing prisoners. The army and its methods were not set up to police the country and take unwilling men alive. The typical paradigm didn't work here. For certain, it would be much easier to simply track the bandits down and kill them. But that would be an endless job, his actions actually resulting in an increase in the number of bushwhackers and bandits he'd have to pursue. Though the new task seemed considerably more dangerous and complicated, it appeared to be the only pragmatic thing.

"You boys up front can relax a little," Douglas finally said. "Doubtful any Rebs will be out in the daylight. It's dusk and afterwards when they operate." He paused for effect. "But it does get dark in these trees at night, real dark. Night's alive with all kinds of critters, friendly and otherwise."

Huff smiled.

Douglas raised his voice. "Next open campsite we come to, we'll stop and camp. Catch some rest so we can keep watch tonight. If they hit us, it will be midnight or later."

About two hours after midnight, Douglas saw the two torches, slowly moving down the road, bouncing up and down, still a hundred yards away. The fragile patrol had camped in a small opening, about an acre, at an often-used site along the road lying adjacent to a natural spring. They had built a fire, now just barely flickering, twenty feet off the road. The five men sat near the fire, leaning against a small rock outcropping.

Douglas elbowed Huff beside him, and whispered to the two sergeants and Cyrus, all awake but sitting quietly, "Somebody's coming. Probably the night riders. Who else moves at this time of night?"

The four bodies around him shuffled. Hammers cocked on their rifles. He gripped his shotgun firmly, lifting it up and slowly cocking its two hammers. His stomach turned, and his skin got numb as he stared into the night. Amid the incessant fireflies, the two torches got closer. Beneath their fluid flames, he saw the silhouettes of the riders, all clad in sheets or burlap, their details becoming more precise by the second. The light colors of the costumes pulsated powerfully in the glinting gold light. Douglas's muscles tightened as he stood, his comrades following suit.

In awe, he now stared at the cavalcade as it approached. For years, he had hunted these men with barely a glimpse into their clandestine world. Now he saw the cloaked riders up close and personal. A high-pitched whistle blew. The six horses all slowed, turned in the little campsite, and approached the dying fire. He had heard legends about the sinister whistles, used for commands to disguise the clans' voices. Live and in person, the eerie, high-pitched sadistic noise, like the hoot of an owl, permeated the night and ran a chill down his spine.

Douglas's heartbeat reached a crescendo. Almost like magic, the riders came into view a few feet from Douglas, the black voids of the eye slits clearly visible. All carried weapons, a few shotguns and rifles, either in their laps or in their hands. Two riders had their rifles haphazardly pointed at the army patrol.

The lead horse reined up five paces from the soldiers. The other five horses halted, a half-length behind, two on one side of the lead rider, three on the other. A dozen seconds of tense silence passed with only the soft sounds of tack rattling and the fire hissing.

"What do you want?" Douglas finally asked. He raised his shotgun and put its sights on the lead man, feeling his own hands get cold. Beside him, he heard the movement of the other soldiers raising their weapons. Two of the night riders steadied the aim of their rifles on the four soldiers as two more started to turn their weapons on the army patrol. "Easy, we see the barrels of any more of those weapons, we'll pull these triggers." Douglas spoke directly to the lead man. "Might not get all of you but I'll get you before I go—a few more, too." Speaking down his shotgun's barrel, Douglas moved his sights from the man's chest to his head. He tried to keep cool, but felt his exterior betraying the upheaval in his gut.

The lead rider moved his cloaked gaze over the soldiers slowly. He put a hand under his mask. "Don't want nothing," he finally said in a muffled voice.

"Then what the hell you doing out on the road in the middle of the night? Drop those weapons, all of them. I'm taking you all in."

"What for?" the man replied. "We ain't done nothing. Riding the country armed, or riding concealed ain't no crime, not even up North. We're just ensuring the peace. Looking out for the best interest of our people, promoting ideas for their benefit. Most people in these parts approve of it, too."

His mind racing, Douglas thought for a second. His plan had a flaw. The man had a point; they hadn't yet done anything, though he suspected their intentions. He had figured there would be gunplay at the inception of any encounter. He thought he recognized the voice, not one of the Garretts or the sheriff, but someone he had heard somewhere, probably just in passing. He strained, but couldn't place the voice in the endless sea of people he saw everyday.

"I guess you could kill a few of us," the faceless rider continued. "Haul the rest in and say you were ambushed. That's how you damned soldiers operate most of the time. You're a dishonest lot of heathens. If you do, we'll get you first. Even if you eventually kill all of us, one day, you and the army will be gone, for good. And the natural order of God will be restored." The man turned to Cyrus. "I thought the army claimed the highest moral bearing. Seems you don't have any problem riding with infidels."

Douglas let out a long breath, keeping his sights on the man. A sense of utter frustration fell over his soul. He wanted to pull the trigger. Do just what the outlaw had evoked. It seemed the only rational action. If he did, he'd have blood on his hands, blood that would never go away. His mind was constantly haunted by similar episodes in the war when he'd done things. Things accepted by the army, but not by his conscience. Shooting these men would violate his code, his rectitude, what made him different from the outlaws. Secondly, he had men around him, soldiers under his command. Huff certainly would revel in the action, but probably not the sergeants.

"Pull off those masks, now!" Douglas yelled.

The lead horse wheeled around and raced into the darkness, the other five behind it. Douglas followed the figures with his barrel, wanting to fire. He applied a little pressure to the trigger, almost hoping the gun would ignite, or one of his men would open fire, and the shooting would start. But the rumble of hooves only grew fainter by the second.

18

An hour after noon the next day, Douglas and his four subordinates crossed the Red River via ferry on the outskirts of Natchitoches. They had departed the campsite at dawn and completed the seven-hour ride back to town without incident. Douglas instructed the two sergeants to go ahead into town to the army post to get some much-needed rest. He'd be along shortly.

He lifted his hat and ran his hands through his hair, exasperated. He had spent the morning in the saddle, not thinking or scheming, not even really on the lookout for enemies, but almost lifelessly staring into the green haze around him. He felt almost beaten, almost wanting the outlaws to storm out of the bush and settle up in a final shoot-out that would end his ordeal, one way or the other. That was what he and his troopers were trained to do, reconciling in the open, honorably, like the war, not the endless game of chasing ghosts. He looked forward to this evening. Hannah had promised to cook him dinner when he returned. She seemed to be his only refuge.

The day was ordinary, sultry and breezeless, as Douglas looked over at the Cotton Palace, the only structure near the ferry. A few citizens walked about the rutted, red road. Two idlers, typical in appearance, rugged, middle-aged, and unsavory, loitered on the porch of the bar. He turned to look at two Negro kids, not even ten years in this world, running, laughing, and playing in the deep ravines along the riverbank. Both the young lads carried the gullible bliss of youth, untouched by the tyranny, the hardships, and injustices their black skin would curse them with when they grew older. They had little knowledge of the pushing and shoving around them.

Douglas smiled. He had genuine concerns for their predicament. He knew their smiles would wane over the years. The war and its aftermath had been the cruelest to the area's freedmen. With no homes or social structure, many had simply starved to death after the war, and most now barely eked out an existence sharecropping or at odd jobs, many living in the same quarters and working for the same masters as before the war, now not by law, but by necessity. Douglas had long since quit worrying about the prejudices and the plight of these people so blatantly flashed in his face every day. He was only one man, he couldn't alter the world. The Northern Army had changed the land and laws, but done little to change people's convictions in four years of war. His practical side told him the world wasn't fair. That was just the way it was. It wasn't the government's job to care for these people, only to ensure their rights.

He turned to Huff and reined his horse toward the two-story Cotton Palace. "Let's check on Basil." He swung his foot over the saddle and stepped down. With an affable tone, he continued, "Grab your rifle and come on . . . in case we run into any drunk Rebs."

The spacious bar looked rather tame when the two soldiers entered. In the early afternoon, an employee banged on the keys of the grand piano, more in practice than anything else, and a lone customer, a humble yeoman, sat at the bar over a glass of whiskey. Douglas's entrance caused the piano to pause, and the captain immediately noticed the bartender's shifty, startled eyes. Eyes that signaled alarm that something was awry.

Douglas's stomach squirmed with a nervous twitch. "Upstairs, now!"

The two soldiers ran upstairs. Douglas turned to Huff, put a finger over his lips, then tiptoed down the hall. When he drew close to Basil's room, he heard two loud pops and a powerful grunt. He heard a man talking, almost yelling, authoritatively. As he reached the door, he wiped the sweat building on his face, pulled his pistol from his holster, and pointed to Huff's rifle.

More thunderous pops that induced a muffled squeal of a woman seeped through the door.

"Bitch, we'll teach you to double-cross us!" a voice shouted from the other side.

Douglas softly felt the doorknob, locked snug. He inspected the entrance, a flimsy set of planks that opened to the inside. He sucked in a deep breath, held up his pistol, and pointed to Huff, who lunged into the door, smashing its handle and flinging it open.

Huff fell to the floor in the doorway with the collision. Douglas ran into the room, pistol extended. A room full of busy flesh filled his eyes. Two men stood beside the bed, one flaunting a long leather whip. Both men turned, reaching for their pistols. Before either man got a gun up, Douglas instinctively pumped a round into each man's chest. Crimson circles formed on their shirts, as each twisted, almost lifeless, to the floor.

As the sounds of the shuffling feet and gunfire dissipated, the room got still, only the rattle of one of the outlaw pistols twirling on the floor and Huff rising to his feet. Death moans came from the two men. Then more whimpers. There was disorder on the bed.

The gunfire still ringing in his ears, he looked to see the two naked, sweat-laden bodies, both with mouths gagged and tied to the bedposts, lying face-down on the bloodstained sheets. Dozens of deep gashes carved up the backs of Basil and the beautiful whore. Douglas winced, almost shaking, as he looked at the girl's soft, luscious skin, now a gnarled mangle of blood and torn flesh. Thick areas of chafed skin surrounded the two's ankles and wrists, a testament to their torment. The girl turned to look at him, exposing the abundant, deep, black-red knife slits in her face set against now almost lifeless eyes.

The bed then shuddered and vibrated ferociously, moving a few inches on the floor and bouncing up and down as Basil jerked on the ropes confining his hands and feet. He shook and quivered like some type of caged beast.

Hands shaking, Douglas grabbed his knife and reached over to cut Basil's hands and feet free. The gunfighter slowly rolled over on his side, his eyes more alive than Douglas had ever seen them.

Face totally lathered, Basil struggled to his feet. He hobbled over to the two bodies on the floor. He grabbed Huff's rifle and began to bludgeon each of the men with the gun's butt, expending all the energy in his blood-covered body. His anger charged the air, and he grunted like an ape as he swung the rifle. Below, the two expired outlaws' lifeless skulls became contorted into something without shape, their brains now spilling onto the wood floor.

Douglas stepped back, still in a state of shock. One of the men had been the deputy from Winnfield, Weaver, the other he had never seen. "They're already dead," he finally mumbled.

Basil flopped down on the floor, his exposed rear landing first. He sat up straight, let the rifle fall from his hands, and ripped off the mouth gag wrapped around his head.

Douglas slowly walked back to the bed. He tried to hide his gaze from the bloodstained wounds as he cut the girl free. She didn't respond. She didn't even remove the gag from her mouth, but balled up on the bed in the fetal position.

Douglas's stomach turned, his hands shook. He had seen plenty of innocents suffer, and many of his own troops meet their maker, but most of those had been hidden in the bigger haze of a repugnant war. But his current actions, those of his men, had consequences, unspeakable consequences for people who had no interest in his cause, any cause. If this girl lived, she was doomed to a hideous existence: an unsightly, disfigured shell of a woman. This vicious, pitiless land would have little sympathy for her.

"Huff, go fetch the doctor," he said.

19

It was dark, a steamy night, hot and full of the sounds of birds, bugs of all description, and a few whispers behind him. Douglas, on his knees, felt the dirt below, its dampness soaking through his trousers. Off in the woods, the branches and foliage flickered with a cherry glow from four or five torches. His feet were secured, snug with a rope. Another rope, pulled taut around both wrists, secured his bare chest to a large pine; its bark uncomfortably jabbing into his ribs.

Huff was bound to an adjacent tree, his blue soldier's pants pulled down to his knees, resting on the ground. His throat was lacerated, his head cocked back and limp. Half of his severed penis protruded from his mouth. Below his chin, blood seeped down from the mouth and neck to the soldier's blood-stained and grimy chest—farther down, around the groin, more blood and gore.

Douglas trembled with fear. To his right, a faceless man stood, his strange green eyes dancing below a large, big-brimmed hat. Perspiration gushed down Douglas's neck and onto his cramping, tired back.

The eerie man stepped forward, unraveling a long leather whip, its lashes about three feet long and made of rough, rawhide strands. He extended his right arm, and let the tip of the long whip dangle over Douglas's naked back.

Feeling the coarse leather slide over his back, Douglas shook uncontrollably, his skin turning cold, the hair on his neck rising.

The man slid the long whip down Douglas's back, slowly, gently. He paused a few times, smiling, before stepping behind Douglas, his shadow still visible on the ground. The shadow rolled up the sleeve of his muscular right arm.

Letting out all his air, tensing up, Douglas forced his sweaty chest into the rough pine bark. "Please, no," he mumbled.

The shadow recoiled the whip, bending back his upper body. An earsplitting pop pierced the night. Douglas winced, spitting out a high-pitched squeal. Breathing hard, his mind dizzy, he heard a few laughs from the darkness. He hadn't been struck. The sadistic bandit had only cracked the whip over his head, but the torturous effect of this was probably worse than the inevitable blow.

Douglas looked over his shoulder.

The man grunted. The leather sliced the air. A penetrating roar, like the crack of a pistol, ripped into Douglas's ears, before echoing off through the trees. He flinched as the hard lash crashed into the pine tree just above his head, sending apple-sized chunks of bark flying off the trunk. The snap of the whip had a violent, powerful ring, earthshaking.

Tears now running down his cheeks, Douglas pressed his eyes shut, his entire body shaking violently, his stomach nauseated. He wished he was dead. Nothing he'd ever experienced compared to this.

The night got quiet. In front of him, he looked down at the shadow of the man behind him, securing his footing and gripping the evil instrument again.

"Please, no!" Douglas yelled. "Please! I'm sorry. Whatever you want, I'll do it. I swear."

A distant voice chuckled loudly. "He sounds like a baby. A Yankee piglet. Don't use him all up. Leave some for me."

"I'll leave a little; just a little, though," the shadow said.

Douglas wanted to ball up in a fetal position and die. How, how had he managed to end up here? "Dear God, no! Please, sir, don't do this!" he mumbled through his tears. "Just kill me if you want to get rid of me. I will leave all of you alone."

"God's not going to save you," the voice behind him said in a stern tone.

The arm of the pulsing shadow rose, arching backwards.

Douglas trembled with horror as the rasp of the whip, cutting the thick night air, raced into his ears. The night erupted. "Nooooooo!" he yelled.

Then he felt a hard slap on his face, night turning to light. His vision blurred, he saw a face leaning over him. "It's all right," the feminine face said, softly running a hand through his hair. "It's only a dream."

His heart pounding, his mind jumbled, his vision still hazy, Douglas looked down at his rapidly rising and falling chest, the sheets saturated beneath him.

Hannah put a soft hand on his chest, gently massaging it.

Douglas looked at Hannah, shaking his head. He felt the bed, then grabbed a light cotton sheet and mopped his face. He lay silent for a few moments as his heart calmed, and he ran his hands through his hair.

"Was it that bad?" Hannah said softly, pushing her hair behind her ears.

"Just a bad dream."

"It's all right now," Hannah said softly, continuing to rub his stomach and ribs. "It's almost nine. You never sleep this late, but you passed out as soon as you reclined last night."

Still shaken, Douglas thought about the last forty hours. He looked around the room, the reality of his location only now becoming completely real.

"You want some breakfast or coffee?"

"Sure," Douglas said, standing, his breath still heavy. "I need some nourishment and daylight. And I need to get to the garrison." He grabbed Hannah firmly by the arm. "Anytime you think I'm dreaming, wake me, immediately."

20

At his desk back at his office, Douglas looked over some paperwork and a few army manuals that were sandwiched between two bookends. He propped up his polished boots on the desk. Four men, two parties of two Negro men each, all probably in their forties, bickered on in dispute around him. Douglas looked out the window at a squirrel eating a nut on a tree branch just a few arm lengths outside. Despite the commotion inside, he couldn't wean his gaze from the little creature partitioning and consuming the tiny acorn. Occasionally, it turned to look him in the eye. Around and above the tree, the fall sun, high in the sky, beat down on the oaks, wilting their leaves. The dispirited voices of the men continued on almost like a hum in his ears. One minute, one of the parties politely let the other speak until he didn't like the words, and the four men would begin to squabble in such a manner that nothing came across.

Three days had passed since the grotesque

whipping at the Cotton Palace and his horrid dream. Nightmares had haunted him for years, especially during the war; their backdrops were always different, but all were gloomy and fatal. Many times he would realize they were dreams and forcibly wake himself, but the recent dream of his flogging by bandits had been too real, the tribulation too great. He cringed, his back tightening at the thought of the lashes. Worse, in the dream, he had cowered, begging for his life, calling the outlaws "sir," and agreeing to capitulate. The dishonor and horror of it forced his right hand to start shaking. He now feared going to sleep. During the day, he tried to keep busy, doing anything to push the terrible thoughts from his mind.

In recent days, he had spent hours trying to place the lone night rider's voice he had heard on the trail with a face, without luck. The deep, drawn-out tones of the hill-country men lacked the uniqueness of the Northern accents. The doctor had bandaged up Basil and said he would be back on his feet before a fortnight. The whore's final condition was still in question. Douglas still shuddered as he thought of the woman's image, turning her cut-up face and sad eyes to him on the bed. This haunting sight was likely to never depart his mind.

The incident had made Douglas worry about Hannah's safety. Basil had told him she would likely never be a target; such an act would be in violation of the Southern code of honor that would damage any support the highwaymen harbored. Still, Douglas wondered what he could do to protect her. He didn't have enough troops to guard people. For everyone, there was nowhere to hide. Hannah, like everybody else outside a major city, lived in the open and unprotected, like an animal in the woods and subject to the predators' whims.

With this in mind and to soothe his aching spirit, he now spent as much time as he could at the Butler house. Hannah now seemed the only one he could turn to, her arms his refuge, but her caring words and caressing touch had given him little solace or reprieve from his state of shock. In bed, they neither made love nor confided in each other. But it had now been three days, and Douglas felt his senses returning. This afternoon he planned to take Hannah for a buggy ride, the thought of it his only pleasurable deliberation for days.

Douglas turned back to the four men, all dressed similarly, in light homespun cotton shirts and trousers, all sharecroppers. They were arguing over the compensation for some work, but the babbling also diverged into all sorts of other issues to include drunkenness, family matters, and even swearing. For years, Douglas had spent his days settling trivial quarrels, and even a few serious crimes and claims.

For almost four years, he had been the official and only judge and jury on all such matters, at least as far as the blacks, unionists, and carpetbaggers were concerned, or anyone else who respected his authority. Since Louisiana had adopted a new constitution and officially rejoined the Union a year earlier, these matters were supposed to be handled by local authorities. The army only remained to aid and abet the new Republican government and ensure its laws got carried out. But many still

brought their troubles here where they thought
they could get a fair shake, or at least a hearing,
especially on Wednesdays. Due to the arbitrary
nature of these proceedings, and feeling a need to
have his sanity spared the daily, almost endless
grind, he had declared this day, Wednesday, the
only day of the week he held court.

Douglas rested his elbows on his desk. "Let's see,
Jeremiah, you say you paid this man for a day's work
he didn't perform."

"Uh-huh."

"That not true, Captain," one of the other men
retorted. "I work all day, in the heat."

"Buts you'as drunk."

"Was not."

Douglas lifted a hand to silence the two and
looked at all four. "How come I got to settle this?
This shouldn't be something I'm wasting my time
with. If you have to, you can go see the constable.
I'm too busy trying to round up the white militia
before they hang us all."

All four men stopped. A second of silence passed.

"Naw. That man hates us," Jeremiah said.

Douglas shook his head, trying not to smile.
"Jeremiah, you say Winny was drunk, but he says he
worked. I'm assuming you had something to drink?"
Douglas turned to the man in question.

"Just a little, but I work fine with a little."

"Now, Winny, you know you're not supposed to
come to work when you've been drinking. But I'm
guessing you did something . . . though probably
not all you were paid for. Is that right?"

"Maybe, if you put it that way," Winny replied.

Douglas turned to Jeremiah. "What's a day's wage?"

"Twenty-five cent."

"That's settled." Douglas slapped his hands together formally. "Jeremiah, you pay him fifteen cents for his day's work. Next time, don't let him work if you think he's drunk, and we won't have this problem anymore." Douglas stood up in a gesture of finality, and to his amazement both parties made no objection. "Now you men get back to work, and I will, too. And now that I'm not the official authority for this type of stuff, only come see me when there's something really important."

Just as Douglas walked out from behind his desk, Huff arrived in his office.

"Gots your buggy from the hotel," Huff said. "Mr. Long sends his regards. There's no charge for usin' its, so long as you have it back by morning."

"You get the two sergeants on the ferry to Shreveport?"

Huff nodded. "Wishes they would have stayed. We could sure use 'em."

"I inquired, but that major in Monroe said they had to be back by the end of the week. Overland from Shreveport back to Monroe will only take a couple of days. Little out of their way, but they won't have to deal with any night riders." Douglas stepped to the door without hesitation or further conversation, now having a reason to depart before further rows needed to be settled. "Huff, go see that Mr. Taylor who keeps our horses. Have him turn them out, in good pasture. They've turned into worn-down hags. The damn guerrillas have better-looking steeds than we do."

"This just came today by telegraph." Huff handed Douglas a piece of paper.

Douglas lifted the paper and read as he walked outside.

Captain Douglas Owens,
Commander, Company D, 4th United States
*   Cavalry*
District of the Upper Red River
Natchitoches, La.

Captain Owens: Having received your more detailed account and thoughts on the killing of Judge Butler, I am initiating the administrative process to have some additional troops placed under your direct command, the exact quantity and makeup not known at this time. I have also forwarded your requests to have more troops sent to Louisiana, such action being interpreted by local interests as a "national action," to the highest levels of the army, and have only this morning received word from Washington that these requests will be passed to the uppermost levels of the Federal Government for consideration. Any information on this subject will be conveyed to you immediately upon any action taken.

Respectfully, Colonel M. J. James
Assistant Adjutant General
Headquarters, District of Louisiana

Outside, a disproportionate number of people were on the street, all rather quiet. Before he had a chance to ponder their motive, he saw the open wagon, slowly, dramatically moving down the almost silent street, its wheels squeaking. Two coffins lay in the back. Douglas spied the onlookers, reverently paying their respects to the two men Douglas had gunned down at the Cotton Palace by bowing their heads or removing their hats. Douglas's mood regressed to something more grave as he read some words hastily painted on the side of the wagon: MURDERED BY THE ARMY.

Douglas brought the buggy to a stop in front of the white porch and redbrick façade of the Butler house. The late-day sun at his back brilliantly illuminated the residence and its wooden porch that was in need of a new coat of paint. The house's landscaping contrasted the dwelling's lack of upkeep and proclaimed its occupants as women. Immaculate hedges and flowers, all trimmed and concentric, ringed the house, making it look like an oasis. Lush hydrangeas, crepe myrtles, dogwoods, and boxwoods all surrounded by colorful periwinkles and daisies presented a wonderful kaleidoscope of color.

The afternoon ride had been splendid; Hannah's gentle touch and thoughtful inspiring words had assuaged his tension. Their interludes provided him with his only escape, be it fleeting, from his work and worries, like attending the theater. He never wanted them to end. As he stepped down to the driveway, hitching the horses and helping Hannah from the carriage, a sense of anxiety oozed back over him. Hannah's sister, Caroline, had arrived back from New Orleans that morning to tend to some business for a week before returning to the city where her mother still resided. Caroline had a rather bad opinion of the Federal government and didn't mind expressing it.

Hannah, her face hidden under a big-brimmed hat lashed down with a scarf, led him up on the house's porch, holding his hand. Just inside, the two found Caroline standing in the large living room.

"Well, Mr. Owens," Caroline said, not looking at Douglas. "I had hoped my naïve sister's fancy for your courting might pass while I was away. I'm starting to wonder what they taught her in that school in Maryland." Caroline's tone carried no attempt at humor.

"Good evening, Caroline," Douglas said in his most debonair voice, bowing slightly. At least in outer appearance, Hannah's older sister displayed herself as one of the most refined and attractive females he had ever laid eyes on. Tall, thin, with long black hair, intelligent amber eyes, she always dressed smartly and moved easily and eloquently. If ever a woman commanded attention, she did with her stylish, upper-class looks and ageless complexion. In those physical attributes so sought by gentlemen of education and blood, she even surpassed Hannah.

"Mr. Owens," Caroline continued, turning to cast

her gaze on Douglas. "You will not stay at this house anymore. Do you understand?"

Douglas stuttered, "Caroline, has it ever occurred to you that my intentions may be honorable?"

"Don't tell me about *honor.* I've never *met* a Union soldier yet with just a drop of honor. You know nothing of it. You're destroying Hannah's reputation. If your transgressions continue, no good Southern gentleman will ever have her. Hannah's a fine girl, from fine lineage. She's not a tramp. You and your soldiers have already ruined our lives. I'm *not* going to tolerate you destroying what's left of my family."

Douglas felt a little queer, unsure of how to respond. Caroline had never been chummy to him, in fact often condescending, but he had never been party to such an open reprimand. Maybe his overnights at the house had been a little offensive? He finally mumbled, "I think Hannah is quite capable of determining her own course. And the United States Army spends its days and resources trying to restore this area, help you."

"*Restore?* You have no *idea.*" Caroline's voice lost its polished accent. "I can't even begin to describe the hardships you've bestowed on us, and what you've taken from us. You detest our old system, but you made that system legal, not us. We made this land one of the richest in all the world. Then your soldiers showed up here, burned our farms, took all we worked for. You've now made us the slaves. After the war, we ate rats, had nothing, were constantly subjugated and defiled. You provided us with no protection. We did not lose to a greater cause, only to a greater force."

Caroline focused firmly on Douglas, her voice growing high-pitched and urgent. "Do you know what it is like to hide in your room all night, shaking, for fear the drunk soldiers outside might burn down the house with you in it? If that wasn't enough, now you've forced these Northern vultures on us. As so often happens in turmoil, the scum, the white trash, and opportunists are trying to exploit the situation and rise above their station at our expense, taking what we've worked for. The lowly white demagogues are always among the ignorant, naïve Negroes, stirring them up with unreal expectations, trying to turn them against us, all for their own nefarious intentions and personal gain. They incite the slaves into these armed uprisings that our brave Southern men have to put down. Then, the Northern papers exaggerate our men's methods to turn the country against us. Now these freedmen and a few Northerners run the government, everything. The black militia rides around at night killing white folks. Our taxes are fivefold what they used to be. It takes everything we make just to pay them. You Northerners buy up the bankrupt farms like you're trading stock. If you have your way, it won't be long before we're working the fields for them, the fields *we* created. . . . We are God-fearing Christians here, Mr. Owens. You godless people have destroyed our harmony, the inherent way things are ordained. God's laws supersede the laws of the fraudulent radical Congress, and God will visit retribution on you for your sins. And you can put away any inclinations you might have about Hannah. They will *not* come to fruition."

Douglas had heard the sermon in different forms, from countless people in an endless array of settings. Southerners often cited God or religion as their motivator, the basis for their actions, especially when those words or actions disagreed with Northern rule. But this land couldn't be further from holy, at least what he saw as holy, but this call seemed to give the orators an unquestioned loyalty to, and backing for, their actions or words.

Caroline stood erect, imposing, unrepentant.

Douglas pondered what to say. Should he just walk away or confront this woman? He turned to Hannah, her face red and mouth open. He loved her. She believed in him. He didn't want to disappoint or upset her. He wanted to stand up for himself, everything his government stood for, but this was a delicate situation, the emotions in the room about to explode. He didn't want to do or say anything he might regret later. He put a hand over his mouth to clear his throat. "I'm sorry I've upset you, Caroline. It's not the proper way of a gentleman."

Douglas sucked in a deep breath, still looking at Caroline. How could such backward selfishness take on the form of such beauty? Worse, she was educated, not like the thousands of mindless lambs being herded around. "In the last three years, the Northern government has built schools, hundreds of schools, in this area so all children can get an education. This parish didn't have a single school before the war, for whites or blacks. I don't care where you're from, that's not destructive."

Caroline walked to the front door. "Please spare me Mr. Grant's opinions."

Douglas turned to Hannah, almost expecting her to follow her sister outside.

Instead she lifted both her hands and placed them on his cheeks. "Keep in mind my sister lost her husband, and much, much more to the war. Her and Mother were here alone at the plantation during and after the war. She's suffered much, and has always had much more of Father in her than me. The army soldiers didn't do much to change her and anybody's mind when they occupied Natchitoches."

Hannah's words and her cool hands on his face gave Douglas a sense of relief. He searched for the right words, but just as he began to utter a response, Hannah put a finger to his lips.

"Let me go talk to her." Hannah gave him a small kiss on the lips. "I had a wonderful time today. I'll stop by and see you tomorrow."

21

The next morning a thick fog covered the delta, hovering only a few feet above the ground and making navigation arduous. The early day's soft, balmy air held a slight nip, the first of the fall. The rising sun's rays lit the fog, illumining it and by the minute burning off the damp air. Down the dirt road, between the cotton fields, Douglas now saw a few hundred yards.

Ahead lay Hiram Vaughn's enormous cotton gin, two stories of wood planks. Overhead, a plume of smoke from the gin's steam engine rose to the sky, a steady stream of white smoke piercing the horizon. Beneath the smokestack, the gin resembled a beehive. The noise of the steam engine and overseers rumbled across the earth and over the thousands of loose cotton bulbs scattered over the ground, giving it all an air of havoc. A row of wagons, pulled by two mules each and piled high with loose cotton, lined up in front of the gin, the black drivers waiting patiently under their big straw hats.

As Douglas rode closer to the gin, he heard the steel machines inside, gnashing and squeaking as they tore the seeds from the bulbs. Freedmen carried baskets of the seed out behind the gin, piling them in a large mound. This constituted the only industry for several days' ride, except for a few scattered sawmills, brick factories, and salt mines. Douglas viewed the painting-like setting. How many generations of these same people had congregated at this very spot at this time of year, for this annual ritual? The only difference now was the roar of the steam engine and the fact the workers now got paid, though meagerly.

Douglas was here to see the owner. He had crossed the Red River at daylight and made the two-hour trek into the heart of the fertile plain north of Natchitoches that stretched out on each side of the river until it gave way to the hills. Although he had misgivings about this meeting that Cyrus Carter had suggested, he was at a loss for anything else.

His mission seemed hopeless, almost impossible now. His only two white soldiers had been killed, and Basil seriously wounded. What more could he do? It took the entire army four years to defeat these people that they outnumbered four to one, nine to one in manufacturing capability, in an open fight. Now he was tasked with taming an entire region with just three men.

This very morning, in fact, he had a tense moment on the road. At daylight, he had heard the thunderous sounds of a posse on the trail in the dark fog. Fearing the night riders swooping down on him in the twilight before dawn, he had hidden in a roadside thicket, only to witness Juba Sampson and ten of his colored state militia ride by, probably coming home from a night of marauding themselves.

The episode had rekindled the vision of his recent dream, inducing a fit of shaking. It still seemed too real. The horrific thoughts of his whipping had changed his outlook on his setting. He now saw the world like the hapless masses, maybe even the freedmen. Instead of the hunter, he now felt like the hunted, like everybody else, his life dependent on the whims of his enemies, especially if he didn't behave properly.

Over the last few days, Douglas had been thinking about all this and his feelings for Hannah that had evolved into something more than just a passing fancy. For the first time in years, his callous world devoid of feelings had gained some color and given way to an urge to live, now that he had something to live for. Was all this worth it, worth dying for? Though the Dallons and Garretts needed exterminating, did he even believe in his bigger mission, especially since the army seemed so reluctant to do what it required?

After Basil's flogging, he had actually thought about just giving up. He had killed three bandits and the deputy sheriff, and ran another night rider out of the country. He thought about just writing a report to headquarters describing these facts and stating that vigilante activity in his dominion had subsided to a tolerable level. He could cite the fact that the gold and the two sergeants had made it through the country unmolested, despite the journey being well-known in the area beforehand.

But the reflections on his nightmare had changed his psyche, his mind-set on the army's mission, humbling him, and putting him in the place of the masses instead of the protection of the army. Over the days, he had found himself no longer wanting to vanquish the bandits because he had been ordered to, but for a new desire to eradicate the clans, what they stood for. Their vigilante violence and the circumvention of the country's laws had to be stopped. And he had hope, the telegraph he had received yesterday.

"Can I help you?" a man said from behind Douglas.

Douglas looked over his shoulder to see a white overseer, in his fifties and dressed in light cotton clothes, his pants held up with suspenders.

"I'm looking for Hiram Vaughn," Douglas replied.

The man stared at the army soldier for a few seconds without words. Instead of his adapted field uniform, Douglas had worn his official blues, trimmed in yellow and laced with gold buttons and shoulder boards. He thought this might add to the formality of his visit.

The man then pointed to a small office adjoining

the gin. A moment later, Douglas walked into it.
Two of the walls were covered with field maps, two
more with chalkboards listing gangs of men and
charting their days worked, schedules, prices, et
cetera. Behind a desk stacked with papers sat a
harsh-looking man, parched red with a wrinkled
toughness.

"I'd like to see Mr. Vaughn," Douglas said, folding
his arms behind his back formally.

The man sneered at Douglas with intense brown
eyes. "He's at home, having breakfast. That's his
custom this time of day."

"Can you give me directions?"

The man let out an aggravated breath and stood.
He looked at Douglas again, and the pistol on his
hip. "I'll have to take you, but I'm busy right now."

"I'm busy, too, and I've got the authority to go
anywhere I want. You can take me now, or I'm going
to find him myself."

The man swore a few times then stepped out
from behind his desk. "All right, let's go."

Ten minutes later, Douglas trotted down the long
drive leading to the Vaughn house, which was
perched on a small ridge and commanded wonderfully over the land even from a distance. Sided with
huge oaks, the road's gravel had been meticulously
edged in an exact straight line. Down below his
horse's feet, the drive shone so clean it looked like
it had been swept.

Douglas rode on, following the overseer, past the
workers' quarters and several inauspicious sights, no
longer in service but still standing: a large pole once

used to tether slaves for whippings, and beside it, the spacious dog pens that once restrained a pack of hounds for tracking runaway slaves.

The two men reined up near the front steps of the enormous two-story house. Without conversation, the overseer led Douglas up on the porch, four feet off the ground, and to a table covered with a white cloth at the corner of the house. The grounds were as spotless as any military post he'd ever seen.

Douglas walked up to the table where a man dressed in nice but casual clothes sat drinking coffee and reading a newspaper. A beautiful young mulatto girl, outfitted in a proper black dress fronted with a white apron and topped with a mobcap, picked up a plate from the table without a word and disappeared into the house.

"Can I help you?" the man said and paused, putting down his paper and looking at Douglas's insignia.

"Captain Owens."

"Hiram Vaughn." The man pointed to a chair. "Would you like a cup of coffee?"

"No, thank you."

"Please sit."

Douglas slowly took a seat in one of the chairs. After carefully scanning the impeccable grounds again, he looked up at the porch's ceiling, twenty feet above. He spied the house's enormous living room through one of the windows and saw a large portrait of General Lee in his butternut uniform hanging on the wall. This was a step back in time, or at least what Douglas imagined of the old South.

He looked back at Mr. Vaughn. Well into his sixties, the planter had a perfectly symmetrical lean face, but without the sadness of the years, and serious, aged, clever eyes.

"To what do I owe the pleasure of this visit, Captain Owens?"

"I'll be frank," Douglas said, sitting up straight and clearing his throat. "I'm sure you've read this in the papers, but the army is having a difficult time subduing some of the more delinquent elements of Southern society. I'm here to ask for your help. I know you hate my presence in this parish and what I represent, but the army is going to clean out these bandits. If I don't get them, then the army will send more men until it's done. It looks as if you're doing well for yourself, so I'm sure you don't want a few companies of troops around here administering the letter of Republican law. If you will help me bring these men to justice, that won't happen. Then we can all go about our business, and I can go back to doing what I do somewhere else." Douglas paused to catch his breath. He pointed to a pitcher of water on the table.

"Help yourself."

Pouring himself a glass, Douglas continued, "What I'm trying to say is the army is going to bring these bastards to justice. It's just a matter of how much of the army north Louisiana wants shoved down its throat. You may have some ideas or be able to help me, thus preventing further bloodshed."

"You little son-bitch," the overseer said. "Are you threatening us?"

Douglas turned to the man who still stood, his large frame now towering over him.

The overseer's facial muscles got tense as he continued his blustering. He pointed his finger at Douglas. "You priss around in your uniform, thinking your shit don't stink, looking down on all of us. Everybody knows you're fucking Colonel Butler's daughter, disgracing her, hanging around over at his plantation that was built by the world you destroyed. You're just a carpetbagger with a uniform. Probably got your eye on the colonel's plantation."

The overseer's words rang out with a deep-seated passion, but the man's flat eyes gave the impression his insides were hollow.

"Can you excuse us, Honus?" Mr. Vaughn said in a calm but firm tone.

A few silent seconds passed as the overseer made his way off the porch and to his mount. As the sounds of his horse's rattling strides ebbed, Mr. Vaughn turned his attention back to Douglas. "My apologies, Captain Owens." Mr. Vaughn picked up a napkin to wipe his lip. "Frankly, it's none of my business. I am aware of your troubles, and I have nothing to gain by taking sides in this fight. And I know nothing that might be of aid to you."

"Mr. Vaughn, surely you can't be so vain as to assume I think you got where you are without some practical knowledge of what goes on around here. So you won't help?"

"Nope. Don't give a damn about the army any

more than I give a damn about the vermin you're pursuing."

Douglas studied the old planter's pale eyes, his reactions, everything about him in an attempt to extrapolate the man's position and opinions. He got the feeling this man feared getting embroiled at all. He currently flourished on the status quo. Though he was certainly one of the most powerful landowners in the region, Hannah had been right, he only nourished and protected his position.

Douglas slowly stood. "I can understand your caution. I am going to bust up the ruthless night riders that prey on innocent citizens. If you want to wait around until the tables start to turn, that's fine with me." Douglas focused on the planter's face. "I only ask that you don't resist me. Let me do what needs to be done. If you do, you can expect to see me back here, with more troops. And I've essentially got a free hand to do just about whatever I want around here. I'm exempt from the local laws and officials' actions."

Mr. Vaughn sat silent for a few seconds, scratching his cheek with his forefinger as his eyes roved quickly. He stuttered before speaking. "I can assure you, Mr. Douglas, I only have a desire to see peace and prosperity for this land. Not myself, nor anyone I hold sway over, will impede that."

"I'll hold you to that," Douglas said, turning to leave. Before he departed, he couldn't help throwing something else in the old man's face. Something that reminded him the times had changed.

"I better be on my way. I have an afternoon dinner scheduled with a Southern belle, the colonel's daughter, as your overseer mentioned. Wouldn't want a Yankee officer to disappoint her."

A few hours later, Douglas approached the ferry he had crossed that morning. To his chagrin, as soon as he topped the little ridge on the river's bank, he saw the ferry departing the little toll station. He would have to wait at least twenty minutes for it to return. He looked across the river to the Cotton Palace. Basil had moved out and into the safer confines of the little army post on the outskirts of town.

Douglas had spent the last two hours methodically deciphering the morning visit. In reality, little came out of it. Mr. Vaughn's voice seemed to carry a false ring. Were Douglas's current duties just a waste of time? There seemed nobody willing to help him. How could these people, who claimed honor above everything else, who had fought so valiantly in the war, not have the stomach to stand up for what was right? Were the defeatist thoughts he brooded over earlier in the morning his only logical sequence? He was running out of plausible options to pursue, and had almost grown tired of worrying about it. What more could he reasonably do?

All of these people totally confounded him. At the academy and in his service, he had intermingled with all walks and races, from every corner of the continent. He had learned there wasn't a trifle of difference in any of them—just about all of them were capable of the same good or bad, internally or externally. Taken individually, the measure of Louisianans equaled the finest stock. The people from these sunbaked, dark bayous and vast fields exceeded Northerners in charity, humanity, and the willingness to help or extend courtesies to strangers and acquaintances alike. But their zealous nature pushed them to the extremes and allowed manipulation by promiscuous elements, especially in times of crisis. He saw this at both ends in their disingenuous deeds and also grand celebrations. It was a puzzle that tore at his soul. In fact, over the last month, as his concern and anxiety had grown, they had started to affect his actions and appearance. He had already gotten drunk twice this week, something he never did, and hadn't shaved in four days. He seemed to have even lost his taste and want for food.

Passing the time, Douglas cantered back down the road in the direction he had come. A few hundred yards later, he veered his horse off to the left on an unkempt drive under a two-acre stand of hundred-year-old oaks. There, he inspected the remains of a once marvelous, spacious, three-story house, its grounds grown over with thick foliage. What remained of the burnt structure, some of the brick facing and several columns, poked up through the new saplings and brush. The grand residence and all its support structures had a lonely feeling, and Douglas wondered at the vast activity that had surely occurred here just a few years earlier. How spectacular the grounds must have once been. Where were the owners, dead or now bankrupt? The entire river basin south of Natchitoches was pockmarked with similar edifices, burnt or destroyed, relics of a bygone era and a testament to the waste of the war. They resembled the ancient ruins of Mexico or Greece he had read about in books or seen in paintings.

The ferry master blew his large horn. Douglas wheeled his horse around and rode back to the riverbank. By the time he arrived at the small toll station, the ferry had moored at the dock. He got off his horse and urged his hesitant mount onto the fragile vessel, handing the operator ten cents. In just a few seconds, his footing got unsteady, and the ferry eased out into the river. Douglas grabbed his horse's bridle, the animal breathing heavy and uneasy, uncertain of the setting.

The henequen rope tethering the ferry to each bank whined over the craft's steel pulleys. The damp wood under his feet squeaked. The water jostled below. The strong, stocky ferry operator with enormous forearms now transferred all his energy to a large wheel, equipped with handles and connected to a set of wooden gears and spokes. The contraption tugged on the rope and pulled the ferry slowly across the murky water. Below, the ferry's planks rested on twenty or so wooden barrels.

Out over the water, all got strangely quiet. Douglas gauged the time from the sun, halfway between its apex and rising, as he looked out at the tall hills and steep outcroppings surrounding the east bank and some decrepit Confederate breastworks high on a ridge. He hated ferry rides. A competent marksman could take out an entire cavalcade before anyone on the ferry ever located the perpetrator.

As the ferry got a hundred yards into the river, the craft's momentum pushing it along, the operator took a respite and walked up beside Douglas.

"Name's Josiah Banks."

"Captain Douglas Owens."

The ferry driver, almost timidly, briefly inspected both banks. He lowered his voice to a whisper. "I'm a veteran of the war of Yankee aggression, 18th Louisiana under Taylor. But me and lot of other folks, the kind not inclined to speak up or make a fuss, is all for you getting rid of some of these folks."

Douglas's ears pricked. He led his horse over to the wheel where the operator had returned. Other than his tight, masculine frame, the man carried a rather mediocre appearance: mid-thirties, of average height, commonly dressed, with unenthusiastic and uninteresting brown eyes and expressions, and a sun-beaten complexion.

"Really," Douglas said. "Which men are those?"

Josiah looked at both banks again quickly as he slowly and effortlessly turned the wheel with little effort. "Sheriff Thaxton and Moses Garrett and his band. Now don't gets me wrong. I don't mind them keeping the niggers from getting too uppity, or running out the damned Northerners." The man paused. "No disrespect intended. But they walk around like they above everybody . . . well, I'll tell ya, folks getting tired of it. Nobody knows, but I thinks it's them who's killing all those good white folks for nothing we hear rumors about."

Douglas added some confidence to his voice, but also spoke softly. "Don't worry, I'm going to get them. You reckon anybody might be interested in helping me out?"

"Maybe, if they thought you might make a difference."

"How many?"

"There's eight or ten that might."

"Men who might ride with me? Who wouldn't be cowed down at the first sound of lead?"

The man produced a truncated smile, exposing his yellow teeth. "These same men ran you bluecoats outta here, didn't they? Don't know if they would ride with you, but they might be willin' to do something to help you."

Douglas looked up. His blood pumped faster, the ferry now two-thirds of the way across the river. "If you know of anybody who might want to help, I can have them appointed deputy marshal. They don't have to be deputized, just help if they can. I pay in gold. Or anybody who might know something, wants to be a witness, come see me. Of course, I couldn't pay witnesses. Might taint their testimony. I'll meet them somewhere more discreet if they prefer."

"I'll do some checking around," Josiah said. He worked the wheel with more zest and raised the tone of his voice. "I do believe it's going to be a fine evening. Might have a drink before I go home. Done a good business today."

The Cotton Palace grew larger in Douglas's vision by the second. He looked at the man again, wondering if he could be trusted. Something told him yes. His mind raced with a thousand thoughts. He wasn't totally sure what the conversation meant. He wanted some time to think about it, piece it all together. Could this man be beneficial, a key to helping him catch the outlaws? His spirit perked. At the least, he now recognized that some people around here sympathized with his cause, at least partially. He had never heard a common man, a working man from the lower classes, say anything even remotely comparable to what he had heard on the ferry. The conversation gave him hope, reassured him that others noticed his work positively. A shot of confidence and zeal rushed over him, and he felt a need to hustle off to Hannah and discuss all of this. As the ferry docked, he jubilantly mounted up and rode off onto more sturdy footing.

22

"Just what I had in mind," Douglas said to the young blacksmith, before grinning at Huff. He turned his attention to the blacksmith's just-completed work, an army wagon, its bed now fitted with a five-foot-square, five-foot-high iron cage. He reached out and firmly gripped the half-inch iron bars, shaking the cage and wagon to ensure their stiffness and integrity. He swung the sturdy little door a few times, making sure its hinges operated efficiently and the opening closed snugly. He turned back to Huff, who also wore a big white smile. "Next time we catch one of those bandits, let me see him escape from this."

"Two mules or horses will pull it fine," the black-smith added.

Basil stepped down from the army captain's office and gingerly ambled toward the wagon.

"How you feeling?" Douglas said, inspecting the gunslinger and the dark yellow flesh around the healing bruises on his face.

"Getting better every day. I'll be back at full speed in two or three days. Worst of it is bunking in these shoddy quarters."

Douglas chuckled. "You may have gotten rid of two of those damn Garretts, but they sure ran you out of the Cotton Palace. Ran your whores off, too."

"Whether the army pays me or not," Basil said, "I'm going to plant those bastards. It's going to be a slow, painful process too. This has gotten personal."

"Maybe you ought to take up honest living for a while," Douglas said.

"*Damned* if I will," Basil snarled. "That'll be the end of me for sure. Just as well let one of those bushwhackers shoot me and put me out of my misery."

"How's Nancy?" Douglas asked.

"Looks like the poor girl's going to live," Basil responded in a serious tone that caused all four men to pause their movements.

A gloomy, somber feeling fell over Douglas. "Can you ride?"

"Yeah, so long as it's not a long trip," Basil answered, raising his eyelids. "What's up?"

"We've got to go up to Lake End tomorrow and investigate the murder of a local colored politician a few days ago. He was found lying in a ditch full of bullet holes. We're to take the steamer first thing in the morning. Don't think it's got anything to do with Garrett's clan. Sounds like just your standard political murder. Probably a waste of time, and we'll ask a bunch of questions, look around, but nobody will know anything or say anything, but I've at least got to fill out the paperwork, file a report. Should be back tomorrow night. I guess some good will come out of it. I hear there's an old Confederate dentist up there. I'm going to get him to pull this aching tooth of mine."

"You should have a gold cap put on it next time you're in Shreveport or New Orleans," Basil said.

"It's killing me, and it's in the back. Nobody will ever notice, not even Hannah when she kisses me." The noon church bells from the town's center sounded. "I've got to go. Want to see Hannah when she lets her class out. Huff, move that wagon around back where nobody can see it."

Douglas walked over to his horse, untied his reins, and mounted up. He had not seen Hannah the previous afternoon when he had gotten back to town from his trip to the Vaughn plantation. Nonetheless, he felt in the best of moods today. Late the previous afternoon, he had received some good news in the form of a telegraph from New Orleans. A squad of cavalry, under his command, was to arrive on a steamer in three days.

A few minutes later, he arrived at the brand-new one-room school constructed on the perimeter of the Butler plantation. The white children were dispersing, walking playfully down the roads and trails spanning out from the school in all directions. Anxious to see Hannah, whom he had not seen since his confrontation with Caroline, he reached to his saddlebags and retrieved a bunch of daisies he had picked that morning. His stomach tumbled with concern. Was Hannah upset with him?

The schoolmarm stepped down off the school's steps onto the ground.

He whistled loudly and waved his hat in a circle over his head. "I brought you some flowers," Douglas said, riding up beside Hannah. He lifted up the daisies and turned to look at a basket tied to the back of his saddle. "And lunch—fried chicken, sweet potatoes, watermelon, and biscuits."

Hannah smiled and Douglas dismounted. Without hesitation, he grabbed the teacher, cradled her in his arms, and placed her on the front of his horse, sideways, her legs and petticoat almost covering his mare's entire side. As she giggled, Douglas handed Hannah the flowers and swung up into the saddle, riding off a few hundred yards to a little meadow on the bank of the Cane River.

There, Hannah hopped off the horse, smelled the daisies with a big sniff, and grabbed the basket from behind Douglas. "I just love flowers. If you're trying to win me over, you're certainly doing it."

Douglas quickly dismounted. When he hit the ground, he couldn't refrain from kissing the schoolteacher, who looked so irresistible in the glare of the midday sun. He loved the taste of her soft, red lips.

"My gosh," Hannah said, recoiling.

Hannah's continued reticence for his affection in an open setting bothered Douglas. "What's wrong?"

"I'm sorry. I'm still not totally comfortable with all this. It will just take time. We should give people a chance to get used to us. Kissing in a field outside the schoolhouse would not be proper for any Southern lady. But I must say, you're awful spirited today. This is just too much after a morning of misbehaving kids."

Douglas retreated and sat on the ground, leaning back in the grass, still cool from the morning dew. "I'll give you a ride home after we eat . . . if that's okay. Maybe your sister won't give me another lecture."

Hannah reached over and brushed his hair with her hand. Her voice got more solemn. "Don't hold what she says and her fits against her. She's not so devious. She's no different than you or I. She only believes what she does because it's what she's been taught her whole life, what everybody with authority has told her. She's never been anywhere but here. She went to finishing school in New Orleans. If you or I were in her place, we'd probably think similarly. I know this violates a common Northern misconception, but on our farm, we never whipped a single slave. All our workers were treated humanely. When there were slaves who ran away from other places, they often showed up at our doorstep. Some of the slaves we owned even showed back up after the war, not even wanting to be paid, just to be fed and have somewhere to live. No one in the Butler house ever violated a single law. Under the old system, you either participated in the system or became one of the vanquished. Those were the hard facts, but many people here fear the freedmen and what they might do after what was done to them. It's only natural."

"I know," Douglas mumbled. "But why does she have to be so hard on me?"

"The army officer we had here before you was very corrupt. Took whatever he wanted. Treated everybody like prisoners. He was generally hated by all. His actions make it difficult for you. I know some of the soldiers in the east behaved honorably, but the Union soldiers here in Louisiana raped, stole, and burned when they weren't hunting down people and settling scores, with bullets. It's hard to imagine how bad we had it here. We didn't even have postal service for almost two years, no currency either. We had to barter to subsist like some type of primitive, native tribe. People in this land of widows and orphans have had their hearts trampled on. Heaven weeps for us. The women here live only in the past, the men only in the present. Simply surviving makes the future impossible to ponder."

Hannah reached over and put the palm of her hand on Douglas's cheek, caressing it softly. "You know I support you, and your efforts here. The South has to modernize to survive. But you have to understand how many people here can't stand the North's hypocrisy. The Northern states wouldn't be so eager to levy black suffrage if they were minorities in their states like we are. New Jersey, Delaware, and your Ohio, just to name a few, don't allow blacks to vote, nor have they passed the Fifteenth Amendment. But the Northern government wants us to cede our government to mostly illiterate freedmen and a few Northern adventurers. You can't expect anything else but resistance from these people."

"But in Northern states, government officials and blacks aren't murdered."

"That's why your job is so important. You have to ensure that law and order come to fruition here. That's what's critical."

Douglas tried to put himself in her position in an attempt to comprehend her thoughts that were almost foreign to him. Though he believed Hannah thought as progressively and liberally as most Boston debutantes, she was possibly the kindest and most benevolent person he knew. Still, she abhorred just the thought of Abraham Lincoln's name with every ounce of her mind and body.

"A squad of new troops will be here Thursday," Douglas said, taking an upbeat tone in hopes of changing the topic. "No new judge; the colonel said he'd send one if I had somebody who needed trying. . . . You know a man named Josiah Banks? Owns the ferry at the Cotton Palace."

"No, never heard of him. Why?"

"Ex-Reb, but told me yesterday, he and some of the small farmers and merchants might be willing to help me root out these night riders. I think he was sincere."

Hannah put a finger to her lip. "There are probably plenty of people who want to see the killing stopped. They're scared, and few are exempt from the rampages. But I wouldn't let them draw you into an open fight. That's what they want."

"I just have to catch a couple of the ringleaders. Get rid of them, and the rest will disband. It's the only way to do it in my estimation." Douglas sat for a few moments. He wanted to change the subject again. The line of conversation was not the reason he had taken Hannah for lunch, but he was having trouble finding the right words to initiate his intended discourse. He looked away to a large patch of sunflowers beside the meadow and then to four egrets sunbathing in the river. "Got something else I want to ask you that's much more important." He put on a bright face, but paused, searching for the correct words.

"What is it?" Hannah said, her eyes getting big above a large smile.

"Well," Douglas stumbled again with his words, his insides churning. He felt his face growing red. "How long have I been courting you? Your sister is right. I shouldn't be staying over at your place, what without us being married and all."

Hannah produced a large smile. "Douglas Owens! Are you about to give me the big proposal?"

Douglas felt an ecstatic, relieved sensation inside. "Well, I've been thinking about it. What are your thoughts on this, a marriage proposal?"

Hannah wrapped her arms around him. "Oh, Douglas, of course I would like to marry you."

Douglas emptied his lungs of air before rattling away excitedly. "You're all I ever wanted. And I'll get a ring next time I'm in Shreveport. When do you want to do it?"

Hannah grabbed both of Douglas's hands. "Darling, not so fast. My answer is yes, but we'll have to do some planning. Let me talk to Caroline first, and then see if you two can reconcile before she goes back to New Orleans in a few days."

"Does this mean we'll have one of those big Southern weddings?"

"I'm a Southern lady, but under the circumstances of the time, we should have a small wedding. We're too broke to have a big wedding anyway." Hannah shook Douglas's hands. "Let's keep this hushed until I discuss it with my family. But you're going to have to take me to New Orleans for a week for our honeymoon." Hannah paused again, and her smile faded. "And also there's one other thing. You're going to have to promise me you're not going to get yourself killed chasing these hooligans. I mean it. I know this country and these men. . . . Nothing you can do is worthy of dying."

23

The next morning, Douglas sat under a small grove of gum trees on the top bank of the Red River, his back against one of the trunks. His horse stood above him, hobbled. From the isolated promontory, he looked down the river where a small steamer had just navigated a bend, the smoke from its two boilers reaching for the heavens.

Douglas checked his watch. The boat was almost an hour late. He turned to inspect the docks below. Basil and Huff were to meet him here to catch the steamer, but they were nowhere in sight. Douglas figured they knew the boat was late, and would be along shortly. He took another bite from a pear, then cut off a large slice of the fruit and fed it to his horse before returning to the papers in his lap.

He had spent most of the last hour going through his twice-weekly ritual: reading a dozen army reports from around the state, and half as many week-old newspapers. Every week, a few political murders occurred across the state, some in the cities, others in the countryside. New Orleans was the worst, a boiling cauldron ready to explode, the opposing forces often fighting pitched battles in the streets with large, organized forces. It was almost a literal second War of Rebellion.

Douglas regaled in reading the differences between the army reports and the propaganda in the dailies. All of Louisiana was in turmoil, one big political tug-of-war. The Republicans needed the Negro vote not only to hold on to power in the state, but also in Washington. To date, the Northern coalition still held a firm grip on the government, but this was tested daily on the city streets and rural back roads. A black congressman had even been murdered recently in Arkansas. Occasionally, there would be investigations of the crimes, and even rarer, a state or even congressional inquiry, but these usually led nowhere, producing only piles of papers to be filed away in some building to turn yellow over time.

Feet shuffled behind him. An icy metallic click sounded. His spine tingled. Beads of sweat formed on his forehead.

"Don't you move," a strange, almost squeaky voice said, only ten paces away.

Douglas froze. He stole a glance down at his pistol, a lifetime away on his hip. Five terrifying seconds passed, the worst of his life. Sweat poured from his skin. His vision got white. His breath got quick and heavy. Was this the end he dreaded? What a dreadful way to go. He finally summoned the courage to slowly turn his head, tightening up, almost cringing, waiting for the quick blast and the impact of lead into his flesh.

Basil came into view, his hands on his hips and a sick smile stretched across his almost normal face. "Just funning with you." He chuckled.

Every inch of Douglas's body and clothes were drenched in sweat. He let out a sigh of relief. His mind still spinning, his vision returning, his anxiety transcended into utter anger as he reached over and grabbed a two-inch rock and threw it at Basil. "Don't be doing me that shit!" he yelled.

Basil laughed louder and longer, a genuine smile forming on his face. "Just joshing you. You oughtn't be hanging out in isolated places by yourself not paying attention just a few days after we gunned down a couple of bushwhackers." Basil produced another evil laugh. "Maybe I taught you a lesson. Didn't mean to stir you up so much."

Still overcome with disgust, Douglas gathered his composure. The last minute had added a year to his life. It was just luck that the man behind him had been Basil. If it had been someone else, he could easily be floating down the river at this very second. He put those thoughts aside and hustled to his feet. "Let's go down to the dock. We're already an hour late. Don't ever do that again. You scared the shit out of me."

Just before noon, Douglas led his two subordinates into a little Negro community a few miles west of Lake End, a small river port with only a few structures. The three-hour trip had been typical, a crowded ride on a steamer, then twenty minutes on horseback through a land populated with dangerous-looking men and the empty faces of women and children. The boat ride had been a blessing in a way. The endless days of riding were enough to wear a trooper's pants thin.

Douglas reined up on the edge of the ten-structure settlement occupying an abandoned plantation. He inspected the pine- and cypress-board buildings, almost all former slave quarters that were now utilized as homes. Little Negro communities had popped up all through the area over the last few years. They almost all centered around their former quarters, with many of the residents now either sharecropping or employed on the same land they had toiled over prior to emancipation.

Most of the communities contained a tight-knit society. After the war, they evolved from the sheer necessity to survive, to prevent starvation, or ward off the other ills of the area. Upon gaining their freedom, the ex-slaves had no money, no property, no government handouts to rely on, and no physical location to flee to. With limited skills and virtually no economy, only the strong and flexible survived. Douglas turned to the cemetery. He saw the fresh grave, and the more than thirty wood crosses that served as testament to the hard nature of life here.

He took a deep sniff; the area had a strange but familiar sweet smell. In the distance, men sang in the fields. He loved the sound of the deep, rhythmic voices bellowing the ageless songs. The wonderful melodies filtered through the trees and over the fields as they had done for generations, a delight to the ear. He had seen no form of self-expression that gave these people more joy.

This very morning, five or six people mingled or worked over the grassless area. The days here were filled with work and few social amenities. Two men chopped wood for cooking, and an elderly woman boiled some water in a large, black kettle as two cute but sleepy-eyed young girls stood beside her.

Another woman weaved a straw basket as she sang: "I want Jesus to walk with me. In my trial, Lord, walk with me."

A large garden, a pigpen, and a livery provided the residents with sustenance as well as goods they could barter or exchange for currency.

All the little communities had a sort of unofficial government, and all had a different personality. Some were docile and nonconfrontational, generally led by a preacher, a schoolteacher, or maybe someone appointed to a local civil position by the carpetbagger government. Others were more rebellious, generally under the sway of a fiery leader, or even whites. These communities turned out to vote and espoused a full piece of the economic, governmental, or social pie, a righting of all the old wrongs. Douglas was a little familiar with this community, sort of a mix of the two extremes. It generally kept to itself, but the local Republican officials had managed to get its residents to turn out en masse at the polls to support the Northern government, both local and statewide.

"What's the name of the fellow who got shot here, and who was he?" Basil asked.

"Jupiter Howard, and he was a politician, elected to the parish government," Douglas said.

"Reckon there's anybody we can talk to?"

Douglas nodded down the little dirt street to a newly constructed schoolhouse. "Probably the schoolteacher." As he spoke, two mangy dogs circled their horses and began barking. Both of the unruly beasts channeled their anger at Basil's mount, causing his horse to get antsy and rear up.

Basil pulled his pistol, ready to plant the rude mutts.

"Don't shoot 'em," Douglas said, laughing as he bumped his horse to ride off. "Probably stir up everybody. . . . Wonder if we could get some hounds to chase down these Confederate raiders."

"That won't work," Basil said and sniggered. "They make too much noise."

Douglas angled his horse toward the men chopping wood. One of the men, shirtless, a rope belt holding up his cotton trousers, looked up.

"Where's the schoolteacher?" Douglas inquired.

The man pointed to the school. "There."

The group rode over to the schoolhouse where Douglas dismounted, instructing Basil to join him but Huff to remain with the horses. He stepped through the school's open door, where he found a man behind a desk at the head of the room. He knocked on the wooden wall twice. "Where are all the kids?"

The middle-aged Negro behind the desk looked up, taking notice of Douglas's military insignia. "Gone home at noon this time of year. They help to get the crops in. If you're here to protect us, you're late." The teacher sighed.

Douglas stepped inside. The schoolteacher wore nice, factory-spun attire, spoke much better English than most of the other freedmen, and had a deep, polished voice to go with a firm, masculine body and graying sideburns.

Douglas removed his hat. "I'm Captain Douglas Owens, Fourth Cavalry. Here to see what I can find out about Jupiter Howard's murder."

"Wish I knew something," the man answered, standing. "All we know is he was shot dead one night walking home."

Douglas pulled out a little writing pad and lead pencil. "What's your name?"

A few silent seconds passed.

"I'm just a teacher," the man finally said. "Education means everything. It's what lets the white man keep his foot on our throats. I don't buy into all that forty acres and a mule, the so-called promise of Reconstruction. Nobody's going to give anything to us. These white folks around here will never change, at least my lifetime. And I got no call to get caught up in the white man's business, his wicked schemes and pursuits of power and profit. And I can read the papers. I know the army ain't staying forever. I'm just a teacher and want it to stay that way. Maybe I make a difference."

Douglas slowly lowered his pad and put his hands on his hips. "Okay, you know if anybody had threatened him? Any trouble he'd been in? Any debts? Things like that?"

"None, other than there were certain elements around here that wanted to get rid of him, what with him being elected to the parish government. They don't like Negro politicians sitting side by side with whites, and electing a few Republicans is not going to change that."

"Don't take this the wrong way," Douglas continued, "but would you say Howard was the antagonistic type, you know, politically? Not that there's anything wrong with that, but it helps me determine if this is a personal or political matter."

"No, he was just a man, a good man, doing his job. I told Jupiter many times to stay out of all that politics. Let things be. It takes time for changes. But he wouldn't listen. But it's not right that they shot him."

The teacher's cynical tone weighed on Douglas, reminding him of the bigger setting, that many people, black and white, thought his work here was a waste of time, just a charade. "Anybody else around here who might want to comment on this, on or off the record?"

The teacher put his hands in his pockets and cast dark eyes on Douglas. "If they thought something might come of it, they might. But since historically that's unlikely, I doubt it. You might say the risk is not worth the reward."

"What about the whites, the Republicans?"

"The state representative, Mr. Foster, possibly has some insights that might be of help, but I believe he's in New Orleans. I can give you his address if you'd like to send him a letter."

Douglas handed his pad to the schoolteacher, who scribbled the address on it.

"Any other major landowners around here?"

"Just a couple other than Mr. Foster, but they're hostile."

Douglas turned to Basil, then walked back outside. He studied the thick, dense woods for anything out of order. The day seemed tranquil. "Let's ride back to town. See if anybody knows anything. Then I'll see if I can find that dentist." He cynically added, "Maybe we'll be lucky enough to get back to town without anybody shooting at us."

24

Twenty minutes later, the three troopers arrived back at Lake End. Douglas felt uneasy here. This area was one of the most contentious under his administration, majority black and officially ruled by Northern carpetbaggers. These bastions of the Northern government had in recent years produced the most frequent and violent clashes between opposing political forces. Like many of these areas in the state, a plan was currently being put in place by the Republicans to create a new parish here, carved out of several surrounding parishes.

Just to the south, the current government had recently succeeded in this unabashed gerrymandering, slicing off portions of Natchitoches, Winn, and Rapides Parishes to form a new and more favorable government entity. To further rub it in the face of the locals, they had named the parish after President Grant and its parish seat after his vice president, Schuyler Colfax. More than a half dozen new parishes were on the docket, most to be named after members of the Northern government.

Approaching the river port's five small buildings, Douglas noticed some commotion in front of the general store. The little community stores in the delta were a source of constant frustration and strife for most of the freedmen and poor whites. They had come to represent the new face of bondage, the store owners exercising a new power—the credit and supplies the sharecroppers required in the altered, post–Civil War economy. The local stores kept their patrons in constant debt with overpriced goods and high interest. Through this, they were transforming themselves and their owners into the hub and control of the land, replacing the plantation houses, and even acquiring significant land tracts as payment for debt.

Pulling up a hundred paces short of the store, Douglas rested his forearms on his pommel, looking and listening. Two white men currently stood in front of the store overseeing two more black men loading barrels into a wagon. One of the black men had busted one of the barrels and its corncobs had scattered into the muddy road.

"You know better than look at me, boy!" one of the white men yelled as he wielded a long wooden cane. "I'm going to dock you a day's pay for that, if not worse." The man raised the cane high and then rapped one of the black men across the back.

Annoyed, Douglas looked at Basil and Huff before slowly riding forward. He reined up in front of the wagon and leaned back in his saddle. "What's your problem, sir?"

"Ain't *got* no problem," the man with the cane said as he looked up at Douglas. "I got business here. That ain't against Republican law."

Douglas let out a long breath, unsure what actions to take. He inspected the two white men thoroughly. Both looked in their fifties, small and stocky, with short necks and manes of shaggy hair. "What's your name?"

"Bubba Smith, from Pleasant Hill. That's James Smith," the man said and nodded to his partner.

"And why did you hit this man?"

"Just trying to teach him to be a good nigger. Black radicals around here got them all stirred up, think they don't have to behave." The man paused a second. "We doing fine around here without your outside meddling."

Douglas produced a smile. "Well, maybe I'll pull out my Henry and whack you across the head a few times. Teach you how to be a good citizen." Douglas reached down and jerked his rifle from his scabbard. He flung it up, cocking the lever as he did.

The two white men's faces contorted, and their eyes roved over the three soldiers, but the scene induced no anxiety in Douglas's gut, only irritation. He almost got tired of these daily episodes, more often than not finding amusement in his reprimands.

The two black men stood by the wagon with their jaws dropped. Douglas felt an urge to reach over and slap the insolent man, or worse, make him and his partner get down on all fours in the mud and pick up the corncobs. He looked back at the two black men. He'd enjoy ridiculing these Rebs, but it would probably result in some adverse retribution against the two freedmen later when the group had headed back into the bush. He didn't want to be the instrument of that. Instead, he pulled out his little pad and began to scribble.

"Bubba and James Smith. I hear of you two misbehaving in any way, I'll come look you up. And I won't be so forgiving next time. Matter of fact, I get over to Pleasant Hill every now and then. I'll stop and check on you to make sure you're being good citizens. Now get this cleaned up. We're going to go in here for a spell. When I come back out, I don't want to see your ugly faces again."

Douglas dismounted, then walked over to the maze of buildings: a few residences, the general store, a saloon, and what appeared to be a warehouse. He tied his horse to a weathered post. "Basil, let's check the bar. Might be somebody in there who knows something about Jupiter's murder, or at least knows where I can find that dentist." He turned to Huff. "You stay here and keep alert. No telling what type of drunk riffraff we might find inside."

Basil led the way inside, opening the wooden door to the small saloon. Inside, two seedy-looking men, both bearded, in their forties, sat at the bar, drinking and munching on a large plate of fried frogs' legs as they conversed with the barkeep, who was similar in appearance.

The two soldiers' entrance caused the conversation at the bar to stop. The two customers turned and inspected Douglas's captain's bars and Basil's sidearms.

"I'll take a drink," Basil snapped, walking up to the bar. "Whiskey."

Douglas sat at a table just inside the door. He removed his hat and nodded to each of the men.

"Any law around here?" Basil inquired.

"Just the sheriff, down in Natchitoches," one of the men answered with a drunken slur, turning up his shot glass. "He don't get up here much. Ain't nothing here, just this half-ass bar, and that group of uppity niggers outside of town. Done got them a teacher from New Jersey. They wants to read, thinks it'll solve all their problems. Make them like white folks."

Basil filled a shot glass from a bottle the bartender had just placed on the bar. As he turned up the whiskey, he continued, "Anybody here know anything about the murder of Jupiter Howard a few days ago?"

The talkative man at the bar turned to Basil. "Probably shot by his own people. They're a jealous, bloody lot."

Basil grabbed the bottle off the bar and walked over to sit down at the table with Douglas, just out of hearing range. "Sounds like everybody's got a sudden loss of memory. Could be just a murder, maybe amongst themselves. Don't know why anybody would give a damn about this wretched place anyway."

Douglas sized up the men at the bar, analyzing their words. He'd probably never find out about the murder. Basil had a point. The Negroes did have a history of taking matters into their own hands. The lack of civil structure and law enforcement in their communities often lent itself to perverse crimes, but this all seemed too convenient, especially for an elected freedman. He quickly tired of his analysis, realizing it made little difference. He had been through this routine before. He had done his duty and had enough information to fill out the necessary reports. He turned his head back toward the bar. "Isn't there a dentist around here somewhere?"

The bartender looked up. "In the store next door."

Douglas looked at his watch. "This shouldn't take long. Ferry will be here in three hours. I'll be back if the old Reb doesn't kill me." He stood and strode outside to the one-room building with a weathered sign hanging over the door that read: Cox's General Store. Inside, he found a short, feeble old man in his sixties sweeping the floor.

"Can I help you?" the man said without looking up from the broom.

"Looking for the dentist."

"That's me," the man said.

"I need a tooth pulled."

The shifty, gray-haired man cast his busy gaze on Douglas, inspecting him. He then turned and nodded to a large handmade wood chair near the window.

Douglas walked to the chair.

The little dentist followed him, then maneuvered the chair so the light from the window fell on its headrest. "Have a seat and let me look. Where's it hurt?"

"In the back, top right," Douglas said, taking a seat. The chair's back angled up at a forty-five-degree angle. He reclined, squinting from the sunlight as he removed his pistol and set it on his lap.

The old man looked at the weapon and then Douglas suspiciously.

"Don't worry. I ain't going to shoot you."

The dentist grabbed his little leather bag, opened it, and retrieved a plum-sized block of wood. "Open up." He slid the block into Douglas's mouth to prop it open and then studied the mouth a few seconds, mumbling to himself. "Pretty bad, rotten, needs to come out. Fortunately for you, that's my specialty. I took a nasty one just like it from General Kirby Smith during the war. Be four dollars." The dentist opened up his bag to expose a dozen steel instruments.

Douglas stared at the sinister-looking tools.

"Ever had a tooth pulled?" the dentist asked, removing one of the large instruments in a businesslike fashion. This one had a sharp hook and lever on one end and an ivory handle on the other. "Lean your head back, going to strap you to the chair."

Douglas shook his head, leaned up, and looked

down at the chair. Two thick leather straps hung from the headboard. He looked again distrustfully at the dentist.

"This will only take a second. You need to keep your head and mouth still, very still. If you think it hurts now, it will be much worse if I break it off and don't get all of it. Now lay back. Don't worry, I can be a gentle old man."

Douglas temporarily removed the block of wood from his mouth and smirked, anxiously leaning his head back. "I've never met a gentle ex-Reb." He felt the old man's soothing hands secure the two leather straps, one over his forehead, the other over his chin, as he replaced the piece of wood back in his mouth.

The dentist then raised the wicked-looking prong to Douglas's mouth. "Be still. There'll be a sharp pain, but quick. Grab the chair with both hands." He then snickered, "Else I'll pay you back for all the army's sins."

Douglas squirmed. He tried to relax, loosen his muscles as he watched the instrument approach, the shiny silver glinting in the sun. Just as he closed his eyes, ready to endure the terrible pain, he heard some screaming outside, several loud, angry voices, one of which sounded like Basil's. He shook his head and raised his hands to restrain the dentist. He reached into his mouth and pulled out the wood block, then secured his pistol in his right hand.

"Cut me loose, now!" Douglas screamed, raising the pistol.

The dentist nervously released the leather straps, and Douglas dashed to the door.

Outside, Basil and Huff stood over the two men from the bar, both now in the street and on their knees, each staring at a hostile gun barrel and wearing complete horror on their faces.

Basil quoted scripture: "All go unto one place; all are of the dust, and all turn to dust again."

"What are you *doing*?" Douglas yelled.

Neither Basil nor Huff turned. Confused, heart racing, Douglas looked around. Not a person occupied the area. He spied Huff, his muscles tensed up and rifle firmly butting his shoulder.

Basil cocked his pistol and quickly fired two shots.

Douglas winced in disbelief, staring in amazement. Neither of the men fell. Basil had missed, obviously on purpose, but both men now whimpered and prayed, begging for their lives.

Basil cocked his hammer again. "I love this, torturing you two lowlifes."

"Put the guns down, now!" Douglas yelled, raising his own pistol and pointing it at Basil.

Basil finally looked over his shoulder to smile at Douglas. "We're not going to hurt these cowards." The gunfighter returned his gaze to the poor men on their knees, continuing to stare them down. "But I'd love to clean up the local blood. These two started this. They'll never pick another fight with me." He finally lowered his pistol. "You two rednecks get out of here. Get back to mule skinning or whatever worthless tasks you keep yourselves busy with. And don't ever cross me again."

Aggravated, disgusted, Douglas let out a long breath and lowered his pistol. He looked back at the dentist, who was standing in the store's doorway watching the events. Douglas had already suffered through the agony of having a tooth pulled, but now had to do it all over again. "Get saddled up, everybody, and get down to the river to wait on the ferry." He stepped back toward the dentist.

25

The warm sun of the October morning shone through a cloudless sky, halfway to its summit. No wind spoke in town, and all the dew had burned off the grass and streets. A line of nine soldiers, mounted, stood side by side on Front Street in Natchitoches. Douglas got his first glimpse of his new troops from his horse. Looking straight at the men, fifty yards away, he turned a corner and rode toward them.

In front of the squad of nine Negro soldiers sat a young white officer, his long, bright yellow hair flowing liberally from under his kepi. He stood in complete contrast to the colored troopers behind him. At the end of the line of horses, one soldier held their guidon. The bright red and white flag of the regimental colors stood out against the sea of blue uniforms and ebony skin. Douglas trotted up to the officer, a lieutenant, who saluted. He returned the salute as he eased back on his reins.

"They're all yours," the lieutenant said in a flat, unemotional voice. "I'm getting back on the south-bound ferry this afternoon."

Douglas looked at the new troopers, all sitting quietly atop their horses with perfect military posture. Gathered around the soldiers, thirty or so residents stared at the line of men. The town sat eerily quiet. The presence of black soldiers here re-sounded, reverberated through every inch and soul of the region, like a churning volcano. The troops' arrival sent a message that the area was now being punished, and the presence of a squad of Federal Negro troops, tasked with policing the area, would have a polarizing effect. Half of the population would behave better, hoping this action might bring a quick end to the humiliating occupation as they were sure to see it, but the other half would be in-cited to utilize all their resources to resist this, force the Yankees to show the white feather and go back from where they came.

Douglas saw no color, only troops under his com-mand. He sucked in a deep breath and shouted, "By the numbers, squad, forward, single column, walk." He turned his horse and slowly led the column back to the small army compound on the outskirts of town. The air was so quiet he only heard the sol-diers' horses' footsteps and their saddles and tack rattling behind him.

Douglas led the column behind his office, to a small parade ground. These troops weren't caval-rymen, but infantrymen on horses. All the col-ored cavalry in Louisiana had been sent to west

Texas to combat Indians. Douglas had requested this. Infantry in this country was useless. He had been informed that all these troops had once served in the now disbanded 4th Colored Cavalry.

He barked a few more orders to confirm the men's ease and prowess on a mount. "Flank right, column of fours." Douglas kept his tone firm and serious. He wanted to see the discipline and training of his new men, but also to convey his competence. He was in charge. He understood how relevant this was, with any command. He yelled again in his most gruff tone, "Countermarch!"

Satisfied with what he saw, Douglas stopped his horse in front of the troops. "Single rank, parade inspection."

With quick, precise movements, the men fell into a perfectly straight line, two paces apart and facing him. A single soldier, a sergeant, trotted forward, stopping six paces and centered in front of the squad. Douglas rode forward, stopping six paces in front of the lone soldier. "To arms."

All the black soldiers dismounted in unison, grabbed their bridles, and stood with stiff stances beside their horses' heads. Douglas slowly rode in front of the line of men and beasts. He looked every soldier in the eye. The men varied in size and age, most black as night with only one being of mixed race.

"At ease." Douglas paused as the men shuffled about briefly. "Post the colors out front. Sergeant, have the men take the horses to the stable across the street. Then release them to the quarters behind me to get settled." Douglas pointed to the building. "You meet me in my office, immediately."

Dismounting, Douglas handed his reins to the sergeant and marched into the building. In his office, he sat behind his desk. The sergeant entered, snapping to attention and saluting.

"As you were," Douglas said casually, without returning the salute. He took a minute to inspect the NCO. He always had difficulty determining the age of the colored troops. They didn't wear their years like whites, often staying healthy well into their seventies. This soldier looked to be in his fifties, maybe sixties, but his short, athletic frame still stood sturdy and strong. The man's eyes seemed flat and without excitement. His big, lean face was adorned with a scruffy beard and mustache. The man didn't look at all vexed or dismayed by this new environment. "What's your name, Sergeant?"

"Dixon, First Sergeant Trotter Dixon, sir."

"Get your men settled in. There's barracks down that hall." Douglas pointed. "We don't have the space for segregated quarters. The men will bunk in the back, you closest to the front. Fall in on the parade ground in one hour. I want to speak to the men. Then we're going to have some target practice. See what your men are made of. The targets are in a closet in the back room. Get them set up on the parade ground as you see fit, set at a hundred paces. Got it?"

"Yes, sir."

"Any questions?"

"Uh, how many soldiers are stationed here?"

"There's just three of us. Another colored troop named Huff, and our scout, Basil."

"Anything else I should know?"

"Mess will be here, three times a day at the standard hours. Our meals are catered to us by the locals. I'll go over everything else with the men this afternoon. Just to let you know, our scout is, well . . . not so agreeable to Negro soldiers in the ranks." Douglas fashioned a small smile. "Your troops look top notch. I've commanded black troops before. And don't worry about Basil. He won't be a problem. I just wanted to give you an honest assessment of everything."

"Yes, sir!" answered Dixon, who then turned and went about executing his orders.

A few hours later, Douglas stood on the parade ground, arms crossed, watching the soldiers fire their Henry rifles. Their marksmanship sufficed, although these troops had been stationed in New Orleans for several years and their military tactics wouldn't be as honed as those of the soldiers in the bush, black or white.

Douglas enjoyed watching them go through the firing drill, stacking arms, and uttering orders between themselves. Being no stranger to colored soldiers in recent years, he thought he understood their traits and tendencies. Unlike white troops, the Negro soldiers seemed to revel in the pomp, the parades, the cadence, always issuing orders with deep, crisp, lively voices. They carried out even the most trivial movements with a theatrical snap in their step.

These troops were of the highest caliber, most probably Civil War veterans, and many literate. Due to Louisiana's early capitulation during the war, the state had the highest ratio of black war veterans in the South, and New Orleans had been a center for raising Negro regiments during the war. The large concentration of colored veterans in the city and the poor Southern economy meant the army had the luxury of choosing only the best for the postwar army. Though there was no scarcity of able colored troops in the South, finding white officers to command them remained a systemic problem. Even though it was widely known that white officers who volunteered for these commands were advanced in promotion, a significant shortage of officers still existed. Blacks still had not been allowed commissions as officers.

One of the paramount benefits of black troops was their general nature of subservience. For all the gusto they displayed on parade, individually, most were quiet, docile, obedient, and much less likely to get drunk, rowdy, and obnoxious, compared with their white counterparts. The drawbacks, though, were vast. The public rarely respected their orders or actions without the presence of a white officer. Even then, the public often got unruly, the troops actually being counterproductive in the mission of pacifying the populace and ensuring tranquility. And to Douglas's constant consternation, most of the soldiers were superstitious. All sorts of odd things caused them to shirk their chores, things as trivial as a red moon or seeing a plucked rooster served as omens to them and induced intransigence to army directives.

Cyrus Carter stood beside Douglas, hands on his hips, watching the troops drill. His gaze got big, and a smile stretched across his face. "We'll get those no-accounts now. 'Bout time the Federal Government pitched in. These troops look top notch. Almost makes me wish I was back in the army."

"Let's hope so," Douglas answered. "I got your paperwork in yesterday. You're now officially a deputy US Marshal." Douglas walked forward to Sergeant Dixon. "Sergeant, assemble the men up. I want to have a word with them. No need for a formation."

Sergeant Dixon shouted a few orders, and in moments his seven soldiers gathered around Douglas.

"As you all can see, you're in Natchitoches now." Douglas crossed his arms over his chest in an informal gesture. "You've been sent here to help apprehend a band of outlaws that recently hung a Federal judge. These hills are full of tough men, not the type of foe you've been policing in New Orleans. Most of the population here hates coloreds, especially colored troops. You may never see your adversary here. They'll kill you without a thought, in an instant, and nobody within a two-day ride of here will give a damn or hear from you again. This ain't New Orleans. New Orleans fell to the Union Army in the first year of the war, without a fight. Despite tenfold the effort by General Banks, these Rebs ran the Union Army out of here. The only way we'll succeed is to maintain constant military integrity. Nobody leaves these grounds without orders. Nobody does anything without orders. You step out there at night, you may not come back. Is that clear?"

His words put a look of gloom on the jovial faces he had seen just moments earlier. "I didn't hear anybody. Is that clear?"

"Yes, sir!" the men all shouted, their deep voices echoing over the green grass.

"I'm a fair officer, and I don't have any problem commanding black troops. In fact, I volunteered for it. I can see you are a quality outfit. But I want it known that I will use every punitive mechanism at my disposal if any troopers don't adhere to my orders. Now, you troops take the rest of the day off, get some rest, and relax. Mess is in two hours. Dismissed."

Douglas remained still as the men slowly dispersed. As he watched their thick, healthy bodies move, he wondered if they had any real idea about their current predicament. Were they just sheep being led to the slaughterhouse? The future dead in this endless, nonexistent war in the middle of nowhere? He would expend all his talents to safeguard them. That was his job, both professionally and personally. Was he up to the task?

26

The next day, Douglas walked to the parish courthouse, where a political rally for the upcoming election was to commence at noon. Due to Republican gerrymandering, the district had a large black majority and had been easily carried by the Party of Lincoln two years earlier, but everyone in the parish believed the seat would now be hotly contested.

The previous year's presidential elections had convinced much of the white community, and its sinister elements, that they could sway the electorate in their favor, even in areas where they theoretically had a significant numeric disadvantage. The old-order political leaders and night riders had perfected their trade and learned how to employ tactics to achieve these results. Their methods included every form of political chicanery and intimidation imaginable: bribery, economic and employment reprisals, whippings, and even murder of potential voters. The chilling visions of Douglas's own dream, the nightmarish whipping at the hands of the clan, which still wetted his palms, reminded him of the persuasiveness of violence, even for third-party observers.

Both parties exploited the political machine itself to their means. The Republicans moved polling places or used the election commissions to sway the vote totals or tamper with the ballot boxes, while Democratic officials often required proof of residence or age that few freedmen could produce or tricked illiterate ex-slaves into voting for the wrong candidate. The Republicans were equally fraudulent in their intentions, but not as skilled, determined, or desperate as their opposition.

In recent days, the local papers had given the election, still three weeks away, front-page coverage, and it had become a hot topic on everybody's tongue. Even with the underhanded tactics, the election would be close. So close that the local Republican leaders had convinced the freedmen that their best chance at victory was to run a white politician who espoused their beliefs.

The large, tree-lined parish square was abuzz with activity as Douglas stepped onto the green grass and leaned against a tree. Almost every wall or fixture around the square held a political poster. Surrounding the square, operatives of both parties handed out pamphlets. Men stood under five or six large tents passing out foodstuffs that ranged from grilled treats fresh off large cooking pits to hard candy. The appetizing smoke and background murmur of conversation drifting through the air gave the scene the ambiance of a festival.

More than two hundred people jammed into the square. Douglas looked to the temporary stage in front of the courthouse, covered with red, white, and blue regalia. In front of the stage, the throng gathered impatiently. To Douglas's surprise, he calculated that almost a third of the potential voters were Negro, the remainder a good representation of the white populace.

Across the square, Douglas saw some of his enemies. He didn't see Sheriff Thaxton, but Moses Garrett mingled around quietly with four or five more toughs. Douglas studied the faces, recognizing a few from somewhere. Had any of them been under the sheets that night he'd met the bandits on the trail? During the elections of previous years, he'd often brought his soldiers to rallies like this to ensure peace and harmony, but now all he had at his disposal was the squad of black soldiers. He'd like to have shown a larger presence here, not that there was any threat of violence, but the sight of army troopers gave the appearance of political stability. However, black soldiers here would be counterproductive to that goal, and Basil hadn't been hired on to oversee the democratic process.

In the past, his men had patrolled the polling stations on Election Day to curb the misdealing, but for this election the freedmen would have to fend for themselves for the most part. Even with his new troops, the quantity of his men had been drastically reduced, and what few he had would likely have their hands full with their daily duties.

Even if he had ample troops, injecting the army into the political process was a delicate matter. Officially, the army was not allowed to prevent public disturbances, but only thwart death and violence if it commenced. Murder was a state crime, and the army's involvement in any part of the political process, other than observing, was strictly forbidden. Butting up against this policy could ruin an officer's career.

Still, he'd try to send out two or three parties of soldiers on Election Day to watch a few of the polls in the colored communities. Maybe he would get some of the additional troops he'd requested. The Democrats' favorite method of intimidation during the election season was to bring large groups of armed men from adjacent states. Since this was the only election in the state, the armed gangs would only have to come from other parishes instead of states. Due to the cloaked nature of their crimes, it'd be difficult to apprehend them even in Northern states.

The frenzy of the crowd grew silent. On the stage, a man dressed in a nice suit and top hat stepped to the front of the wood planks and introduced the first speaker, the Democratic candidate, a large, heavyset man named Bernard Jones, who served as the local postmaster.

"The time is now for change!" Mr. Jones's commanding voice echoed over the heads looking up at him. "We should put the past behind us, forgive and forget. We can't change the past. The new Democratic Party has only one goal: to look after the best interests of all the people."

A few in the assembly applauded.

"These radicals," Mr. Jones continued, his voice growing animated, "these strangers, these Northern thieves and adventurers that are infesting the parish have led us nowhere. Under their leadership the economy has collapsed. People are unhappy. Lawlessness is rampant. What have they given us? What have they done for us? A vote for the Republican ticket will be a vote for more of what we've had for almost a decade: deprivation and poverty. They rule this land like kings and they alone are to blame for the current state of affairs."

The speaker paused to wipe the sweat from his forehead with a rag. He looked down at the crowd, first to the Negroes segregated off to his left, and then to the whites. "I can hardly pay my taxes. The governor and his minions want us to pay for black schools. If the freedmen want schools, that's fine, have them pay for them, or make the Federal government pay for them. Don't take my meager rations for this."

The white gathering let out loud, boisterous applause, and Mr. Jones turned to his prospective black constituents. "And to our new citizens, I say I will work for your needs. The idealistic policies of the Republicans have led you nowhere. I say forget these romantic dreams of reading that have led you to hunger. Go to work in the fields or in your businesses to be productive citizens. I will help you.

I will treat you fairly. The Northerners believe the government can give you wealth, riches. It cannot. Only you and your hard work can make you productive citizens with a stake in society." Mr. Jones raised his hand, pointing to the sky. "I warn you, these invaders lead you around like donkeys while they make themselves rich off of your sweat and toil. They promise you everything. You and only you are the master of your domain. I make no promise to you of handouts, but I will not spare a moment working to give you what you really want, to help you become self-sufficient, empowering you to provide for your families through the only way you can, hard work."

Mr. Jones turned and pointed to his opposition, sitting on the stage behind him, then slid his finger over the entire crowd. "These men will go home one day, but only after they've robbed us of everything. We'll then have no choice but to work together, black and white. I say we start working together now!"

The white mob erupted again with a few shouts from the crowd. Douglas looked to the blacks and a few poor whites in the group. Many nodded silently.

The crowd settled down as the second speaker rose and walked to the front of the stage. Douglas didn't know him, but had read he was a farmer, new to the area, who worked a couple of hundred acres of sugarcane near the southern tip of the parish.

The hopeful politician raised both hands, urging the mob to silence, and turned to the freedmen. "Mr. Jones would have you believe he holds your interests in his heart. The Democrats say they are your friends, but it is they who suppress your vote, sending out parties of terror under the moon. They are the party of slavery and subjugation. They are the party that will do everything in their power to have you, white and black, work the soil for them at as little cost as possible. It was the Republicans who freed you, registered you to vote, helped get Reverend Smith elected to this seat. It is the Republicans who built the new schools for your families, white and black. The Democrats don't want you to read, but *they* can read. The Republicans are the party of free men, working free soil."

Douglas didn't need an education in the local political rhetoric, nor did he care about it. This man didn't have the flair of the first speaker, but seemed more grounded. Though articulate, the short, slight man appeared to be a humble creature of the land, someone who worked with his hands. Most of the Negroes and even some of the whites nodded at his words, but unlike the whites, they did not break into long bouts of cheering.

"We have made much progress," the speaker continued. "No, our actions have not always been correct, but our hearts are filled with genuine concern for the plight of the people of this parish. If elected, I will work for more schools, better teachers, improved credit not just for the wealthy but for everybody. The Republican way is the way of the future. That has already been determined. We must move forward, reconstruct Louisiana, move it back into the Union."

As the speaker continued his bland monologue, Douglas quit paying attention to the words, again focusing on the observers. The rally was more of a charade than anything else. Sadly, the election would be decided not by ideas, but by a force of will. He stared at several of the town's first citizens, most standing on the periphery of the crowd, or on the wooden sidewalks fronting the buildings surrounding the square. Scenes like this reminded him of the importance of his work. They pounded home his enormous responsibility. If he and his men could succeed in exposing the outlaws and their gruesome deeds, they could do more for these people than either of the hopeful candidates' wildest dreams, no matter their core constituency.

27

Before daylight the next morning, Douglas found himself riding the dirt streets of one of the Negro areas just outside of town. He had risen a few hours earlier, and his brief inspection of the barracks had found Huff absent. Suspecting the private had slipped out for a night of drinking and womanizing, a transgression the soldier had twice committed in garrison in Shreveport, he had saddled his horse and ridden here.

The dark morning air sat calm as Douglas inspected the rows of squalid houses abutting each side of the wallowed-out dirt road. The houses were small, many only constructed of discarded lumber nailed together over dirt floors, some resembling nothing more than large boxes. Sewer, trash, and abandoned foodstuffs, discarded around the little community, gave the area a terrible stench.

Douglas, like most whites, avoided this area, its unsightly conditions something society didn't like to look at or think about. Most of the scattered, urban Negro communities had started like this one, on a five-acre plot of low-lying, frequently flooded land purchased by the Freedmen's Bureau after the war as a camp for ex-slaves that had nowhere else to go. A few of the freedmen had purchased adjacent plots, now deemed worthless beside the unsightly shantytown.

The little communities had grown fast, forming their own economies with general stores and even houses of sin. The colonies were a necessary evil for the landed gentry. The freedmen held most of the knowledge of the little details of bringing in the valued harvest, and without their skill, what little wealth that remained would disappear quickly. The colonies kept the valuable labor close, and easily accessed.

Douglas saw a few gas lanterns glowing. He didn't like being out alone, defenseless, especially here this late at night. The clans often visited the Negro communities. He had heard the terrible stories of the masked men entering a residence and dragging someone out of bed to administer twenty or thirty minutes of persuasion, before the helpless individual, begging and praying, promised to vote the Democratic ticket.

These thoughts and the full inspection of the nasty settlement reinforced his recent conversion to the Republican cause. He had once accepted the view, held by even many liberals in the North, that Negroes should be left to obtain social equality through their own merits, and then economic and political equality would follow. But how could someone ever obtain social equality without a political voice?

Two men on foot appeared down the road, breaking Douglas's thoughts. Initially startled, his breath getting quick, he slowly and quietly eased his horse off the road. Relieving his worried heart, he heard the mumbling voices, their distinctive accents revealing them as residents. He clicked his heels and cantered back into the street toward the men, apparently field hands up early and readying for work.

Reining up, the freedmen looked up at him, both squinting their eyes.

Douglas tipped his hat. "I'm looking for a soldier, a black soldier."

Both men stared silently, taking two steps backwards, their faces confused and eyes big.

"One of my soldiers, a big man, black, in uniform," Douglas whispered louder. "I'm just trying to get him back to town."

One of the men pointed down the street.

Douglas rode on down the street another block until he saw a bigger building, just as shoddy as the houses but much larger and illuminated by two large lanterns. He heard voices, growing louder as he approached.

He stepped down from his mount and tied his reins to a hitching post as he eavesdropped. Inside, three men shouted. Drawing his weapon, he stepped into the hastily nailed-together pile of boards. In the middle of the room, lit only by a single lantern, Huff and another large Negro stood, shirtless. Around them, six other men stood, cheering. Huff, his face bloody, held his fists upright, weaving and ducking.

Douglas lowered his pistol and stepped forward, into the light and a few feet from Huff.

The room got silent, and Huff lowered his hands.

"This party is over," Douglas said calmly, flashing his eyes at Huff and then at everyone else. "Get on your horse and let's go, now."

"Let him finish, General," one of the spectators said.

"Yeahs," another young man added.

Douglas grabbed Huff by the arm, pulling him forward, before pushing him to the door. "The fight's over. Let's go."

A young black woman, covered only by a small yellow dress, rushed from the shadows and grabbed Douglas's arm. "Sir's, you got to let him stay. He owe me some of this money he win tonight."

Douglas looked at Huff, standing in the doorway. He reached out and grabbed a wad of scrip tucked into the private's waist belt. He dropped it on the floor, grabbed Huff's army-issue shirt off a chair, and pushed the private out the door.

Two hours later, Douglas rode out to the Butler Plantation. Hannah's sister was scheduled to go back to New Orleans that afternoon, and at Hannah's request, he planned to discuss his wedding proposal with her. For most of two days, he'd thought about how to handle this, hoping he could say or do something to smooth the tension his presence seemed to incite in Caroline.

Douglas planned to be at the Butler house for breakfast at seven, but he was now almost an hour late. As he approached the Butler estate, he looked over at Huff, riding beside him. "I should have you flogged, and may yet, when I have time to bring formal charges. That is, if we're both not dead in a week."

Huff looked at Douglas, speaking with a slight slur. "I's sorry, Captain, but I likes a woman every now and then, just likes you. And likes a drink, too."

Douglas stared at Huff, his blood boiling, his eyes focused firmly.

"Basil get drunk all the time, shoot everything up, and nobody care."

"The rules are different for Basil. You know that. He's white, and he's not a uniformed soldier." Douglas pulled up. The Butler house had come into view, down the road another half-mile. He reached over and grabbed Huff's reins and pointed. "Go over there to that little meadow, lie down, and take a nap. I can't take you back to the barracks like this. That would cause a stir, and the whole damn squad would think they can sneak out and get drunk or go to a brothel. It'd be a mess by the end of the week." Douglas looked down the road, then at the morning sun, and pointed to the meadow. "Right over there, under that tree. I may be a couple hours. I'll take your horse, so no bushwhackers will come by and shoot you. You be there when I get back here, whenever that is."

"Yes, sir," Huff said, dismounting.

Riding up to the Butler house, Douglas saw Hannah standing outside the large barn and administrative building adjacent to the main residence. Two elderly Negro women sat on a bench in front of it shelling peas.

Hannah waved as Douglas dismounted and walked into the barn. Inside, Caroline, who had her hair pinned up and was wearing a red dress topped with a tall, stiff collar, sat at a table. Across the table, which was covered with a few stacks of paper, two black laborers gestured with their hands as they spoke. Mr. Jones, in his sixties, with a hard, leathery face, stood in his overalls beside Caroline. Three more laborers stood against the wall, waiting.

"Come in here," Hannah said, leading Douglas into a small office. "Caroline is trying to negotiate new contracts with the Negroes." She grabbed Douglas's hand. "I'm sorry, this is not the best time, but Caroline is going back to New Orleans tomorrow morning. She's been busy most of the day, and I don't think she's enjoying this."

Douglas peeked through the office's small window. Tension filled the barn. Caroline's face had drained of color, and her voice rose as she waved her hands. Mr. Jones lifted one of the papers and scribbled on it before returning it to the table. The two laborers shook their heads in disagreement, and Caroline stood, fanning herself. She picked up the papers, handed them to Mr. Jones, primly turned her back to the laborers, and walked to the office.

Slamming the door, Caroline sighed deeply and fanned herself again. "I can't take this anymore. They just don't understand."

"What's the problem?" Hannah said.

"They all just want contracts to rent the land for a share of their yield. What happens if their crop yields are low? I tried to explain to them that the bank does not care about that. The mortgage is a fixed rate, no matter what, and we need a set amount for every forty-acre parcel. I hate this. I can't negotiate with them. They don't understand the realities of the world."

Douglas stood silent. An awkwardness filled him, he an outsider stuck in the middle of the family's troubles.

"Let us not talk of this now," Hannah said. "I've asked Mr. Owens to come out. As I told you, he's asked for my hand, and I've accepted."

Douglas removed his hat as Caroline flashed her gaze at Hannah.

"Yes, yes," Caroline said. "I will discuss it with Mother." She stepped closer to Douglas, looking him in the eye. "You are an hour late. When a Southern gentleman visits the hostess of the house, he is usually on time."

Biting his lip, Douglas wanted to remind Caroline she no longer commanded over anything of importance.

"I'm not going to get my blood up," Caroline

said, "but frankly, I don't see any way this will ever work. And, Mr. Douglas, I think in time you'll come to understand this as much as I do."

Douglas stood erect, placing both of his hands behind his back. "I plan to make this work. I'm in love with Hannah, and I can't imagine anything that will change that. Caroline, I know you detest me, but I'm not sure you even know me. You only detest my uniform."

Caroline interrupted, "And where you're from."

Douglas produced a small grin. "Caroline, I'm prepared to resign my commission from the army if need be after Hannah and I are married. I could be of help around here. You need a man to run this place and you know it." Douglas turned and looked back out the window at Mr. Jones and the laborers, then to Hannah, her eyes big. "My record with the army will make it much easier to work and negotiate with the Negroes, and I do have some business sense. I *did* graduate from the United States Military Academy, just like Generals Lee and Beauregard, and most of your Confederate war heroes that you all think are incapable of wrongdoing."

Caroline put her hands on her hips, the tight lines of her face loosening. "I will discuss it all with Mother."

"Can I even get you to acknowledge my intentions are sincere?"

"That is '*may* I even get you to,' Mr. Owens." Caroline's gaze moved up and down Douglas. "And if we're going to have our blood soiled, we do plan on getting something out of you. I'd like to see you lazy Yankees dirty your hands for once. And the next time you pay us a social visit, please do it without that hideous uniform, and clean those dirty boots. We *are* a cultured family."

28

The next morning, Douglas looked down at the gray, powdery remains of two skeletons, lying a few feet apart. Not a trace of flesh remained around the bones. He touched the femur of one and it fell apart like the ashes of a burnt log. He let out a deep breath and looked around at the charred remains of Cyrus Carter's four-bedroom house on the plantation he had recently purchased a few miles outside Natchitoches. It was now a pile of ebony cinders surrounded by a green lawn and under what remained of the house, a chimney, a wood-burning stove, a few pots and pans, and personal items.

Though the smoldering monolith still remained warm, expelling small tendrils of gray smoke, the thick morning dew had fallen on the remnants of the residence, allowing a close inspection. The house was nestled up in a lovely bend in the Cane River, on a tall bluff under towering oaks, and overlooked the tranquil water. A local newspaper reporter surveyed the scene, scribbling on his little pad. Beside the reporter stood three torches, stabbed into the yard, their tops covered with soot, the symbol of the Knights.

Isaac Wright, the editor for the largest newspaper in town, the *Natchitoches Times,* decidedly a Democratic institution, covered the story. Isaac hated Douglas, mostly because of his own infatuation with Hannah. Douglas suspected Isaac belonged to the Knights and had ridden with them during their reign of terror a year earlier. Slight in stature, nervous, and quick-mannered, the reporter looked to be one of the least dangerous creatures on the planet.

Douglas pondered what the headline would probably read: "Local Northern Farmer Dies in House Fire." Anytime the army arrested someone or did almost anything, the headlines often read: "Federal Cavalry Intimidates Local Officials," or "Wholesale Arrests, Army Impedes Local Voters," et cetera. Though Douglas had often looked condescendingly on the man, like a fly that needed swatting, at this moment, in this burnt house, he thought how gratifying it would be if Isaac threw down on him. An inexplicable hate came over Douglas, almost a want, a desire. How pleasurable and satisfying it would be to fill this man full of lead.

"Cyrus's brother?" Douglas asked, pointing at one of the bodies as the reporter walked off and took a seat under a distant tree in the yard.

"I reckon," Basil replied. "They have any family?"

"He had a big family and was planning to bring them down this spring to work the farm."

Squatting, Basil pulled out his knife and delicately extricated some of the burnt material from around the bones. "Hard to tell if they were shot, or just couldn't get out of the house—probably shot first, I'd say."

"Not hardly enough to bury. I'll send the undertaker out here. See if he can gather up enough to bury. . . . This mean anything?"

"I'm thinking on it." Basil stood, put his hands on his hips and looked around. "Probably not. A carpetbagger like Cyrus, one that's so vain and outspoken in taking up the Radical cause and ramming it down these people's throats. This is the result of his actions. This would have most likely happened if me and you had never even set foot in Natchitoches Parish. The day he bought this farm, he was probably doomed. Anyway, it's just one less rider in our cause. These raiders may not even be the ones we're chasing." Basil turned to look at the front lawn. "But judging from those tracks out front, it was a big party, maybe a dozen. . . . By the way, how's your tooth?"

Only Basil would ask a question like that at a time like this.

"Getting better . . . I may get those additional troops I asked for, maybe white ones, and enough to make a real difference." Douglas looked sternly at Basil. "What about the Butlers, Hannah? You reckon there's any danger of something like this happening to them?"

"Not likely. Not Colonel Butler's family. That would be very desperate even for a bunch of outcast militia. It's you they want to plant. Ain't much you can do anyway. You can't guard everybody. If they want somebody, they'll eventually get them."

"That's reassuring." Douglas walked over the ashes toward the front yard and the reporter. He paused, turned to Isaac, and pointed to the ground. "You see all these horse tracks and those torches . . . you going to include those in your story?"

Isaac continued to scribble on his pad without looking up as he responded, "A good journalist only reports facts, not hearsay or conjecture." He stopped his writing and looked up at Douglas, inspecting his uniform, then looked down at the pistol on his belt. "The pen is more powerful than the gun . . . or any army."

Hannah's voice drifted behind Douglas in the Butler house's large kitchen. He looked over his shoulder from the dinner table at his fiancée. She was preparing some cornbread. Not paying attention, Douglas wasn't even sure what she said, but the sound of her voice as she made his dinner soothed his soul. She rambled on about how much she missed playing the piano. The Union soldiers had destroyed their treasured old grand piano one night in a drunken frenzy during the war. He looked out the window at the setting sun, laying a wonderful burgundy mantle of light over the Butler plantation.

His day had been long. He hadn't spent it mourning, distraught, or analyzing Cyrus's senseless murder the night before. Maybe Basil was right. It had nothing to do with him and his new soldiers, who had now been in Natchitoches for two days. He fretted more about who or what was next.

Douglas had spent the afternoon drilling his new troops for two hours, but decided more of this would probably be bad for morale. The squad appeared to be a fun-loving bunch, often spending their spare time singing, clapping, clattering tin cans, and playing energetic harmonicas in rhythm with their deep voices. They enjoyed sitting in small groups telling overdramatized stories that concluded either with a chorus of laughter or heated debate. Initially, all the soldiers looked the same, and he only saw a collective image of the unit, but now he began to get to know the troops as individuals, getting a sense of each man's personality and qualities.

The constant noise in the barracks had forced Basil to take up residence at the City Hotel downtown. This amused Douglas, for the proprietor of the hotel was a devout Baptist and tolerated no indiscretions on the property. The army captain had decided to seek his own form of solitude at the Butler plantation.

He needed to do something with the troops. Nothing degraded morale more than idle time. The countryside had been quiet lately. He figured in a day or so he'd take the squad into the hills for a night patrol, hoping he might discover some impropriety. Maybe he just needed to wait. Basil had said the bandits would come after them and not vice versa. Cyrus's plight reminded him he always needed to be ready.

As Hannah cooked, Douglas pondered Huff, what to do with him. He had grounds for almost anything, but he had bigger problems. He needed men. Huff had to be punished, to the full extent of the military code, but could he spare him? As often was the case, and much to his constant dismay, at his isolated post he had no other officers to discuss critical command decisions. He was the master of his actions, failing or succeeding on his skill and merit only.

As he weighed his options, he noticed some movement outside and stood, focusing his eyes. From the kitchen window, he saw the silhouettes of two men on horseback slowly riding up the drive to the Butler house.

"Hannah, you expecting anybody?" Douglas's voice crackled. "Two horses approaching out front."

Hannah turned, covered the fire on the stove, and moved to Douglas's side where she looked out the window. "No."

Douglas removed his pistol and handed it to Hannah. He then grabbed his shotgun and leaned against the wall, straining his eyes. The men on horseback, still only silhouettes, tied their horses to the rail on the front porch.

"You think there's more of them?" Hannah whispered, voice trembling.

"I've been told, daughters of Confederate war

heroes aren't usually their targets, but you never know, your house may be next on the list, after Cyrus."

A pair of footsteps rattled on the front porch, followed by two soft knocks on the door. Douglas, his throat getting thick, lifted his shotgun and stepped in front of the door, five paces from it. He raised the weapon and pointed it at the door, gesturing for Hannah to open it, standing out of view.

As Hannah slowly turned the knob and opened the door, Douglas looked down his barrel. In the half-light, he recognized the face of one of the men, Josiah Banks, the ferry master he had talked to that day after his meeting with Hiram Vaughn. Douglas slowly lowered the shotgun, but kept it at the ready.

"What do you want?" Hannah asked.

"Miss, I's lookin' for Captain Owens."

Douglas stepped forward.

"Captain Owens," the man said, "it's Josiah, from the ferry, Josiah Banks. Got somebody who wants to talk to you. You told me to come see you if I knew of anybody who might know something about the night riders. I didn't really want to go to the garrison with all the peoples watching, but I seen you heading out this way earlier and I's seen you here a few times. Figured you might be here, or I could leave you a message."

"You found me. Come in, where I can see you."

Both men slowly ambled inside. With the glare from the house's lanterns, Douglas deduced that neither carried a weapon. He lowered his shotgun farther, its barrel now pointing at the floor. "Sorry about that. Can't be too careful nowadays, especially after what happened to Cyrus Carter last night. This is Hannah Butler, the mistress of the house."

Hannah extended a hand and smiled. "You men want some coffee? I've also got some fresh cornbread and bean soup. Please, have a seat at the table."

"Why, thank you, ma'am," Josiah replied, tipping his hat and following Hannah to the table. "This is Sidney Crow, and he may have some information for you."

Douglas reached out and shook the other man's hand, noticing the dirt under his fingernails. He appeared similar to Josiah, but very short, maybe five feet three inches at best, with long blond hair, sporting a rough, bland farmer's makeup and outfit.

Hannah set three cups of coffee on the table, and the two guests each took small sips.

"Yes," Douglas said. "I would most certainly be interested in anything you might know about the night riders, or who killed the judge or Cyrus. Anything."

"Well, I-I," Sidney said, slightly stuttering. "I was really scared to talk to you because of what they might do to me. But it's just gotten too bad lately. I just felt I needed to talk to somebody."

Douglas leaned forward. "Do you know any specifics about Cyrus's death?"

"No, not about any of that. But, 'bout a month or so ago, me and my son were sitting out on the porch one night. I lives 'bout one mile other side of the ferry, across the river, 'bout a quarter-mile off the road, just before the flat plays out. You may know it, little brown house north of the road. I farm hundred-fifty acres, and it's my own land. Tell you, farming's been tough lately, what with all the floods and caterpillars and Yankee taxes. Even with all the good prices, I barely get by at all."

"Yes, it's been very tough the last few years," Douglas said.

"Wells, anyway, this exact night, we's up on the porch, say around midnight, waiting on the moon to come up for we's aiming to go coon hunting. Lot of people say I got the best hounds in the parish. Anyways, we heard some shots from back in the hills. Three shots. So's being a good neighbor and all, I decided to walk over and see what all the fuss was about. Likes I said, the moon was now up good, so I could see a fair piece. When I crossed this little hill, where the road came into view, right there where they say Mr. Smith used to have a gin long time ago, I saw two men dumping three bodies in an old well. I hid behind some trees and tried to see who it was, but both men wore masks. I stayed still. I was scared and didn't want them to see me. I know what they do. Anyways, after they threw the bodies in the well they got back on their horses. They took their masks off for a second to fire some tobacco, and I saw it was Clinton Dallon. The other man was his little brother, Amos. You know, the one that's just a pup, maybe nineteen years or so. Didn't see him, but I know'd it was him. Real small, and I heard him talk, sounded just like him. One of the people they threw in the well was an army soldier, had a uniform just like yours, but the others were just normal folks."

"And you'd be prepared to tell a judge and jury this?" Douglas asked, taking a large gulp of coffee.

Sidney's eyes roamed nervously but seriously. "I don't really want to, but I will. That Sheriff Thaxton has it in for me. Figure he's going to get me one day, anyway. So does Moses Garrett. He's the den captain. See's, I used to ride with them back during the elections. But I quit afterwards. He don't like that I quit, and he's always pushing me around, trying to get me to do things I don't want to do. And he owes me a hundred dollars for some hay he took from me last year. I didn't never mean no harm, but I didn't want General Grant to be president, not after what he done to us. But these dumb black folks around here just vote how the carpetbaggers tell them. We can't have that. I seen things back when I rode with them they don't want nobody to know about, but I ain't going to talk about that stuff if that's okay. These killings lately have gotten too bad."

"You have any family?" Douglas asked, trying to figure his next move and the applicability of all this.

"Just a son. He's up in Shreveport now, looking for work. The fever done took my wife, and my eldest son died at Antietam, Ewell's Division. Stopped those Yanks cold, sent them running."

Douglas turned to Josiah. "Anybody see you come here?"

"No," Josiah replied. "I ride out this way all the time, Sidney here, too. We buy oats from Mr. Stanton on down the road. But like I said, I kept a good watch."

Douglas nodded to both men. "I'm going to go to town, get a few more soldiers to come out to the house tonight. Josiah, you get on home. I'm going to check all this out tomorrow. Telegraph Shreveport for the judge. Sidney, best you stay here for now."

About eleven that night, Douglas gently knocked on Hannah's bedroom door. He had spent the last few hours riding back and forth to the garrison, bringing two soldiers to the house to guard Sidney. He had settled the guards in and given them orders that someone was to be awake and watchful at all times.

What did it all mean? It was certainly a turn for the good, but this only magnified his worries. This all seemed almost too good to be true. Could it be? Everything in his mind grew more urgent, adding a sense of anticipation to his concerns. Was Sidney genuine? Would he testify? Was this some type of trick? Possibly some elements of the clans or society had fed him Sidney, in hopes the army might clean this mess up for them, sparing them the dirtying of their hands. Was there an internal struggle within the secret groups? Did the clans or anybody really know who the night riders were? Tired of pacing, and trying to settle his psyche, he slowly opened the door to find his bride-to-be sitting in bed, reading by the light of a gas lamp.

"Well, this is a surprise," Hannah said, her face turning red. She lowered her blanket, put her book aside, and stood. "Didn't know it was proper protocol for an officer and gentleman to indulge in front of his soldiers."

"It's not. I just needed a break." Douglas stepped forward. "It's been a long day."

Hannah grabbed the gaslight beside her bed and hurried over to a little nightstand with a mirror where she began to tidy herself up. "Let me make myself presentable." She pulled a blouse over her head and turned her back to Douglas. "Can you give me a hand?"

Douglas reached over to the two buttons on the back of the blouse. "I can, but I'm much better at unbuttoning you than I am buttoning you."

Hannah laughed. "Captain Owens, I bet you're rather witty when you're not so serious all the time."

"I look forward to a time when none of us is so serious all the time," Douglas mumbled, pulling back the curtain and looking out the window.

"I let Mr. Jones know there'd be some men staying at the house tonight."

Douglas removed his holster and sat on the bed. It felt good just to remove the weapon from his waist. "I bumped into that reporter who's so smitten with you at Cyrus's this morning. Wonder what he'll have to say in tomorrow's paper."

Hannah smiled as she combed her hair. "I'd never pretty myself up like this for him. You should feel honored."

"He's harmless," Douglas added.

"No, he's not. He's a slimy, cold killer—as bad as Moses Garrett. More dangerous with that pen of his and all of his radical rhetoric." Hannah flashed her gaze on Douglas through the mirror.

"How do you know that?"

"Just speculation, but trust me. Women know these things."

Douglas stood and stepped forward, behind Hannah, and put his hands on her shoulders, gently massaging them. "He sure sells a lot of papers. How's that? I'm certain the majority of folks around don't adhere to his beliefs."

"He certainly has a rivalry with you, not just over me. He fuels the people's venom, and they're easy prey for him." Hannah stood and put a finger to her mouth. "After all we've been through, becoming minorities in our own communities and being ruled by outsiders is unendurable. It's just too much, too fast. Even the common man wants to hear that. Until they regain control of the government and have no one to blame, they'll be easy prey for these newspapermen."

Douglas thought about pitching a rebuttal. To a person, almost every native white citizen in the state assumed that the regaining of white, home control of all forms of state and local government was a foregone conclusion despite the fact that simple mathematics made this impossible. He ran his hands through his hair. "I used to think all this was a lot of trouble so a bunch of ignorant Negroes can vote, but I'm learning there's a lot more to it than that. I can't just let everything be . . . I just can't, but it's all so confusing. Good or bad depends on your point of view. I was probably chasing Josiah and Sidney last year, and may again sometime."

Hannah looked over her shoulder. "You've got to get these men. They'll stay after you. Their blood is thick. It's probably you or them."

"Ah, I'm just thinking out loud. I'll finish this. I've got orders, and I always follow them, no matter what."

Hannah walked to her bed and sat. "Quit trying to fight these outlaws by your rules. It won't work."

"I'd feel a lot better if I'd get those additional soldiers I've asked for."

"What about Senator Dunn? I thought he was going to find some men for you to deputize."

Douglas sat beside Hannah. "I've talked to him. Says there's a lot of people out his way behind me, but none that are willing to ride with me."

"Well, let's talk about something else, something not so dreary."

"What did you have in mind?"

Hannah caressed her neck. Like a jolt, this removed Douglas from his troublesome thoughts. She slowly disrobed, then blew out the gas lamp. "But none of the good people around here will tolerate what these night riders perpetrate. And . . . it looks like my daring groom is about to bring them to justice."

29

After a near sleepless night, Douglas sent for both Senator Dunn and the town's mayor, a local Democrat, and his secretary. In front of all three, and with the mayor's secretary keeping a good written record, Sidney retold the story he had told Douglas and Hannah the previous evening.

Douglas had left the two soldiers to guard Sidney, and now, late into the afternoon, he sat horseback as the crew of hired Negro laborers, guarded by four of his soldiers, worked to remove the bodies from the abandoned well Sidney had told him about. The old water source sat hidden in an overgrown thicket just off the Winnfield Road. The men had placed a long ladder into the well, and set up a series of ropes and pulleys to access the dark, damp crevasse and remove the corpses. The foreman of the work gang had already informed Douglas that the well contained a trove of carcasses.

Three bodies already lay stretched out on the ground. The town's undertaker, wearing a cloth

mask over his nose, currently stood over them,
pouring lime on what remained of the rotten cadav-
ers. The young army corporal, who had come up
missing seven weeks prior, was easy to identify in his
uniform. The three bullet holes in his chest were
still visible. Not enough remained of the two other
disinterred souls for identification.

The scene had an urgent, busy air in the late day.
Despite objections, Douglas had coerced Natchitoches's mayor to come to the well. Senator Dunn
also inspected the work, and an artist and notary
from town were both now engaging in their trades.
The artist busily sketched the dead as Douglas inspected his work. The army captain wanted to make
sure he had everything documented meticulously.
To Douglas's delight, no crowd had showed up at
the well site, not even a reporter. He'd only seen
two farmers ride by, and neither seemed acutely interested in their exhuming. Looking over the scene,
he joyfully thought he might finally have enough
evidence for a conviction, even with a hostile jury.

"What, or rather who, else is down there?" Douglas asked the crew foreman, a tall, thick freedman in
his fifties, as he climbed up the ladder and over the
three-foot-tall brick wall casing the well.

Finding his feet, the foreman lowered the rag
wrapped around his face, wiped the sweat from his
dirty brow, squinted from the bright glare of the
sun, and set the gas lantern on the well. "Probably
four or five more down there, maybe more, but
they's just bones. No flesh left. Say they's been down

there a while. We'll try to get them out best we can, keep them separated for proper burial."

Douglas turned to look over his shoulder as his troopers pulled a wagon up, readying it to load up the bodies. He turned to the undertaker. "I want to bury them in town."

A purple dawn broke against the tall trees and maze of hills the next morning. The peaceful ground lay covered with dew, the air full of mosquitoes. From the saddle, Douglas looked up at the complex of houses and barns, the Dallon farm. He felt tired this morning. Despite the fact he had exerted little physical energy the last few days, he hadn't slept well the last two nights, spending all his gusto scheming and fretting. A surge of excitement and satisfaction almost overwhelmed him. He now stood at the precipice of all he had strived for the last few months.

It had been a long morning. He had left Basil and Huff at the Butler house to protect Sidney. He'd like to have had Basil at his side, but the gunslinger had a long-standing feud with the Dallons. He wanted the Dallons alive.

The cavalry line of eight soldiers had departed Natchitoches an hour before daylight, arriving at the ferry at Campti ten miles north of Natchitoches in time to catch the first ride of the day. They crossed the Red River in the portentous still of dawn, the only sound the rumbling water and cocks crowing.

Douglas had planned to arrive at the Dallon

Farm, a mile into the hills on the edge of the delta, just after daylight in hopes of finding the outlaws asleep, possibly worn out from a night of unruliness. But without Basil to lead the way, the column had gotten sidetracked for an hour and a half, taking a wrong turn on one of the trails, one of the many that composed the infinite labyrinth in these hills.

To the east, the sun now peered over the trees, brightening the day with first light. A few clouds carved up the horizon, placidly turning from violet to crimson. In the pasture beside the road, some good-looking cows stood almost lifeless, like statues. He heard shuffling, but it was only a raccoon, scurrying through the pine straw. He listened diligently in the half-light of the wilderness as his mare quietly grazed under him. This bewildering land of green made you see things that weren't there: deceptions, illusions, mirages. The more you stared, the more you saw.

Douglas looked down at a hand-drawn map and surveyed the ground again. Everything matched. He looked up at the farm. Maybe its occupants were still asleep? Hope filled him. Five troopers and their horses sat behind him in a line, side by side. Two more sat atop the wagon, holding the makeshift iron cage behind the horses. The men looked powerful and competent in their blue uniforms.

"Sergeant Dixon," Douglas said in a low voice. "At arms." The five soldiers all removed their rifles from their scabbards, worked the levers, and held the rifles across their laps. "We're going to quietly ride up there. I'm going to take two of your men into that house on the right, the big one. You and the other three will keep a watch outside, dismounted, on the corners of the house in case we need you. Try to stay concealed best you can. We won't bring the wagon up until we have the criminals in custody. We want to take them *alive.*"

Douglas led the five soldiers to the house that was a hundred yards away. He hugged a treeline at the edge of the open field to cover his approach. As he neared the residence, he saw nothing amiss, not a soul in sight, but the farm's five buildings left plenty of areas out of sight. He thought about circling the house, surveying all the buildings, but decided against this. It would increase his chance of being seen and might stir up some dogs or chickens.

Reaching the front door, all the men dismounted without a word. Douglas waited for Sergeant Dixon and his two men to deploy to the front corners of the building, where they knelt behind some tall shrubs. He then hunched low and tiptoed to the door, his feet moving softly over the worn porch. With two of the soldiers covering him, he checked the latch of the entrance. To his surprise, it wasn't locked.

He opened the door and led the soldiers inside. The house was small, only four rooms. Not a human sound came from it. Douglas strode through the dining room and kitchen. He inspected the first bedroom, the bunk unmade, but unoccupied. He stepped to the other bedroom. As he peeked across the threshold, he saw a body, a teenage boy, snoring gently on his back under the sheets.

On Douglas's cue, the two soldiers raised their rifles at the youngster and Douglas stepped forward. He grabbed the lad's arm and jerked on it hard. Young Dallon uttered something incomprehensible. Douglas put a hand over the teenager's mouth as he pulled him out of bed.

The young man finally got a grasp of the situation and began to resist, fiercely. Douglas raised the shotgun and struck the teen across the face with its butt. "Where's your brother?"

With less vigor, the young Dallon, dressed only in his long johns, continued his struggle. Douglas turned to the two soldiers. "Give me a hand. Let's get his hands bound behind his back. We'll get some answers out of him then."

The soldiers scurried forward. They placed their rifles on the bed and wrestled with the captive, who now renewed his resistance with all his fortitude, ranting loudly.

A deep voice boomed from the door like a bolt of lightning out of nowhere. "And the Lord said: sit at my right hand, until I put your enemies under your feet."

Douglas turned to see the barrels of a shotgun locked on his chest. Behind the barrels stood a rangy, slim man with greasy black hair and a big, sick smile above a long, full beard. The beard reminded him of those so popular with Confederate officers during the war, but rare in the Louisiana climate. Douglas had never laid eyes on Clinton

Dallon, but this man matched his description. On one side of the assailant stood a tall, middle-aged, attractive woman with fair skin and a fine, vigorous figure. On the other side stood a black man, solid and healthy, probably in his thirties.

"God damn you to hell," the man holding the shotgun said. "Touch him again and I'll kill you before I have the amusement of wounding you a couple of times first."

Douglas slowly stood erect from his hunched position. He held out his arms and scanned the two soldiers, scrambling for their rifles on the bed, urging them to freeze. Looking back at the shotgun, he waited for the impact. He tried to stall, hoping the soldiers outside would come to his rescue. "We're taking him and you in, to stand trial for the murder of Corporal Taylor. You can't get us all. You've only got two shots."

"I can get you," the man said and grinned. "I'll take my chances with these two, probably get my pistol out before I go down. If not, I'll go to the pearly gates with a big crown."

Douglas looked to the black man standing beside Clinton. "We've got witnesses, even if you get us all."

"Not Buck," Dallon said. "He's a good nigger."

"Drop that gun!" Sergeant Dixon said, out of sight. "Now, or go see the devil."

Clinton stole a glance over his shoulder. Then returned his gaze to the shotgun aimed at Douglas.

Sergeant Dixon and another soldier came into view outside the bedroom's door, behind Clinton.

"I says drop it," Dixon said again, but louder.

A few gut-wrenching seconds passed. Douglas's collar got wet and sweat beads poured down his back. Clinton's eyes roved wildly and his body shook, his hands quivering a few seconds before he lowered the shotgun.

Sergeant Dixon stepped forward and kicked Clinton in the ass, violently, sending him a few paces forward. "You's under arrest."

Completely relieved, dizzy, his vision almost blurry, Douglas tried to reestablish his composure. He and both the soldiers near the bed rushed for their weapons and put everyone in the room in their sights. "Go fetch the wagon. Let's get them loaded up. I want to go back to town the back way, come in from the west. And . . . I don't want a big ruckus. Does everybody understand?"

30

Douglas walked through the stable across the street from his office to inspect the army stock. In the barn, four or five soldiers tended to the horses, inspecting their hooves and shoes and girder burns, and trimming the manes neatly. A few soldiers mended tack or uniforms.

Douglas loved being around the barn; the sweet smells of manure, hay, and leather were invigorating. He was, after all, a cavalry soldier and this reminded him of it, what he had been trained to do.

He looked at the happy soldiers. Douglas had now been with them almost a week. After having spent so much time around them, surrounded almost every minute of every day, he almost forgot he was white. The men's faces were a delight this afternoon. Despite his near undoing, the morning raid to get the Dallons had been a success; the captives were now interned in the little jail in Douglas's office across the street. Though Douglas forbid the troops, all but Dixon, from entering the room that accessed the cell to gaze at the prisoners, the ranks buzzed with talk of the raid. The soldiers' stories varied, from vivid tales of the brave white officer or Negro sergeant to detailed, dramatic accounts of the captain's near downfall.

The soft chattering in the barn paused as Douglas looked down the corridor that led to the street. There stood Hannah, lifting her dress with both hands to avoid the dirt. She hopped along joyfully toward Douglas, passing a few greetings to the troopers.

"Thought I'd come down and see the intrepid soldiers that brought in the Dallons," she said with a smile.

"We's a sure brought 'em in," one of the soldiers said. "And brave Captain Owens was in the lead."

Douglas led Hannah back to the street, not comfortable with her around his troops. He grabbed her hand and pulled her out of the barn.

"I needed to get out of the house," Hannah said. "Don't you want to take me for a balloon ride? It's down at the ferry. Everybody says it's grand fun."

"Well, now," Douglas said. "Why not? It's a wonderful day." He inspected his bride, her fair skin, curves, and red hair shining sumptuously under the bright sun. Just looking at her pleased him. He still had trouble believing she was his.

"It's a quarter each. Am I worth a quarter?"

Douglas grabbed Hannah's horse and extended his hand to lift her. "I reckon," he laughed. "A quarter isn't much for the best-looking gal in town, especially when your sister's out of town and I've got business that will require me to come out to the Butler plantation several times this week."

The large hot-air balloon sat tethered to a dock on the bank of the Red River. Around it, dozens of citizens of every background looked on curiously. A man dressed in a black suit, topped with a bow tie and black hat, paced around the dock selling tickets. The little circus apparently moved up and down the river via steamboat, stopping for a day at the population centers to collect fares before moving on. "See the wonderful Red River Valley, thousand-foot safety line. Don't miss it. It's a once-in-a-lifetime chance!"

Douglas stepped forward and handed the man fifty cents.

A few people in the crowd pointed at the two, mumbling in French, a habit the natives used to disguise their disapproval.

Douglas and Hannah then followed a little Chinaman over to a wicker basket that was tied to the ground.

"Step here," the Chinaman said, grabbing Hannah's hand from Douglas and helping her up a set of wood steps. "Thousand feet, five minute up, five minute at top, five minute down. That's it."

Hannah smiled as she boarded the basket, tucking her dress inside. Douglas followed, the large, white cotton balloon hovering overhead. An oversized gas

burner sat in the basket, its flames burning at the
base of the balloon.

The Chinaman then climbed into the basket,
untied some ropes battening the contraption to the
dock and some sandbags, and turned a large handle
on the gas burner. "You ready?"

"Yes, yes!" Hannah said.

The basket jerked free of the ground and zoomed
up. Startled, Douglas grasped the wicker box, his
stomach churning. He looked over the side at the
ground falling away rather rapidly. The heads on
the ground turned up, arms waved, and everything
grew smaller by the second.

The sun shone on the land from the side, producing silver reflections from the metal rooftops of
town. A few plumes of smoke rose from the chimneys. Off in the distance, the Red River meandered
through the land, and the brown water of its tribu-
taries blended in with the burgundy river. Miles of
cultivated fields and scattered farms, surrounded
by sun-splashed hills, produced a wonderful mon-
tage of color. The fertile plain cased the river, maybe
five miles wide. From the air, this composite view,
even including the farms, almost looked untouched
by man.

Hannah let out a few deep breaths and a long *ooh*
over the sound of some birds cutting through the
clean air.

Douglas grabbed Hannah's hand. How had he
managed to find the woman of his dreams in this
seemingly deserted landscape?

The Chinaman looked down from the basket to

a man feeding the balloon rope. What seemed like only a few seconds passed, and the little man turned to Douglas then looked at his watch.

"Oh, it's just stunning," Hannah said. "Look, there's the Butler plantation. It's just exquisite from up here. We used to pick flowers in that field when I was small."

Douglas pointed to the Butler house and then his office. "That's where the good guys are and that's where the outlaws are, all locked up."

The temperature had dropped. The cool wind stirred Douglas's hair as it brushed across his cheeks. This was somewhere between heaven and earth, he and Hannah alone, above the world and its burdens. He wrapped his arms around her, holding her tight. "I love you," he said, giving her a big, deep kiss.

A quick burst of air jetted by, jostling the basket. The balloon and its passengers rocked and dipped, quickly displacing Douglas from his fairy-tale thoughts and reminding him of his dubious location.

"Time we go down," the Chinaman said. "Go down slower than come up."

Hannah giggled, and continued the kiss that had been altered by the turbulence. The two stood speechless for a few seconds before Douglas slowly moved back to the edge of the basket to look down. The ground grew closer. A dozen or so white kids played kickball on an open lawn, their faint screams and bantering drifting up. What was their future in this strange land so far from anywhere? What would it all look like in ten, twenty, fifty years? What future did those youngsters have? Would they grow up to be bigoted criminals, swayed by a few bad apples, malicious toward the changing world, or take their own courses that surely promised a bountiful harvest for man and land alike? Could he make a difference here or would his work be temporary, only to be swept under the rug at some later time? The land and people were indelible fixtures. His command wasn't. In a few days, would he be claimed by this land, his body decomposing without a grave or tombstone?

Out of the corner of his eye, he saw the balloon's large shadow racing across the ground to meet him back at the dock.

Hannah grabbed his hand, squeezing it tightly. She reached and straightened the collar on his uniform. "Captain Owens, this was just terrific."

The Chinaman barked loudly at the man on the ground, ending Douglas's magical ride into solitude.

The basket collided with the dock gently and Douglas felt his footing grab hold of the basket's floor. Hannah fanned her now cherry face. An annoying fly crawled up the side of her nose, blotching her beauty. They had returned to the ugly land.

Douglas laughed. "Anytime I turn you red or make you fan yourself, I've pleased myself."

Hannah chuckled and extended her hand.

Douglas grabbed it and helped her out of the basket. As he did, he noticed the hoarse, uninviting, and cynical voices of the people, the pushing and shoving of the world. Dirty work lay in the future, but he now thought he had the bandits on the run.

The setting couldn't have been further from Douglas's tranquil balloon ride with Hannah earlier that afternoon. He looked into the little cell in his office. Only the dark air from the pitch-black night filtered into his office. In the cell, Clinton Dallon sat at a small table, lit by the only light in the room, a candle.

Douglas had instructed Huff to move the younger Dallon to one of the back rooms where three soldiers currently stood watch. He then had the desk and two chairs placed in the cell. He turned to Basil and Huff, standing outside the bars. He struck a match and lit a lantern on his desk before opening a letter that had arrived that day by a secure carrier from New Orleans.

Captain Douglas Owens
Commander, Company D, 4th United States
  Cavalry
District of the Upper Red River
Natchitoches, La.

I apologize for the tardiness of this correspondence in response to the letter you sent Colonel M. J. James on October 3, 1869, but due to the nature of its contents, I felt it essential that this letter be conveyed to you only by secure courier.

I wish you all speed in the pursuit of the perpetrators of the recent violence in your dominion, especially as it pertains to the murder of men under your command. I assure you that you will have my full support in any and all activities as it relates to this matter.

Though the highest elements in the Federal Government, to include President Grant, agree with the general assessment that additional troops need to be sent to the South, the current political situation in the country merits that all attempts should be made to achieve the wishes of Congress through civil and peaceable means, and the army is to be used only as a last resort. Though this doctrine will continue to be applied nationally, local commanders do, of course, have the freedom to use the forces currently under their command as they see proper in carrying out our overall mission. As you and I know, the mission of the army, as established in the Constitution and army protocol, is that, on an institutional basis, it should have no involvement in the political process, and any such activities that might be perceived as such will undermine its Constitutional authority and the support of the citizens of our Republic.

Based on this, I regret to inform you that in all matters outside of the stated objectives given you by written orders on or about September 7, 1869, further assistance will not be forthcoming. The squad of cavalry recently deployed to the Natchitoches garrison is at your disposal

*indefinitely, pending other needs in my department.
At this time, the department has no additional
troops to spare.*

*Respectfully,
General Joseph A. Mower
Commander, Department of Louisiana
New Orleans, La.*

Douglas sighed deeply, folded the letter, and placed it in a drawer. He looked up on the shelf beside his desk at the hundreds of files he'd amassed on crimes and suspects over the years. He stood and laughed at Clinton Dallon. "Kind of makes you believe Mr. Darwin is right about all that evolution and stuff, doesn't it?"

Clinton turned to Douglas with a dead face. "I only see one thing in here that evolved from an ape."

Basil grinned, looking up at the highwayman as he continued to sharpen his knife on a stone. The long, icy strokes produced a demented sound that seemed to be music to Basil's ears but made Douglas's skin crawl.

Douglas ambled into the cell, Basil behind him. He took a seat in the chair opposite Clinton as Basil stood beside the table, looking down on the outlaw. Huff stood outside the iron cage, holding his rifle at port arms.

"Do I need to introduce myself?" Douglas said. Like most of the bushwhackers he had met, this one appeared completely witless.

Clinton just stared at Douglas, squinting so hard his cheeks wrinkled.

Breaking the silence, Basil rapidly raised his fist and backhanded Clinton with all his might, knocking him out of his chair.

"The captain asked you a *question*," Basil snarled. "You answer him, or you'll wish the only thing I'll do to you is to give you a lifelong limp like I gave that pig father of yours."

Clinton climbed back onto the chair, his veins pulsing big and fast. He wiped the blood from his face on his sleeve. "You're Captain Douglas Owens, Fourth Cavalry, defeated and run out of here in disgrace by General Taylor during the war."

Douglas reached into his pocket and removed a hanky. He wiped a big splotch of Clinton's blood off his white undershirt and then tossed the rag across the table. "I've got a proposal for you. No offense, but I don't really want you or your brother. You're little fish. What I want is somebody who will make my superiors happy, get me a promotion or some medals so I won't have to go traipsing off to these godforsaken hovels where there's no running water and sewer. Somebody like Moses Garrett, or Sheriff Thaxton, or that greasy little prick, the local newspaper editor. What's his name?"

"Fuck you," Clinton said.

Basil raised his hand again, but Douglas motioned for him not to deliver the blow.

"I don't see where you have any choice," Douglas continued. "I've got sworn, documented, and written statements that you and Amos helped kill Corporal Taylor. We got his body out of that well. Got both Republicans and Democrats in good standing who will attest to that. You and your little brother will hang."

"If you *touch* him," Clinton barked, trying to stand, but restrained by Basil, ". . . the vengeance of the Lord will fall on you."

"I'm not too worried about the vengeance of the Lord," Douglas persisted. "Here's the deal. I'll let you go. You can walk right out of this jail. Your guns are on the desk there." Douglas turned to point at the weapons. "There's a horse tied up outside. All I want you to do is get a message to me the next time Garrett and his gang of cutthroats make a raid. I'll arrest them and then I'll let you go." Douglas paused and reached into his pocket to pull out two pieces of paper. He unfolded them. "Here's a blank pardon for you. You can take it with you. And here's a statement from the Federal judge of record and governor stating I have the authority to issue pardons."

Douglas pointed to a few places on the paper. "See those seals and signatures? That makes it authentic. Of course, you have to give me some information that leads to a conviction. It's all spelled out in there. You can take it, have it. That way I can't backstab you. Despite Basil's objections, I've spared your father, too, and any of your cousins. It's all in there."

Clinton picked up the papers and studied them, running a hand through his hair.

"Now, you could turn my offer down and get out of here and not do what I tell you. Of course, I've still got your brother, and a warrant for you, and a bunch of written evidence on you and your brother. He'll hang for sure, and you'll have to leave the country. Stay on the run until we get you or the bounty hunters do. I know where you live. That's a nice farm you've got. Be a shame for the carpet-baggers to buy it for nothing. Besides, you'll be easy to find, because that ugly-ass scar on your forehead will show up well on your wanted poster. And then I've still got your brother. He doesn't look like he'll stand up to interrogation very well. Might get what I need from him anyway. I think I can flog him if he misbehaves." Douglas turned to Basil and Huff. "Can't I do that under regs? I bet Huff there can really work a whip. Look at his big, strong arms."

Douglas paused, and Huff shaped a big smile. "Wouldn't that be something, the slave whipping his former masters? But I don't think we need to entertain all that—so long as you act like you should."

Clinton looked around at all three. Without a word, he stood and strolled out of the cell. He grabbed his gun belt off Douglas's desk and opened the door. After he exited, he slammed the door shut, the echo of its collision with the jamb bouncing loudly off the office's walls.

"Think you're making a big mistake," Basil said.

"Why?" Douglas replied, standing. "We've got his brother, and a Federal warrant for him. Not to mention a stack of evidence. All he can do is cooperate or flee. He's got a wife and family here. Worst case is he hauls ass and we try the younger one. Judge Atkins doesn't give a damn about his age. Eighteen is manhood in Louisiana, written in the code and practiced. I've seen Judge Atkins throw younger men to the gallows. It's all we can do. If we don't catch the leaders, we won't do any good—just feel better about ourselves for a few days, then be back on the trail ducking bullets. Damn it, I want a trial and conviction. That's all that will solve the problems in the long haul. . . . Huff, go back there and get Amos. Put him back in this cell. Keep two guards in here all night, and send three fresh men to guard Sidney, now. I want the guards there changed twice a day, so they stay fresh."

31

Later that night, about two hours after midnight, Douglas woke to a loud knock on the door of his room at the military garrison in town.

"What do you want?" he mumbled into the darkness.

"It's Private Jenson. There's a big problem at the Butler house."

"Come in," Douglas said, leaning up. He struck a match and reached over to light the gas lantern beside his bed.

As the door opened, a bright gold tint lit the room. Douglas swung his feet to the ground and pulled up his pants.

"Captain Owens," the soldier continued, his words jittery and brisk, his motions antsy. "The clan raided the Butler house about an hour ago. Think they took Mr. Crow and Miss Butler and Privates Jones and Thompson, also."

"*What?*" Douglas screamed. "I thought y'all were guarding the house. How did that happen?"

"Don'ts know, Captain. I was out front, guarding the road by that big tree. You know that big tree by the drive. Then I heard a couple of shots. Sounded like they hit glass or wood, not flesh. Took cover for a second, no more than thirty seconds, then I made for the house. It's about fifty yards from that big tree. Took me another minute or two. I's bein' careful and didn't want to get shot. I heard some horses running in the back. Went inside and nobody was there. I ain't see no blood. Then came straight here."

"Goddamn guards probably sleeping!" Douglas yelled, pulling his undershirt over his body.

Forty-five minutes later, Douglas, Huff, and two soldiers rode up to the Butler house. The twenty-minute ride had been dreadful, the events unbelievable. The bandits had often outwitted him, their unorthodox methods completely at odds with reason, but they had never done anything like this, if what Private Jenson said resembled actual events. If the outlaws had taken a society woman, something considered uncouth in all realms of Southern society, they had truly become desperate, much more dangerous than Douglas had ever imagined. In the eyes of most, this vastly superseded the murder of carpetbaggers and scalawags, or even burning a courthouse.

From the drive, the Butler grounds stood peaceful, a quintessential Southern night. A few gas lanterns lit the house's windows, like square boxes of light in the dark night. Overhead, the clouds gathered. The breeze picked up, swinging around from the south, turning moist as it skimmed over the Gulf of Mexico. He smelled the air. Rain was imminent.

Before he had left town, he had awoken his seven remaining soldiers and Basil. He wanted to bring Basil to the Butler house, but leery of the night riders making an attempt to free Amos Dallon, he had been forced to leave Basil with four of the soldiers, all with orders to stay awake, on guard duty, with a picket in front and at the rear of the office.

Douglas stepped down to the ground and motioned for his subordinates to do the same. He tied his horse to a hitching post and walked up on the front porch, but found the door locked. At the house's rear, the back door was open, one of its panes broken out. The ground in the area had been trampled by horses.

Huff struck a match and bent over to inspect the torn turf. "Looks like a big posse, ten horses, fresh, two hours old at's the most."

"Private Mercer, you stay here. Private Combs, you go up front," Douglas ordered, and then stepped into the house.

Little seemed amiss despite a thorough inspection. In the kitchen, he smelled the faint odor of gunpowder. He looked up and saw two fresh bullet holes in the ceiling. Then his heart skipped a beat as he inspected the large dinner table in the kitchen. A long bundle of scarlet hair, tied in a knot, lay on the table. He lifted the hair, feeling its silky, smooth texture. It had been freshly cut. He put it to his nose and smelled the scent of Hannah's perfume.

Instead of sadness or worry, rage fell over him, almost making him shake. He spent a few seconds thinking, analyzing his options before putting the bundle of locks in his pocket and turning to Huff. "Let's get back to town, pronto. They're gone. We'll never pick up the trail tonight. Probably not tomorrow either. The rain will wash out their tracks before daylight."

The rain fell from the heavens in sheets, almost horizontal. Two quick flashes of white light lit the little porch in front of the garrison, followed by two earsplitting rumbles of thunder. In the street, under their slickers, four troopers cowered in the rain on horseback. The thunder spooked two of the mounts, who threw their heads back and blew long, loud snorts. Douglas couldn't even see across the street, now just a muddy wallow, covered with almost four inches of water. Overhead, the early afternoon sun could not be located. A big gust of wind pushed the torrent under the little awning. Douglas pulled down his hat, almost to his eyes, and lifted the collar of his coat high up on his neck.

"I told you not to let the son of a bitch go," Basil said over the murmur of the rain tapping on the tin roof. "I know these men and how they react. That's the first time you haven't taken my advice and now see wheres it's got you."

"I'm throwing the rules away," Douglas said, ducking away from the deluge. "We're going to get these bastards, whatever it takes. What do you think?"

"She's alive. That's why they left the hair. It's a sign. They want to swap her for Amos. She's likely not seen her captors so it's an even trade. The others are dead, gone. Never find those bodies. That's how they operate and that's why they didn't kill anybody at the house. No bodies, no blood, no crime, just speculation—except for a few carpet-baggers. They do that occasionally and leave the bodies as a sign. Makes the Northerners want to hightail it out of here, for good."

Since Douglas had gotten back from the Butler house a few hours before daylight, he had been in a surreal, dreamlike daze, almost having to touch himself to make sure he was awake and not in a bad dream, another nightmare. An urge to get Hannah back engulfed him and all of his thoughts. It had forced the Dallons and the night riders to the back of his mind. Throughout the morning, his frenzy had not abated, and his long pondering of the events only manifested into something more like a fury, raging inside him and expanding by the minute. His face as well as his soul was permanently contorted with anguish.

The local paper had yet to mention the Dallons' arrest. This wasn't an accident, Douglas was sure of that. He doubted Hannah's abduction would be reported. As a recourse, he scratched out a narrative describing the capture of the Dallons and the taking of Hannah Butler and mailed it to

Colonel Jones and an editor with a small press in New Orleans, the only pro-Northern paper in the state. But it would be at least a week before it arrived.

"They ain't going to kill her," Basil said. "She's the beautiful daughter of a Confederate hero, one of the most beloved men in this valley, even if she is engaged to a Yankee. That'd be too much for them. They'd lose too much credibility with the locals. And they want Amos back. They'll never get him if they kill her."

"I'm not so sure I agree with you. Like you said, maybe she'll just come up missing. Then there will only be speculation."

"They'll never kill her if they think they can get Amos back. That would solve their problems. You wouldn't have a trial then. Wish you'd take me with you today, Captain."

"Need you here to guard Amos."

"These black soldiers can handle that. I already told you, they ain't going to do nothing in town, especially during daylight."

"What's the name of that bar in Montgomery?"

"Bend in the River."

"Are you sure Sheriff Thaxton will be there?"

"Yep, he goes there almost every day and that's where he'll be in this storm for sure. It's right there by the church. If by any chance he's not there, he'll be in Montgomery somewhere, or at his office in Atkins. . . . What you going to do after you find the sheriff?"

"Don't know yet."

"Fuck those self-righteous rules you always abide by. If you haven't noticed, they don't work. If you want to win this fight, you just have to do it, win it, whatever that means."

Douglas tried to respond, but only stuttered something no one comprehended, not even himself. He reconsidered bringing Basil. For some reason, he thought the gunfighter could ride off toward the bandits and solve his problems, guns blazing, and produce the outcome he wanted. Something inside him forced him to push these thoughts aside.

Basil stepped forward. "Have you decided what you're going to do if it comes down to Hannah or the bushwhackers?"

"Haven't thought it out."

"You damn sure better decide before the lead starts flying."

Another flash of lightning cracked in the distance. The horizon in all directions had now turned almost black. He stepped off the porch, headed into the darkness. "It will be Hannah instead of the outlaws. . . . If I'm not back by midnight, I probably won't be back at all. Make sure Amos goes to trial if that's the case. The judge will be here in three days."

The four troopers and Douglas crossed the river on the ferry at Montgomery around five that afternoon. The rain had slackened, but the day had grown dark and gloomy, the pines whipping wildly. Douglas had decided to make the fifteen-mile trip on the east side of the Red River and cross at Montgomery. He had little choice because the ferry at Natchitoches had been closed due to the storm. The trip had taken longer than expected because the column was forced to take cover from a deadly hailstorm in an abandoned barn for over an hour.

During the ride, a coldness had started to run through his body. His knees had gotten weak, and he spent the time cursing everything: God, the bandits, himself, the army.

From the edge of town, he studied the little frontier village of Montgomery. It was mostly white and the epicenter of anti-Northern sentiment in the area. He turned to look back down at the river from the small hill. The deep, wide watercourse hustled along and created a natural barrier that the bandits could use to keep him from getting back to the safety of town. The ferry here and at Natchitoches were his only exit points.

The Bend in the River sat on the edge of town. The long, slender wood shack had weathered, unpainted boards, a tin roof, and a single visible entrance. No residents roamed the streets in the inclement weather. He turned to Sergeant Dixon and Privates Mercer, Jenson, and Combs, sizing up his forces. He had started to get to know his men better, all by name and manner. He found very little fault in any of them, at least from a professional perspective. He had conversed with all personally, and in so doing, gathered random information about each:

where they were from, whether they had families, their personal histories, and so forth, which solidified their characters in his mind.

A fine line had always existed in the army between the ranks and commanders. The commander needed to get close enough to his men to know their attributes, display his competence, convey he cared for them, but that relationship was never to get to a point where the men considered him a friend or equal. This process was much easier with Negro troops. But with their newfound closeness came impediments as well. Douglas had grown to care for these men, their daily needs and safety. And as a result, it took almost inhuman traits to remain a good military officer. The best commanders, the ones who operated the most efficiently and accomplished their missions with the least cost, were those who ordered their men around like lifeless objects, with no concern for their well-being. A good commander only cared about his objective.

"Privates Mercer and Jenson," Douglas said in a flat, professional voice. "You two stay out front and keep watch. Sergeant Dixon, you and Private Combs come with me. Just stand inside the door, weapons ready. Bullets might start flying any second." Douglas dismounted, leaving his reins with one of the soldiers, and opened the door. The bar's pungent scent, rampant sounds of the banging piano, and busy voices filled the air.

Douglas paused and looked through the thick smoke and down the long, dimly lit room. The bar was on the right. Five or six sets of deer antlers and tanned hides hung on the walls. Twenty or so people occupied the room, five or six at the bar, and twice that number at the tables and the roulette wheel. Four women, scantily clad, paraded around as waitresses or sat at the tables, entertaining the raucous, unsavory looking men. Almost all the men wore sidearms, and a few had long knives tucked into their belts.

The two black soldiers followed Douglas inside and stood at each side of the door, their rifles at port. The room's ambient conversation paused briefly, but the piano music continued.

Sheriff Thaxton sat at one of the tables with four other men playing cards, drinking whiskey, and smoking. Douglas approached, his boots banging on the wood floor, the rowels on his spurs jingling. All five men at the table watched him advance.

"Captain Owens, the local representative of our beloved Federal government!" the sheriff said, his voice booming. "What can I help you with? How about a little gambling?" The sheriff turned to look at one of the women. "Or what about one of our Southern beauties here?" The lawman leaned back in his chair and placed his cards on the table, face-down.

The piano paused. The saloon turned into a room full of whispers. The ticking and clacking of the roulette wheel slowed to a stop.

The sheriff continued, "What kind of trouble are you stirring up today? And where's your sidekick, that lowlife, murdering outlaw, Basil Dubose?" He chuckled and looked around the bar. He now had everyone's attention. "I guess I should watch my mouth. Word is you and your men murder anybody that don't see eye to eye with you. Isn't that right?"

"I'm looking for the Dallons and Moses Garrett," Douglas uttered, putting his hands on his hips. He looked at the sheriff's glassy alcoholic gaze. "And a certain piece of merchandise of mine they have."

"Wouldn't know anything about any of that," the sheriff answered in a phony voice as he looked over at the two soldiers near the door.

"I've got a message for them, and I want you to pass it on. I've got something they might want. I'm going to bring it to the municipal building in Atkins tomorrow night at ten. If they're interested in trading, I'll bring their merchandise, but they've got to bring mine."

The room remained deadly silent.

The sheriff cracked a big smirk. "Well, I can't make any promises, but if I run into them, I'll surely pass your message on."

Douglas turned, using his unadulterated military bearing. As he approached the door, the piano erupted into a loud rendition of "Dixie." The bar crowd followed suit and began belching the words of the song at the top of their lungs: "Oh, I wish I was in the land of cotton, old times there are not forgotten . . ."

32

For almost twenty hours, Douglas had thought about his plans for his rendezvous with the night riders in Atkins. Certainly, the bandits would be waiting on him there later tonight. He had spent the previous night and all day considering the various options. At the very least, he was prepared to trade Amos Dallon for Hannah. Getting her back safely trumped everything, but he doubted it would be that easy. How many desperadoes would they face? How would it play out? Would the outlaws ambush him? Trick him? Or would they simply trade for Hannah? Did something like his nightmare await?

An endless array of scenarios raced through his mind, and he had tried to analyze each in hopes of already having a plan to deal with every one of them. Whatever happened, he stood at the precipice and had come to grips with that. He would get Hannah back tonight, or die trying. His seething, vengeful, and anger-filled body and mind would settle for nothing less.

As he chewed on some salt pork, Douglas blew into a cup of coffee, trying to cool the steaming brew. He looked over to his men on the parade ground behind his office, making ready for their trip into the bush. He would take his full contingent to Atkins, the seven remaining soldiers, Basil, and Huff. Together they would be a formidable force, nine well-armed and well-trained men. The troops were currently loading supplies, ammunition, and spare weapons into either the wagon or their saddlebags. Several sheets had been stitched together and draped over the wagon's cage to hide Amos on the journey out of town. Douglas didn't want anybody to know what was transpiring.

Despite his sullen mood, Douglas almost smiled as he watched Basil step off the boardwalk onto the parade ground to inspect the preparatory activities. Basil doubtless didn't enjoy the company of his newfound colored brethren, but he had gotten to know them, learned to work with them, if only out of necessity. Though Douglas had given the gunfighter a stringent warning that no condescending remarks would be tolerated, he could do nothing about the gunslinger's strange, spiteful facial expressions. The soldiers all looked at Basil like he was some sort of demon, something like a witch doctor or voodoo doll endowed with mysterious, magical, and evil talents. They all stayed clear of him, the silver-headed phantom, if possible.

Though the soldiers seemed convinced of Basil's

skills, Douglas and his paid gun hand still wondered about the troops. They looked competent on the parade ground, but were they reliable under fire? He had gotten to know all of the men, but long ago learned that no matter how hard he analyzed and thought he understood his soldiers, regardless of race or background, nothing gave him a real hint of how a man would react when the shooting started. Only the duress of the ultimate sacrifice brought a man's inner qualities, his mettle, to the surface.

Basil approached Douglas, carrying a small crate. He reached into the wooden box and pulled out five sticks of dynamite, already armed with short fuses. "Put these in your saddlebags."

"What the hell for?"

"Don't know. We've got 'em. Might as well take them with us. Could come in handy."

"How do you think it will play out?"

"Don't know," Basil replied, lighting a cigar. "I doubt the outlaws even know. All I do know is we have to put ourselves in their minds, try to think like they do. They'll all be cloaked, and they have only one goal: to make sure there are no witnesses."

Douglas removed his hat and scratched his head. "I do agree with your earlier assessment. It's likely that Hannah doesn't even know who her captors are."

"Let's hope so, because then they might be open to simply making a trade. From their perspective, if they've got any sense, they probably don't want to harm her. But if she has seen them, their only objective will be to kill her and get Amos back, or kill him.

If Clinton or old man Dallon are there, this may work to our advantage. They'll likely try to save him." Basil looked off to the hills. "What's your plan?"

"Don't know yet."

"Well, you damn sure better be making up your mind. There'll be no time for indecision."

"I'll know when we get there. This may sound optimistic, but I'm not going to rule out bringing in more of their gang if we have a chance, especially Clinton. I've got sworn testimony on the Dallons. I guess we'll have some evidence against anybody else we're lucky enough to apprehend, but that evidence will only be us. It won't carry much weight with a jury, especially if they don't kill any of us. We'll see."

Douglas sighed. Basil's comments only added more uncertainty. He'd only be able to decide their course after he sized up the situation in person, but he would then have to make a quick decision. His stomach turned uncomfortably.

"We'll have to ride right by Moses Garrett's place on the way. He's about two hours short of Atkins," Basil added. "Maybe we should pay him a visit. Might catch him at home. Sidney told us he's the boss. I wouldn't normally suggest that, but you cut the head off a snake and the rest of the slimy bastard becomes confused, useless. Any unknowns are sure to work in our favor."

Basil's proposal caused a hundred more situations to rush into his head.

"Don't take this personal, sir," Basil said in his most ingratiating voice. "But strictly from a military sense, have you considered the chance that she might be in with the guerrillas? Leading us into a trap. She's the daughter of a Confederate colonel, and her sister's a fiery Southern belle. You have to consider that at the very least she's scared silly and worried about her own hide."

Dumbfounded by the remark, Douglas mumbled, "No chance." Had he been so blinded by love to not see this? Visions of Hannah, their wonderful time together, filled his mind. He reasoned this unlikely, only giving it credence because of Basil, who was a man governed only by a totally objective view of the world, almost a man without feelings.

His men got quiet. Behind his office, two soldiers led Amos Dallon out of the barracks. His hands were tied behind his back and his mouth was gagged. The young bandit jerked on the rope, and lunged from his captors as one of the troopers placed a cotton sack over the outlaw's head. Two more soldiers secured a rope around his ankles before they lifted Amos's limp body up onto the wagon and into the cage.

"Get everybody ready to go. We leave in ten minutes. Let's take the back roads out of town. That way we won't stir up any fuss before we reach the ferry."

Much to Douglas's satisfaction, the little army patrol reached the ferry at Grand Ecore without arousing any undue attention. In fact, they had arrived to find the ferry on the near bank and only two strangers milling around the Cotton Palace. Josiah Banks manned the ferry.

Douglas led his mare onto the ferry, the wheels of the wagon squeaking behind him. Once on board, the men chatted as they secured four wood blocks around the wagon's wheels. He looked at his watch. An hour after noon. From here, it was a twenty-mile trip to Atkins. With the wagon in tow, they'd be lucky to go three miles an hour over the primitive trails. Easier routes existed, most notably crossing the river at Montgomery, but this route afforded more cover. He had thought about the timing carefully. It needed to be perfect. They had two hours to spare. They didn't need to arrive early. The two hours gave him a cushion in case they found obstacles on the trail. If required, he could ditch the wagon and put Amos on one of the three spare horses in his column. They would rest and ready themselves somewhere just outside Atkins under the cover of darkness. And they'd stop at the Garrett place. Maybe he would get lucky and find Moses there.

As the craft eased out into the river, Douglas felt his footing waver as he walked his mount to the front of the ferry. A few minutes passed, but when the ferry built up some momentum, Douglas motioned for Josiah, who abandoned the ferry's controls and walked over.

"They killed Sidney, if you haven't heard," Douglas said with a straight face. "Two of my soldiers also, and they've taken Colonel Butler's daughter." He paused and nodded at the wagon. "Got Amos Dallon in that wagon. I'm going to meet them in Atkins at ten, hopefully trade him for Hannah Butler and maybe bring in a few of Garrett's posse at the same time."

Josiah looked at the wagon. His face contorted with an unpleasant frown. "When did all that happen?"

"Night before last. I'm going to get Miss Butler back tonight, one way or the other." Douglas paused. "You want to help, or know anybody who might?"

Josiah continued to study the cage.

Douglas then assumed an austere, serious tone. "I'm either going to get them tonight or they're going to get me. You'll either be rid of them tomorrow or on your own. The time is now."

"Where?"

"Municipal building in Atkins, ten o'clock tonight."

Josiah looked to the west, to the sun. He pulled out a pocket watch and studied it. "I'll turn the ferry over to Bubba, see what I can do. See if I can round up some men."

"How many?"

"Eight, maybe ten."

"That's enough."

"You say they've got Colonel Butler's daughter. There won't be many there, no more than ten. That's all that would participate in that." Josiah looked back at Douglas's soldiers, assessing their strength. "Looks like an even fight." He then turned and walked back to the ferry's pulley wheel.

"How will I know you'll be there?"

Josiah turned back to Douglas. "You won't. No

way to know. Be prepared to go it alone if I can't get any help. I ain't coming alone, Captain."

Douglas and four of his soldiers now sat horseback in a small stand of pines about four miles north of Atkins. The day was late, less than an hour before dusk, around 7:30 in the evening. They had made good time, better than Douglas had planned. They had seen only two parties on the trail, neither of whom appeared interested in their presence. All day, the troops had kept a vigilant eye, but the next two hours were the most critical. The cunning desperadoes preferred the darkness and their home turf. The small village of Atkins sat at the confluence of two small streams, in some of the most isolated land in Louisiana, surrounded by the thickest forest and least-populated hills in the area.

Douglas had spent much of his time worrying about Hannah. Sidney and his soldiers' ordeal came second. The night riders killed indiscriminately, without principle, their only goal profit. The Knights propagated different tactics, most geared to instill fear or rid the state of their political enemies. They had a code, albeit a reprehensible one. Both groups held two goals sacred: they tolerated no witnesses or evidence of their crimes, and they remained anonymous. The party they currently pursued appeared to be a mix of both groups.

Douglas held little hope for anybody but Hannah. Over the years, he had heard rumors about the work of both the night riders and the

Knights. Little information existed about the night riders' techniques, but many stories circulated about the Knights. They administered whippings, and usually left warning notes or burning poles as their signs of accomplishment. Sometimes they lynched and other times they simply shot their victims. One of their favorite pastimes when they assaulted larger groups was to allow one of their victims to watch the murders. After they finished their work, they would permit this wretched soul to flee, which would then provide the euphoria and excitement of a chase. If the condemned somehow escaped, he passed on the tale of his torment to the populace, thus adding to the group's diabolical lore and sending a dour, horrid warning to all.

"We may be in luck," Basil commented after looking through his glasses at a house perched on a hill above. "He may be home."

Douglas inspected the house. A lone saddled horse stood out front, tied to a post. "Looks like he's getting ready to depart for his night's chores."

"Let me shoot him when he comes out," Basil said. "I can get him from here. It's only about a hundred and fifty yards." The gunslinger looked around, then back to Douglas. "This is perfect, the sun's at our back. He'll never know what hit him. We're headed into a one-way fight. Get this bastard now and it doubles our odds."

Douglas had never lowered himself to giving an order to kill someone in cold blood. Moses had surely committed heinous crimes before, but that was only conjecture. He looked at the long shadows, growing by the minute. Overhead, the sky was a strange red umbrella, like a crimson roof transitioning to gray as it collided with the green hills. He now felt a void inside, nothing. He looked down at his shaking left hand and nodded to Basil. "Kill the bastard."

As the gun hand pulled his long, scoped rifle from its holster, the troops looked on in amazement, mumbling a few hushed whispers.

"We'll move around and take cover," Douglas said. "Basil . . . make it quick. One shot. If something goes awry . . . make sure somebody gets Amos to Atkins, and we get Hannah back." Movement from the house caught his eye.

Moses Garrett stepped down on the ground. Instead of saddling up, he walked across the yard toward an outhouse.

"He's gonna take a shit," Basil said softly. "Soon as he gets in there, let's get him."

The five troopers remained perfectly still until Moses disappeared into the outhouse. Douglas then led three of the soldiers off to the side, into some brush where they had a good view of the outhouse but still had the setting sun at their backs. There, they dismounted, and lay prone on the ground.

Douglas looked back at their previous location. He saw nothing. "Be ready," he whispered to his men.

The seconds passed slowly. The door finally opened. Everyone heard it bang against the little wooden building. Moses then stepped out, completely visible, still readjusting his trousers. Douglas froze.

A shot broke the quiet, slicing through the air. Moses buckled back into the outhouse, his left shoulder exploding with blood. He landed on his rear, then quickly stood, reaching for the pistol on his hip. The two soldiers beside Douglas squirmed and murmured with astonishment at the shot.

"Let's go!" Douglas cried, dashing into the open toward Moses. "Fill that outhouse with lead." Two shots flew into the bushes behind him. As he ran, he raised his pistol, firing into the outhouse, still a hundred paces away. Beside him, his men also opened up. The outhouse's wood planks splintered. He continued to fire. Now close enough to see details, he saw Moses's gun, protruding from the door, the outlaw's body hidden inside.

Douglas stopped, took a knee, and quickly reloaded. Beside him, the three soldiers continued to fill the little wooden building with lead. The pistol fell from Moses's hand, and Douglas stood and motioned for his soldiers to follow as he approached the outhouse. His Colt fully extended and loaded, he slowly stepped in front of the door.

Moses lay on his back, his white shirt now saturated with blood. He quivered and recited what sounded like some type of prayer. He finally turned his gaze to Douglas, looking down the captain's barrel. "Providence will see that you get what you deserve, soon."

His arm shaking, Douglas pointed his pistol at Moses's head and squeezed the trigger. The gun erupted, splattering blood on the ground and ceasing all movement from the villain Moses Garrett.

33

Day became night, a still, dark, muggy night. On the horizon, a peculiar red moon hung above the land.

Atkins was just a crossroads with a few side streets, maybe ten wooden shacks. The hamlet's tall pines and oaks blocked any moonlight. In front of the municipal building, two torches blazed, throwing light into the muddy, rutted street and illuminating the small wooden building whose two windows were fogged up but showing a lantern or two inside. A few flies, buzzing around in the light, constituted the only life around. Behind the building, the shadows merged into nothing in the distance.

Douglas sucked in a deep breath. He didn't bother to look at his watch. The group had stopped in a meadow outside of town and waited an hour, departing a quarter short of ten. Now they were here, quicker, easier, and with less anticipation than Douglas had figured. During the day, they had taken a reserved pace, hoping to conserve their horses in case they needed them later that evening. He had told his subordinates if he yelled the command "Fire," they were to kill all the outlaws except Amos and Clinton Dallon. Basil had insisted for days, in accordance with outlaw etiquette, that Clinton had long since fled to Texas.

Before they had departed Moses Garrett's place, they had put the corpse of the dead clansman on his horse and led the animal out into the woods, where they shot the beast. Though the bullet holes and blood of the shoot-out still existed, Douglas hoped no one would find the evidence until morning.

From where he stood, holding the reins of his horse, two torches lit his silhouette. Behind him, his eight soldiers and the wagon remained veiled in the darkness. He still had no plan; somehow he had just let events bring him here. Anything seemed possible in the steamy night. He bent over and grabbed an apple-sized rock off the road and tossed it up on the building's porch.

Two men appeared on the wooden porch, both with their entire bodies, head to boot, concealed with sheets, and both holding rifles by the stock, their barrels pointed downward.

From the street, Douglas yelled in a flat voice, "Where's Hannah Butler?"

One of the men replied, raising a hand over his mouth and squealing to alter his voice, "Where's Amos Dallon?"

Douglas turned and nodded. Three more large torches then lit up, illuminating the street with their pulsating light. All eight soldiers, still mounted, and the wagon, its cover removed, came into view, fifteen paces behind him. Every man in the army patrol held his Henry rifle at the ready.

"I want to see Hannah!" Douglas yelled.

"Let us have Amos first," the man said and laughed. "He's no good to you anymore. I hear your witness fell on hard times."

"No," Douglas replied, his throat becoming dry. "Bring her out."

No one said anything for a few seconds. Finally Basil yelled, "I'll kill the little sack of shit right now. Would love to." He climbed up on the wagon, pistol drawn. He leaned against the cage, pulled out his penis, and began to urinate on Amos.

A third veiled man appeared on the porch, leading Hannah by a handful of hair, her mouth gagged and hands tied.

"You all right, Hannah?" Douglas asked, a sense of utter relief falling over him as he stared at his bride's flushed face and unsmiling eyes. For most of the day, almost terrified, he had pondered Basil's suggestion that Hannah might betray him. That thought hung like a dagger hovering over his heart, ready to penetrate. Her sight quashed the blizzard in his stomach. Any other sight would have crushed him, probably sending him into a tantrum of hysteria, incapable and without a desire to finish the day's work. From his position, she looked no worse for the wear, her skin and pink dress only slightly soiled.

Hannah tried to utter some words through the

cloth gag as she uncomfortably jerked her head, resisting the firm hand pulling on her short locks.

"Cut her gag loose so I can talk to her," Douglas said.

"No, she's fine," the man said. "Give us Amos and you can have her."

"Bring her out to me." Douglas turned and motioned to Basil. "Bring Amos to me. I'll hand him over when I get my hands on her."

Time passed slowly as Basil retrieved Amos from the wagon. Douglas still hadn't decided how this would play out, at least from his side. If no one threatened gunplay, he would let the events unfold, depart with just the swap if that was possible. Were his adversaries aware of Moses Garrett's fate?

Out of the corner of his eye, he saw Basil walk up beside him, Amos on one side, a drawn pistol at the ready on the other. From his other eye, he saw more movement. Beside the building, four more horses, each carrying the white figure of a man wearing a mask with eye slits, stepped forward into the light. Their hammers and levers cocked. Behind him, the levers of his own men's weapons moved in unison. The two sounds brought the tension to a crescendo. On their horses, the soldiers walked forward and stood behind Douglas, facing the building, Sergeant Dixon half a horse in front.

Douglas studied all seven of his opponents. He saw the three on the porch clearly, but the four horsemen beside the building were only vague images. Was Clinton Dallon among them? If the shooting started, he'd like to catch him alive.

Basil had slightly turned, showing his narrow and less vulnerable side to the bandits as he secured his footing. He then raised his pistol and pointed it at the man beside Hannah. "Bring her down here, now."

As Douglas watched the fearless, competent gunfighter, a sick thought entered his mind. Basil could just as easily be playing on the other side of the street. Only army gold had put him in his current position.

The outlaw in Basil's sights raised his pistol, jerked on Hannah, and pulled her forward, leading her onto the street.

Hannah and the man approached. Douglas looked into the slits in the man's mask. Hannah's face flushed red. An urge to reach out and swipe the man's mask off rushed over him, but he couldn't bring himself to do it. Gunfire would surely erupt. Just as he reached out to grab Hannah's arm, almost feeling her smooth, soft flesh, the thud of horse hooves came from town.

"Dear God," Douglas mumbled, a cold chill running over his body. All the men, from both sides of the street, poised to fire, shuffled to look. Death hung in the air. Nine horses, all mounted with men in masks, stormed from the center of town onto the scene, reining their mounts to a stop in front of the little municipal building.

One of the men in the newly arrived posse of masked men stood in his stirrups. "Let her go, you've gone too far. Killing innocents and kidnapping women. None of this aids our cause. You've brought nothing but the firm rule of the Republicans on us."

Everyone stiffened. As the masked men on horses shuffled around, Douglas pushed Amos into the street and grabbed Hannah, pulling her behind him.

"Y'all falling in with the nigger soldiers?" one of the men on the porch said.

Fifteen seconds of silence fell on the scene. Douglas looked around for Amos, but couldn't find him in the half-light. He finally sounded off. "We can make this a white man's fight if that's what you want." He shoved Hannah into the darkness behind him and turned to Sergeant Dixon. "Sergeant, back your men off, down the street."

Sergeant Dixon gritted his teeth and gripped his rifle firmly. "No, this is our fight, too."

Douglas raised his shotgun and pointed it at the sergeant. "That is a direct order. Do you understand? You too, Hannah, go with them."

The sergeant swore a few times and then wheeled his horse around, spurring the gelding hard, and galloped down the street into the darkness. One of the soldiers helped Hannah up on his horse before the other troopers followed, without all the dramatics.

The man leading the belated posse in the road looked at the four masked riders astride the building. "You can go. Last chance."

The four cloaked riders beside the municipal building turned to look at the two men on the porch, then back at the large, unfriendly group of clansmen in the street. One rider backed his horse into the darkness.

"Where are you going?" a man on the porch yelled. "Can't believe you're cowing down to this bullshit."

The three other riders disappeared as fast as they had appeared. The nine horses in the posse from town rode forward, crowding the municipal building. Douglas felt surrounded. Three of the men in the nine-man posse grabbed thick ropes from their saddles and held them high.

A deep voice sounded out from the mayhem. "Captain, this is no business of yours. Go back where you came or suffer your fate."

Douglas and Basil stepped back a few paces into the darkness and watched the late-arriving mob tear off the masks of the men on the porch. He recognized two of the outlaws, one Sheriff Thaxton and the other the preacher from the Montgomery Baptist Church, the one whose sermon he had attended a few weeks earlier. This was the voice he had heard that night on the trail, the voice he tried to place, but never could put with a face.

Basil jumped on his horse. "Let's go. Let's just get out of here, *now.*"

As Douglas mounted, he looked at a few of the men in the group who had arrived from town, all still veiled. Was one of these men Josiah? Or had he simply passed along the word to other clansmen, more powerful than the local outfit of miscreants? Did he play any role in this, or had this been ordained independent of him? Did he and his deeds even matter to this secret society?

The posse threw three ropes over some framing on the awning. He'd never know the answers. Still unable to depart, he watched the gang roughly handle the three condemned. On their way to hell, the three night riders sported crazed faces of disbelief.

Basil reached out with his reins and slapped the rear of Douglas's horse, sending the mare racing into the night.

Head spinning, mouth dry, still bewildered and almost in shock, Douglas brought his horse to a sliding stop a few hundred yards down the street where his troops huddled under a large tree. Hannah sat atop one of the horses. "Sorry about that, Sergeant. Didn't want to do it, but had to. That posse hung those three. Not many times we can get away without a scratch and get that."

"Sure's hope so. Just don't make it a habit," the sergeant replied. "I've got better news. A lone rider just took out of town. Down there." The sergeant pointed. "Headed south. Without a mask. I'd say it's Amos."

Almost unable to believe his ears, Douglas gently goaded his mount. "We'll probably have enough moon to track him. Leave the wagon. Let's move down the road, just out of town, and regroup."

Five minutes later, Douglas dismounted. In the damp road beneath his feet, three torches illuminated his patrol, which was grouped around a set of horse tracks.

On a knee and holding one of the torches, Huff slid his hand over one of the hoofprints. He looked up at Douglas. "Hind, rear shoe has a big groove in it that will be easy to follow, even at night." Huff felt the dirt road, picking up a handful of the moist soil. "Especially on this wet ground."

Douglas turned to his men, then Hannah, her white face appearing like a lantern among the dark skin and shadows. He wanted to go after Amos, but not with Hannah. He looked back at his men. "Basil, I want you to take Hannah back to Natchitoches tonight. Stay with her until we get back."

The words caused some slight unrest among his men. Apparently, though the troopers feared, maybe even despised Basil, they felt more comfortable with him around. Douglas himself didn't fancy the thought of going after Amos without Basil, but he had no choice. He trusted only the gunfighter with Hannah, certainly at night and riding the back-country.

Douglas grabbed Hannah's hand. He led her a few feet away into the privacy of a shadow. He put the palm of his hand on her cheek, feeling her soft skin. "Are you all right? Did they hurt you? . . . I love you."

"I'm fine," Hannah said in a low voice. "Take me with you. You may need Basil. I'm not afraid of these men."

Hannah's trembling voice, her bloodshot eyes, told Douglas she lacked the energy required for the pursuit. He didn't want her to go anywhere but the safety of town, and he suspected her vigor didn't match the zeal in her voice.

"No." In the dark nothingness, Douglas found her lush lips and kissed her. The tender kiss seemed a world away from the daunting, bloodthirsty setting.

"Go get Amos," Hannah said in a resolute tone. "Have him in jail in Natchitoches in a few days for everybody to gawk at. There's nothing you could do for me and these people that's more important than that." With that, she let go of Douglas and ambled to her horse.

Douglas looked down the road, slicing into a valley as it slivered its way through the tall trees and eerie night, leading into the unknown. What lay down this trail? Was he up to the task? Hannah climbed on her horse. They both had hazardous trips ahead. Would he ever see her again?

34

The sun rose over the eastern horizon, just enough of its round, burning glow poking up over the distant hills for its shape to be discernible. The army patrol had bivouacked atop a small ridge, in an open, twenty-acre field. The tired soldiers had gotten a few hours in their bedrolls, and their horses had grazed on a thick stand of grass behind the camp.

Before Basil had departed with Hannah, the gun hand had informed him that old man Dallon had been the third man the posse had lynched.

With the aid of the torches, the army patrol had picked up the trail of the lone rider, only requiring the troopers to stop every mile or so to make sure the tracks remained on the road. They had stayed far enough back to give the renegade no hint of their chase. The night ride had been strange, almost weird, the dark sky overhead blotted with an enormous, hours-long meteor shower, the largest

Douglas had ever seen, a magnificent display of captivating light.

Whoever rode the horse had been in one hell of a hurry. The patrol had followed the tracks about fifteen miles south of Atkins before they turned off on a small side trail leading to a deserted farmhouse. The army troopers had arrived there about two in the morning, and Douglas ordered his men to stop and get some much-needed rest, out of sight, taking turns guarding the house. Huff had wanted to dynamite the house upon their arrival, but Douglas had refused. He wanted Amos alive.

Basil had suggested that Amos was probably aiming for a safe house. After a little rest there, he was then on to Texas, probably with an armed escort. He would likely cross the Red River via a little-used ferry at Colfax, thirty miles south of Atkins. By Douglas's deduction, the outlaw had three or four more hours in the saddle to get there.

Douglas looked at the little abandoned farm. The well-constructed and comfortable house had two nice barns hidden in a thick stand of pines set back from a small creek bottom near the road. How many men did it currently house? He didn't like the picture. The dense platform of trees made visibility poor. Now, early in the morning, he and four of his men surrounded the house, facing all four sides, a hundred paces from the grounds. From where he sat horseback, he saw none of his men. He had sent Huff and two more soldiers down the road about a mile toward Colfax in case Amos managed to slip out unseen.

Despite his doubts, Douglas almost didn't believe his good fortune. He had Amos surrounded. He only had to keep him from escaping. The bandits had killed Sidney, but he still had the written testimony, certified, from upstanding members of the society, both Republican and Democratic. The last few weeks had been expensive. Four of his soldiers had been killed, also the judge and Cyrus Carter. But in exchange, a pair of Dallons and two Garretts had been killed. He had banished two more of their gang out of the state, and disposed of the sheriff and his deputy. If he could just get Amos, try him, then he would accomplish much more than he had ever realistically expected. It might actually do wonders for the peace, prosperity, and political stability of the entire region.

The clansmen who hanged Sheriff Thaxton and his underlings had no interest in seeing Amos go to trial. They probably would kill to thwart it. Douglas's patrol horses were almost used up, and the bushwhackers always had better mounts than the army. The little farm likely kept fresh horses for Amos and whoever might accompany him. Douglas would have to get Amos before he crossed the river and that would probably be right here, if he ever wanted to catch him.

A light wind blew cool, a lingering remnant of the storm two days prior. A large flock of beautiful, colorful ducks swooped by overhead, diving for a small lake behind Douglas. The sound of their wings, piercing the air, drifted over the placid morning.

How could such a serene land be so vindictive and homicidal?

A single shot broke the morning calm. He raced toward the sound that came from behind the house and to his right. Sergeant Dixon fell in behind him. Ducking under and around the limbs and trees, he saw one of his troopers, distinctive in his blue uniform, spread out on his back, blood gushing from his chest. Out of the corner of his eye, he also saw four men on horseback charging roughshod toward the little creek bottom near the road. In the morning haze, one of the riders looked like Amos.

"They're headed for that creek!" Douglas yelled. "Down by the road. We can beat them there. Everybody, go!" He spun around, spurred the mare, and raced into the thick patch of timber surrounding the creek. A hundred yards behind him, two of his other soldiers rode in his direction. "Let's get on the other side of it! Maybe we can get them in a crossing fire!" he yelled to Sergeant Dixon.

Douglas and Sergeant Dixon beat the bandits to the creek, and the two soldiers stormed across the little stream, ankle deep and ten feet wide, its water flush with red soil. On the far bank, Douglas dismounted, grabbed his shotgun, and slapped his mare on the rear to send her into the trees. The sergeant did likewise. They took up a position behind a small red-rock outcropping. They squatted, inspecting the creek, which was spotted with a few birch trees and some wild coffee trees.

Fifty yards upstream, four riders emerged from the trees into the tight opening between the stream's banks. Douglas and Sergeant Dixon fired a few rounds that flushed the riders into the trees, unmolested. On the other side of the creek, on a bluff, two other soldiers arrived. The little stream had high banks, about four stories, but the incline was gradual enough to be traversed on a horse.

"Get off of those horses and get downstream!" Douglas yelled to his two soldiers on the other side of the creek. "Make sure they don't get to the road and don't shoot Amos." He shoved two more shells into his shotgun.

The little slice of earth awoke with gunfire pinging and zinging off everything. Douglas squatted and took stock. The outlaws were trapped in a side draw where it petered out in a ravine, one from which they couldn't escape without coming under unhindered fire, at least on horseback. But the desperadoes held the high ground, firing down on him and Sergeant Dixon.

"They's going to get us," Sergeant Dixon said, as the hostile fire continued to rain down from above. "If nothing else, a lucky shot will find us."

Douglas looked up the hill. Nothing to shoot at. He emptied both his barrels. He tried to forget the situation, the consequences, just treat this as a routine action. He looked across the creek trying to locate his other soldiers, out of sight, but firing. One of the soldiers screamed. The friendly strafing stopped. The bullets from above still pelted everything.

"This is hopeless," Sergeant Dixon said, scanning the area quickly, the whites of his eyes big. "I can't gets a good bead on them from here. I'm going to work my way around. Gets up there where I can see them."

"You'll never make it."

Sergeant Dixon climbed out from behind the rocks, the lead still flying. He splashed into the creek, the brown water gushing around his feet. The sergeant moved upstream. Bullets stormed into the water as the bandits zeroed in on him.

A deep voice sounded from above. "There goes the sum' bitch. Shoot that nigger."

"Get over on the bank!" Douglas yelled.

Sergeant Dixon took a knee, raised his rifle, and fired two quick shots up the hill. Then a bullet splattered into the sergeant's groin, crumpling him over forward. The sergeant regained his composure, lifting his rifle. His eyes brazen, his movements calm and steadfast, the sergeant searched the hill as he carefully returned fire.

"Get some cover!" Douglas screamed, stretching his arms out toward Sergeant Dixon, just twenty paces away. Douglas leaned over into the creek, attempting to help the sergeant—foolhardy and certain death. Helpless, he watched another bullet slam into Sergeant Dixon's neck. His head fell sideways to his shoulders, limp, as his body made its descent to the rocky streambed.

The firing slowly faded. The trickling of the water whispered in the background. The stream now dribbled by with spots of Sergeant Dixon's blood dispersed within.

"God damn, I got his ass," another voice said from above.

Panicky, Douglas looked around. He heard nothing from across the stream where his two other men had been ensconced. He didn't want to go like this.

Twigs snapped. Footsteps thudded above. Two men, almost faceless figures with big wicked grins, emerged twenty feet above him. The sun rising behind the outlaws burned Douglas's eyes. Both outlaws raised their pistols and pointed them at Douglas. Holding his shotgun at his waist, Douglas froze. Everything slowed down. He paused just a second, intending to jerk the shotgun up and send a wall of buckshot at the vigilantes as he braced for the impact of the oncoming barrage.

A loud shot pierced the air. Douglas lifted his shotgun and fired. Both men tumbled over. More gunfire rang out from above. Douglas fell back into the rocks. He looked down at his chest, body. Shocked, he saw no blood, no bullet holes. He felt no twinge of pain as he heard the thud of dashing horses fading away.

Almost not believing he was alive, Douglas reclaimed some spirit, quickly reloaded, climbed out from behind the rocks, and struggled up the hill. From the tiny escarpment where he had stared at death, the two bandits, neither of them Amos Dallon, lay sprawled on the ground, still squirming and grimacing. Douglas finished each off with a head shot.

More groans came from behind him. He wheeled around, his shotgun at the ready. Huff lay stretched out on his back, blood profusely flowing from his gut. Douglas rushed forward and knelt to inspect the wound.

"I gots 'em," Huff grunted. He tried to laugh. "Heard all that shoot'n, thought the daring captain of the Republic had killed them all."

"Hush," Douglas snapped, quickly inspecting the wound, the blood pulsing freely from the gash as Huff's heartbeat slowed.

Douglas removed his shirt, balled it up, and pressed it against the large wound.

"It's no good," Huff growled, spitting up blood. "I can't feel anything down there. My legs won't work. I want some water. Gives me some water, Captain. I guess you won't gets to court-martial me now."

Douglas removed his canteen and poured water into Huff's mouth, sprinkling some on the private's face. He wiped up a fingertip full of dark blood off Huff's tongue, knowing it indicated a quick death.

Huff's breathing slowed more, and he shut his eyes.

"Huff," Douglas whispered.

Huff opened his eyes. "Captain, let me tell ya. It was worth it. I'll see you on the other side, the better side." The private's eyes got glassy and fell shut.

Douglas put a hand on Huff's chest as its movement slowed further. Like all men, rich or poor, regardless of social status or background, Huff was dying alone.

"Yes . . . to the better side," Douglas mumbled. What had this man seen in his life, far more than even he, hardened by a lifetime of war and death, could even fathom. Surely, this man had spent a life of constant toil with little or no relaxation. Huff finally looked at peace, probably happy to be escaping this world of seething anger. Douglas had always wondered about Huff's past. He didn't even know where this man came from or where he'd been born. Did Huff even know this, or anything about his parents? Douglas would never know now.

35

Four candles flickered in the little room. The afternoon sun poured in through the window. Together, the two sources of light lit the gloomy space.

Private Mercer, wrapped in blankets, lay on a cot, his mangled leg now covered with blood, some dark and dried, some fresh red and recent.

The doctor examined the bullet hole, a few inches above the knee, swabbing it a few times with a piece of cloth. He picked up a half-empty bottle of whiskey on the nightstand and handed it to the private. "Finish this, all of it."

The army patrol had gotten to Colfax an hour and a half earlier. The outlaws' trail had been easy to follow here. By Douglas's judgment they had arrived almost two hours before the army patrol, and the ferry captain had confirmed that two men on horseback had crossed the river mid-morning.

Douglas's pursuit had not been speedy. Their tired mounts wouldn't have any part of it. Before he departed the site of the skirmish, he had policed up his three dead men: Huff, Sergeant Dixon, and the private shot behind the bandits' house. He lashed them over their horses and brought them here. A fourth soldier, Private Mercer, had been shot in the leg. He had been one of the two across the creek during the final, deadly engagement. His partner had dragged him to safety and treated his wound, which was probably why he was still alive and would most likely survive.

In the back room of the general store that also served as a hotel and café, the surgeon now inspected the private's wound. Douglas turned to Private Combs, standing beside him. Neither said anything, both fearing the worst: the leg would be removed.

Private Mercer nursed the bottle, helpless in these brief events that were sure to impact the rest of his life. Douglas had seen this many times during the war. His nightmares of the glum field hospitals, the lasting, scarring work that transpired under the rank tarps had been worse than the battles themselves. These victims suffered long after those slain in their quest of glory. This sight would surely reinitiate his horrid dreams.

"Don'ts let him take my leg," the private cried, his eyes glassy, tears running down his cheeks. "I gots no one to take care of me."

"Drink up," the doctor said, opening his little bag. "I'm just going to trim the trousers, clip a little skin. That's it, but you may feel a little twinge."

The doctor raised a pair of scissors and trimmed

the trousers. He severed the man's meat in a familiar routine—the preparation for amputation. The doctor cut free all the skin around the leg, exposing the bone, but left a long flap of flesh attached to the upper thigh to cover the stub.

Only this morning Douglas had felt numb, dead, staring at the gun barrels, but he now felt totally alive, everything clear, exaggerated, completely real. There couldn't be a greater, more pitiless transformation in all the world. The next few minutes would change this man from a strong, vibrant soldier, someone the government depended on, into a weak, feeble soul depending on the government just to survive.

The doctor turned to Private Mercer. "I'm going to give you more, something to kill the pain." He lifted a metal apparatus from his bag.

The private grunted and threw his head back, resisting.

The doctor turned to Douglas. "Give me a hand."

Douglas grabbed the private's head, holding it still as the doctor placed two metal tubes into the patient's nose and squeezed a little rubber bulb that injected the chloroform.

The soldier drifted away. He was still conscious, but clearly not comprehending much.

The doctor pulled his bone saw out of his bag. "I need you both to hold him still, very still."

Douglas reached into the doctor's bag and pulled out a second bottle of whiskey. He turned it up, finishing a third of it. After two more large gulps, he handed the bottle to Private Combs, who emptied it into his mouth. Douglas then placed all his weight on the patient's chest. He closed his eyes and hugged the upper body, securing Private Mercer's arms as he waited for the screams and firm quivers. It came in only a second. Douglas squeezed his eyes hard. The seconds passed slowly, the only sound the surgeon's long breaths and some jingling from the doctor's bag.

"Okay," the doctor said. "That went well. He's very strong. Just a few seconds more, let me close it up."

Douglas opened his eyes, turning his head to the wall. He buried his nose into his arm trying to escape the vulgar smell.

Finally, the doctor stood. "Wound's very clean. He should make it. I don't want him moved for at least a week. He can then go to Natchitoches, but by steamer only."

Douglas stumbled outside. Fresh air. Nearly catatonic, he emptied his canteen into his mouth and spent a few seconds collecting himself in front of the hotel. What was left of his patrol, two of his three remaining men, dressed in their dirty uniforms, sat horseback on the riverbank, looking out across the river from under their forage hats. Beside them, the three dead soldiers remained lashed over their saddles.

"Corporal Foster . . ." Douglas said in a tired voice, looking at a soldier he had grown fond of in recent weeks due to his lively makeup. "You and Private Jenson come with me. Let's ride down to this livery. See if we can buy some fresh horses."

Douglas led his mare a few hundred feet down the riverbank to a stable. Sitting on the steps of a wooden barn, he found a stout, healthy freedman. "You Thompson?"

The man nodded as he leisurely chewed on a piece of straw.

"We need three horses, your best three. Going after Amos Dallon."

The man stood and ambled over to the adjacent stable. "Ain'ts got but two horses. And one of them's not for sale. I ride him home every day."

Douglas reached into his saddlebag and grabbed a little leather pouch. He poured the gold coins in his hand, counted them, and then put the money back in the pouch before tossing the bag to the man. "Five hundred dollars. Almost twice the going price. We'll take both. And I'll need you to lead us to Fort Jessup. I'm sure that's where Amos will camp. Going to get him tonight."

Thompson looked up at Douglas, then turned to the two soldiers still on horseback. "You're a fool to cross that river. General Banks took twelve thousand men over there and came back with barely eight. There's not a stick of law and order over there, Federal or local. I ain't going under any circumstances. You just as well shoots me now. And I told you, I've got one horse for sale, one hundred and fifty dollars."

Douglas stiffened his stance. His hoarse voice got loud. "I'm not asking, I'm *telling* you. I'm requisitioning the horses. Me and Corporal Foster are going to Fort Jessup. You're going to lead us on foot until we get close enough to find our way. Then you can come back."

Thompson started to say something, but paused, turning again to look at Douglas's two subordinates.

Irritation filling him, Douglas grabbed his pommel and climbed onto his horse. He yelled at his men, his loud voice filled with fury, "I'm going to check on Privates Combs and Mercer. Be back in ten. When I get back here, have two of our saddles put on these two horses." He turned back to Thompson. "And you be ready to go, or we'll see if you'd really rather be shot."

Douglas spurred his horse and trotted off back down the riverbank. About halfway to the store, he heard a horse behind him. He turned to see Corporal Foster riding up.

"Captain Owens," Corporal Foster said softly, pulling up.

Douglas locked a firm gaze on the corporal.

Corporal Foster retained a silent stare.

"What is it?" Douglas finally snapped. "Speak freely."

"Wells, I knows you want this Amos real bad. We wants him too, but you sure you wants to go after him with just me and you? Maybe we should wait till we rested and ready. And if you don't minds me saying, you think it's right to order that man to go with us? We's all had a long two days. Maybe none of us thinking right now. You's got a new bride you going to be marrying real soon. You needs to be thinking about that."

Douglas looked up the riverbank to the three dead soldiers still tied over their horses. The Red

River rushed along, its power almost making him feel miniscule and frail. The recent storm had washed all sorts of limbs and debris into the murky waters, accentuating the river's strength and volume. Douglas scanned the rich alluvial soil to the distant hills, the vast wilderness between the mighty Red and the Sabine Rivers. Texas lay just beyond this wild and untamed area almost devoid of civilization and Federal control.

He turned to look at the little settlement of Colfax, a rare Republican stronghold in the area, its six buildings fronting the river. Nearby, a few hogs snorted in a pigsty. The only other life in sight was the ferry driver, currently transporting a woman and a child across the river to the far bank. He was hungry. His men appeared small and meek compared to the land. How skinny and spent the army horses looked.

Tired, his vision almost blurry, he looked back at Corporal Foster. He'd never had one of his soldiers question his orders. Rage washed over him, but Corporal Forster's calm, kind, and competent gaze carried a sobering reality. He wanted to get Amos, more than anything. This was his only chance. He blew out a mouthful of air, shaking as he realized it was not to be, not in his current state.

"I guess you're right," Douglas finally muttered, pausing and thinking. "We'll wait for the steamer. The man at the store says around eight. We can then bury those three in Natchitoches. Amos is more than three hours ahead of us. Probably be a small army of outlaws camped at that old fort that will be waiting on us."

Douglas reached into his coat and pulled out a letter he had removed from one of the men Huff had killed that morning. The letter was addressed to an Ann Thompson in Tyler, Texas. Hoping its contents might give him a hint to the future location of Amos, he opened the letter and read:

My Darling Annie—

I hope this letter finds you well. I received the new shirt you sewed for me. It fits well and I wear it often. There's still little work to be done here. All the people are sad and many still hungry. I check on your father's place often, but dare say it has fallen into disrepair. Everything is shameful here. I long to see you, and knows you is homesick, but at this time I can not suggest your return. The carpetbaggers seem only intent on self-advancement and not the plight of the people. Every day, it becomes clearer that the Northern Government's goal is punishment and wants us to be second-class citizens with no say in any important matters. We are having some luck running them out of the country, though I fear the process will be lengthy and sometimes calls for drastic measures, but we know the Almighty leads our way and we will not let setbacks alter our progress. At present, the Federal soldiers are excessively oppressive, gunning down many innocents, but this will pass. The fight against the Northern forces sometimes troubles my mind for they are God's creatures too, but it is our responsibility. Please write me soon. I hope to come visit you at Christmas, and look forward to the day when you can return to the land and people I know you hold dear.

Your Darling, Joseph

Douglas folded up the letter and put it in his pocket. He then sniffed the rusty, spongy water. The letter reminded him that despite this setback, his work here wasn't done; there would be tough days ahead and many battles still to fight. He looked back around at his men, growing fewer by the day. "Let's ride over to that little grove of trees, let our horses graze and water, spread our bedrolls and get some rest so we'll be fresh in case we run into any trouble."

36

From Front Street, Douglas looked out at the distant hills, spotted with patches of deep green against the gray and auburn of the hardwoods, now without leaves. Now, three days before Christmas, the mild, brief winter was setting in. Overhead, a few cloud fingers swabbed against the edges of the platinum sky, otherwise clear over the land. Though it was late in the day, the temperature still hovered in the upper fifties.

The citizens of Natchitoches moved around the dozens of Christmas trees, all decorated with ornaments, standing along the brick avenue and abutting the Cane River. Heaps of fallen leaves lay scattered along the street, giving the town the hue of fall. Nine weeks had passed since the incident in Atkins. The local papers had touched up the story, spinning it as corrupt officials and ruffians apprehended and dealt with by honest citizens, the Federal government failing in its duties to handle such matters properly. None of the local stories made mention of

Hannah in any of the events. The lone liberal daily in New Orleans had run a few back-page stories, more in line with Douglas's version of the events.

The Democrats had carried the local election, and since, the hills and backcountry appeared peaceful, at least on the surface. Nary a traveler had come up missing or even reported anything amiss in the last two months. Rumors still spread about the work of the clans, though sparingly, practicing their trade that never got reported like wild animals on the prowl at night.

The nefarious clans had suffered only minor setbacks, both directly and in the perception of the people. Despite all his efforts, and much to his consternation, there had been no trial to be covered by the state and national press where the locals got the firsthand details of the night riders' deeds, disgracing the Knights and assuring everyone that the government and its laws ruled the land.

Where had he gone wrong? He had Amos Dallon in his grasp. Instead of the procedures advocated by the legal system, he had let him go because of Hannah, and gotten drawn into bloody gun battles. But what could he have done? Had this been selfish, his personal wants overriding bigger concerns?

In the weeks since, Douglas had personally written several of his military friends serving in Texas, urging them to be on the lookout for, and if possible, pursue Francis Garrett and the Dallons. He still held out hope, but a general sense of failure filled his daily thoughts. The threat of mob violence still reigned over this land, as much or maybe even more than before his arrival. The locals still spent their unquenching energy and skill opposing the Northern government instead of channeling it to remaking the desecrated land into something fruitful again. Surely, more violence lay ahead.

The rugged individuals here hated the heavy hand of any government, and with that hatred came an undercurrent of rebellion, though he felt many yearned for the end of occupation and a return to normalcy. Good pervaded over bad in most. Somehow, he still held a rock-solid belief in the worthiness and character of these people.

Douglas had tried to put all the prior events behind him, but he still woke up several nights a week, his skin clammy as he heard the pitiful screams of Huff's dying moans echoing through the pine forest or envisioned Sergeant Dixon's brave, bloody body falling in the creek. Despite this, he had lately felt a sort of reawakening, as if he had returned from the dead. The local citizens had started to treat him with a little more respect, many possibly but silently appreciative of his work.

Did more gun battles loom ahead? He still walked uneasily, constantly fearful for his life. He'd ridded the area of most of his overt enemies and the worst outlaws, but the clans certainly wanted him gone. He had even written his letter of resignation, but had yet to submit it. Was it safe to stay here without the protection of his uniform? He thought he'd even overheard rumors of his demise. He'd been so traumatized by recent events that he couldn't decide if all this was real or simply his overreaction.

Would he have the resources and wherewithal to bring the outlaws to justice the next time they reared their ugly heads? Though his work wasn't done, he was getting close to putting all of this behind him and moving on to another stage in life.

He strode into the City Hotel and made his way to a first-floor suite. He checked his watch, knocked on the door, and then entered.

Colonel James sat at a desk reading over some papers. He looked over his wire-rimmed glasses at Douglas. "Have a seat," the colonel said before Douglas had a chance to pass a salute. "Talked to the mayor and senator today—a few of the local carpetbaggers also. Seems it's as peaceful as a Vermont morning around here. You've done yourself credit."

"Thank you, sir."

The colonel put his papers down and sat up straight. As usual, he conversed in a very formal tone. Douglas couldn't remember a time, on duty or after hours, regardless of the setting, that he and this man had ever carried on a casual conversation. The colonel never deviated from his official mood or closed the distance between them. "I know this wasn't easy. You had to get your hands fouled. But nothing got stirred up. Hardly a word came across my desk about this area. That's the way the army is supposed to work, and the way we like it to work. We do the dirty work so the political machine moves along smoothly. The people are happy. That's what the people want us to do . . . make the country into the image they have of it. They just don't want to see us do it, or read about it. That's why they pay us. I'm going to write up a letter of commendation for you."

"Thank you, sir."

"I paid Basil the rest of his gold this morning. He said that's all he was waiting on. Think he took a boat to Shreveport this afternoon. Said he had some work in Arkansas. . . . I hear you're getting married. When's the big day?"

"One week from today." Douglas smiled. "We're going to spend our honeymoon in New Orleans. That's why I put in for that leave."

"Oh, yes." The colonel shuffled through some papers. "I approved that. Be sure and bring your new wife by my office and introduce her to me while you're in New Orleans. I depart on the first steamer out tomorrow. I'm surprised the locals let you get away with that."

"There's a few around here who aren't very happy about it." Douglas paused, almost stuttering. "And what about the medals and letters of commendation I put in for Sergeant Dixon and Private Huff?"

"Oh, those," the colonel said. "I've looked over them, but haven't gotten around to doing anything yet. I will in due time."

Douglas continued to stare at the colonel, leery of his words. He doubted anything would come of it. The army all but ignored any real combat in the South—that would acknowledge the real problems— and sweeping citations for dead Negro soldiers under the rug would be an easy task.

The colonel produced a rare smile. "That'll be

all, Captain," he said, picking his papers back up and returning his gaze to his desk.

Douglas stood and passed a few seconds without speaking. The colonel's words seemed to have a terminal taste. Even if things had manifested into something resembling his commander's opinion, they had done so through the blood and toil of his men. The army needed to maintain its commitment to the area to ensure future tranquility. One of the traits of the clans was to retreat, disappear when the federal or state government pried too much, only to reinitiate their activities when the landscape became more favorable. He searched for the right words to convey this.

Douglas finally spoke up. "Sir, will I be getting any additional troops?"

The colonel leaned back in his chair. He removed his glasses. "Captain, I know you didn't get everything you needed here. I sympathize with you. I did all I could. I like to see my men have all they need to succeed, but let me be frank. I know you read the papers. President Grant would like nothing more than to send a couple of divisions here, but's that so unpopular, he fears the Democrats will win Congress if he does. If that happens, the army will be ordered out of the South. We don't make policy. We only represent the will of the people. It's the people in New York and Ohio that won't let us do what we need to do here. So, it's not likely you'll get any additional resources. We're spread pretty thin. Just between us, I'm guessing you'll probably get orders in a few months to cease and desist all activity here. Likely close the garrison and move everybody back to Shreveport or New Orleans. Everybody in the North thinks all these newspaper stories about the violence down here are just exaggerated fiction. Hell, President Grant's under constant fire. These problems and lawlessness are only occurring in Republican-controlled states, and many in Congress and the press think the army is only being used to assure a Republican majority. The army hasn't failed these people. We've acted honorably. The democracy has chosen this course."

Douglas let the words sink in. His forehead got tight, his temples pulsed with frustration. He raised a hand, hoping to make a case against this, searching for the right words. He also wanted to mention his future resignation. Word of it had leaked around to a few people, and he didn't want his superiors to hear about it secondhand.

"Go along, Captain," the colonel finally said in soft, reassuring words. "I've work to do."

Douglas turned and walked outside. The day now waned with twilight, the bricks growing dark and the abundant gas lanterns dotting the town. He walked down the street a few blocks to a bar owned by a friend and local unionists. Two of the colonel's aides, a captain and a lieutenant, had accompanied him on his trip to Natchitoches. Both were Douglas's good friends, and the three had agreed to congregate here after his meeting.

He lamented the fact that he hadn't seen Basil off. The setting sun and long shadows reminded him how uncomfortable he felt without the gunfighter at his side. It also reminded him how much he feared the Southern nights. Douglas sucked in a deep breath and thought about his meeting. The lack of support might change his future plans. He put the stressful thoughts aside. Tonight he need not worry with these. He wanted to do some catching up and recounting old adventures. Maybe the colonel was right. Maybe the worst was behind him.

Four hours later, Douglas walked outside the little bar. The dark, damp air had cooled, falling into the forties. He reached into his pocket and retrieved a few gold coins. His head spinning from all the drink, he handed the money to the establishment's owner, who locked the door as the two stepped onto the street.

"Here you go, Joe. Excellent dinner and wine," Douglas said, grabbing his saddle pommel and climbing onto his horse.

The old barkeep, feeble, gray-headed, good-natured, and in his late fifties, turned his steely eyes on Douglas as he put the money in his pocket. "You get back to your office, straightaway. No need to ride out to the Butler place."

"Not to worry." Douglas urged his mare around, facing her down the street.

Joe reached out and grabbed Douglas's bridle, locking his gaze on him, and taking up a serious tone. "You're a good man. Now get on home, and stay on the main road."

Douglas tipped his hat and gently spurred his

mount as he headed down the street at a slow trot toward the army post. Just a few blocks from the bar on the far end of town, he turned the mare down a side street, really just an alley, through a complex of derelict cotton warehouses that cut the distance back to the garrison in half.

As he ambled along, fifty yards down the street, he saw some movement ahead. Four horses trotted into the street. In the moonlight, he saw the long sheets and disguises draped over the men, like something you'd see at the gates of hell. Briefly, he remembered the bar owner's admonition. Had that been a warning? He pulled back on his reins and whirled around, only to see a similar scene behind him. He looked about. Tall brick walls encased the entire block. No escape.

His horse blew, sensing danger. His vision got focused and honed as he saw the riders behind him turn and slowly walk toward him, now only thirty paces away. Was this it? "Oh my God," he mumbled, a fear shooting down his spine. He didn't want to meet his maker, not here, not like this. It couldn't be.

Douglas wheeled back around. Death marched closer. Pulling back on his reins, he brought his horse to a stop. He scanned the situation again, the reality, the finality of it all settling in. He, even with the backing of the almighty army and all its resources, could not win this confrontation.

Hannah. He saw a mix of her bright smile and grief. He looked to the alley again. Just ahead, some bricks had fallen off the warehouse wall to his left, leaving a small opening. He raised his pistol, fired once at the clansmen, leaned forward on his mare, and spurred her forward.

The night awoke with shots and screams. Something shoved Douglas to the side, almost knocking him off his horse. He grabbed his pommel as the pain shot down his shoulder. His horse lunged through the opening, maybe four feet wide, and Douglas's face scraped against the rough brick.

The voices and shots faded in the darkness. Now dizzy, Douglas lowered himself over the neck of his mount, dropped his reins, and pushed his spurs forcefully into her ribs.

37

Douglas looked out the window of his second-story apartment on St. Peter Street. Surrounding Jackson Square and its vast parade grounds sat some of the city's grandest buildings. The day was clear and bright and the towering Saint Louis Cathedral commanded over the tall trees, well-groomed shrubs, and mighty Mississippi River churning and bubbling in the background. On Decatur Street, a large crowd had started to collect around one of the city's first buildings, the Cabildo.

"Grandpa, will you take me to the parade this afternoon?"

"Sure, Johnny, if you want to go," Douglas replied as his nine-year-old grandson climbed up on a chair to look down at the festivities. Down below, a huge grandstand had been set up to accommodate the speakers—the governor and one of the US senators, among others. Colorful streamers, and dozens of American and Confederate flags stood out sharply against the verdant grounds as four Negro men worked large brooms over the square's gray brick pavers.

Johnny turned to his grandfather. "What is everybody celebrating and what's so important about the Cabildo?"

"The State of Louisiana is turning it into a museum. It's one of the most famous buildings in the state. Several battles took place there during the war." Douglas looked at the impressive building. Its three stories of brick and Spanish arches had now stood for more than one hundred years. After the war, the building had been the epicenter of the local Republican government. On several occasions, pitched battles with the Southern loyalists had taken place there and it had also hosted the famous *Plessy v. Ferguson* trial. The building now served as a symbol of Southern pride and autonomy.

"Who are those men in uniforms?"

"Those are Confederate veterans, celebrating their past battles." Douglas squinted. In the crowd, he also spotted a couple of dozen Union uniforms. He turned and looked to the north. In the last forty years, New Orleans had emerged as a modern city, the largest in the South and one of the premier cities of the nation, a bountiful economic engine that the entire country prided itself in. Where once the roads had been muddy alleyways leading to ramshackle wood shacks, shiny bricks sat under the modern streetcars that weaved through the grand new buildings, Southern mansions, and numerous parks populated with tall oaks. In the Northern psyche, the city represented the Lost Cause of the Confederacy and its proud and brave people. In the country's collective opinion, the latter had been, over the years, transformed into virtuous victims only overpowered by numbers.

Around the square, hundreds of pedestrians walked the streets. The city had come to symbolize the Old South, and travel writers in the North raved about its charms, a Southern paradise filled with wonderful food and handsome, polite gentlemen. Douglas often witnessed the droves of tourists wandering the wide tree-lined boulevards and admiring the abundant memorials dedicated to the South's heroes. Catering to these Northern invaders had become a major financial windfall for the city and its merchants.

"Grandpa, weren't you in the war? How come you don't have on your old uniform?"

"Well, Johnny, I fought for the other side, the Union. I'm from Ohio originally. I was in north Louisiana. That's where I met your grandmother. Her family had a big plantation up there, but some years after the war, they and a lot of other people lost their farms."

"How'd they lose them?"

"The entire area had been destroyed by the war. The economy was very bad, and they had several years of really bad drought. The locals said the land was cursed by God."

"Cursed by God, that sounds really bad." Johnny

looked at Douglas with big, curious eyes. "Those days must be over now."

"Yes, they're over. I'll tell you about it sometime. Now run along. We'll go to the parade this afternoon." Douglas patted Johnny on the shoulder and escorted him to the door. He turned to another young man in the room and strolled over to take a seat at his desk.

"Thanks for allowing me this interview," the young man said, pulling out a pencil and writing pad.

Douglas motioned for the man, probably in his late twenties, to have a seat. "I hear there's a dozen reporters here from Northern newspapers to cover the celebration. Who'd you say you were with?"

"*The Chicago American.*" The reporter took a seat. "The weather here is great in December. I tell you, I went to the ball hosted by the United Daughters of the Confederacy last night. I don't know if I've ever met ladies of such refinement and beauty. It was down there by that wonderful statue of General Lee. . . . I mostly wanted your perspective. It must be strange, you really fought in two wars, one that everybody still revels in its honor, and the other, well, generally now is considered a mistake."

Douglas leaned back in his chair. "I know it's become popular lore that the Federal government's goals in the Reconstruction years were folly, but I think I fought on the right side in both wars, if you want to call the ten years after the war a war."

"Well, it is true that no state suffered more from carpetbagger misrule than Louisiana. Most people think it was a terrible mistake for the irresponsible Congress to force illiterate Negro rule on the educated and intelligent."

"Mistake, huh?" Douglas squinted at him.

"Well, I do agree that some of the methods I've read about were uncalled for, even regrettable, if not downright terrible, but they were necessary and the results were inevitable."

Douglas produced a cynical laugh. "If I had to comment on any of the Southern peoples' methods, I'd say they were *effective.*"

"What about your time during the war. Didn't you fight in north Louisiana?"

"Yes, both during the war and after. I had to leave in late sixty-nine. I was forced out. You see, those were very dangerous times in that area, especially for Northerners. It became too dangerous for me to stay. Many attempts were made on my life. They almost got me once, shot me in the shoulder. I barely escaped, almost bled to death. Then I decided to leave. I'm not sure if it was my position in the army, or the fact that after I married my wife, I planned to stay and run Hannah's plantation. You see, my wife, before she passed away, was Southern landed gentry. . . . Maybe both." Douglas skipped a breath, and his hands got jittery.

"And you decided to stay in the South. I must say, your grandson looks like he's as Southern as General Longstreet's grandson. My readers love to hear about the old war heroes, North and South, but especially the Southern ones. These modern-day novels of the Old South are really big sellers. Do you ever see any of your old army pals or enemies? Do you ever attend any of the reunions? The sons of both sides come to these, and there never seems to be any animosity. We're one nation, completely rejoined again."

"No, I don't go to any reunions. I'm just an old man now, waiting out my days, but I still think about the wild old days all the time. It was really tough fighting, especially after the war, the worst I was ever a part of. The ex-Rebs had no rules. They killed without mercy. They wanted no quarter, and they gave no quarter. When I reflect back, I can see now the country wasn't ready for much of the changes the war brought. It wasn't the Southerners who won home rule, it was the Northerners who gave it to them. It was President Grant himself who said: 'What good does it do to save Mississippi if it means the Republicans lose Ohio?' Initially, I didn't believe in the radical Congress's plans either, but with time I began to see their intent, and what it would have meant for the freedmen if the Federal government would have pursued their plans more vigorously. It's hard to fight and win without the support of the people, but I wanted to catch those outlaws. Not getting some of the militia leaders was what most disappointed me because my men fought hard and died. The army had a lot of good men in that fight. Many of the men I served with went on to be famous soldiers. Many went out west and fought the Indians, even the Negro soldiers. Some even died with Custer at the Little Big Horn. As for my enemies, I still keep track of some of them." Douglas turned to a wall beside his desk where a dozen or so newspaper clippings were pinned up. He pointed to a few obituaries. "A lot of them are dying off. Some of the men I chased for years were buried like heroes, for what *they did for Louisiana*."

The reporter readjusted himself in the chair. "Just one final question. How about you? Have you changed? What are your feelings today about those old days, and everything that's changed in the country?"

"Almost regretfully, I've come to understand the new ways, and new way of thinking about all this. I had to get on with my life, and that's part of it. I can't live in the past. After I moved here, the Republican administration got me a job with the postal service. I kept to myself and put any political leanings aside. When the Democrats took over, I went out west and worked on the railroads for a few years. Later, for my conversion and support, the state Democratic Party arranged for me to be the postmaster here." Douglas paused, thinking for a few seconds. "About a year ago, I took my first trip back to north Louisiana in over forty years. Just wanted to look around, see how things have changed. Even today, I traveled under an alias. Doubt anybody would want to plant me now, but you never know. I walked the old streets of Shreveport and Natchitoches. There are a few people up there that still talk of the old days, but it won't be but a generation or so before no one will have any idea what went on after the war. The memories of those days, those men, the life-and-death struggles that took place, will walk the streets unbeknownst to everybody, like ghosts."

AUTHOR'S NOTE

After a disputed election in 1872, Southern Democrats forcibly took control of the Louisiana governorship and legislature. A Federal judge eventually deemed that they had not won the canvassing, and President Grant ordered the anti-suffrage government be removed from the State House by Federal troops. The army replaced them with a pro-Northern government. The action resulted in an outcry, North and South, for the restoration of states' rights.

Four years later, the presidential race of 1876 was one of the most contested in American history. After the fall election, no candidate for the nation's highest office had an electoral majority. In a back room in the Capitol, Southern Democrats assented to give their support to the Republican candidate, Rutherford Hayes, if Federal troops would be recalled from the South and Congressional Reconstruction ended. On April 24, 1877, and to the cheers of thousands of bystanders, the last Federal troops in the South boarded an outbound steamer in New Orleans.

In just a few years, the Democrats reclaimed complete control of the South. With this, the secret clans all but exterminated the carpetbagger element from Southern society. The newly emancipated freedmen were left to fend for themselves. Under such conditions and constant intimidation, they rarely voted and remained mired in an existence little better than before the Civil War.

No one knows the true magnitude of those slain during the years of Reconstruction, mostly ex-slaves, Southern unionists, and Northerners, but these surely number in the thousands in Louisiana. A Congressional investigation documented more than a thousand political murders in Louisiana just in 1868. The Parishes of Red River, Winn, and Grant were the epicenter for much of this violence.

The history books tell us that local citizens, mostly ex-Confederate soldiers, put the leaders of the West and Kimbrell clans in front of a firing squad in Winn Parish in 1870. For years after the Civil War, army officers, most notably Majors A. R. Chaffee and Lewis Merrill, and Captain N. B. McLaughlin, forayed into this area chasing the mysterious night riders and white militia leaders. They killed many in Louisiana and east Texas, almost always employing clan tactics, simply shooting down the criminals in the open and in cold blood. The army's efforts had little impact. In 1874, US Marshal J. B. Stockton wrote to his superior from Red River Parish: "As soon as I go away with the cavalry, they intend to kill all the prominent white and black Republicans in the parish."

Marshall Twitchell, one of the most famous Northern invaders to the area, arrived in Sparta, Louisiana, as a Freedmen's Bureau Agent in 1865. Though apparently honest, well intentioned, and no doubt a brave man, he seemed to epitomize the word carpetbagger. He married the beautiful daughter of one of the region's first families and bought a plantation. He soon moved much of his family from Vermont to Coushatta in Red River Parish, got himself elected to the state senate, and many of his kin elected to prominent local offices, largely with the support of black constituents. This all ended in 1874 when the Knights of the White Camellia gunned down six of Twitchell's family and friends in broad daylight. Two years later, Twitchell himself had both his arms shot off, again at high noon and in town. Shortly after, he departed Louisiana for good, supplanted in the state senate by one of his opponents, an ex-Confederate captain.

New Yorker Delos White, a decorated Union cavalryman in the Red River Campaign, became a Freedmen's Bureau agent in Winn Parish in 1866 after his predecessor in that position had been murdered. He established numerous schools and rode with the army in pursuit of the area's white militia and outlaws. In 1871, while White slept at the home of Judge William Phillips, a group of vigilantes arrived in the middle of the night. The gang of white terrorists shot White dead and burned the judge's house.

Judge Phillips, a Confederate war veteran, Southern unionist, and Freedmen organizer, prospered during Reconstruction, acquiring several large land tracts. He lived with a mixed-raced woman, fathering a child by her during this time. Unheard of for the era, he gave the son his name and all legal rights that accompanied it. Appointed judge in Grant Parish by the carpetbagger governor, he also pursued the parish's desperados relentlessly. One of the most hated men in the area by the people and press, he survived several attempts on his life, but in 1872 resigned as judge and fled, fearful for his life. Penniless and destitute, like many Southern unionists, Phillips eventually sold out to the Democrats and campaigned for their ticket in 1876 for a nominal fee.

Black political leaders also suffered. Hal Frazier, the black election commissioner in Montgomery, was shot dead by a gang one afternoon in front of his sawmill after the 1868 elections. Captain William Ward, an ex-slave and the colored commander of a black regiment of the Louisiana State Militia tasked with supporting Republican leaders in Grant Parish, fought the Knights for years. Elected to the state legislature, he was later expelled from that body at gunpoint and barred from returning to Grant Parish.

Christopher Columbus Nash was an ex-Confederate soldier and one of the more vocal and violent white supremacists in the area. He shot Delos White, and on Easter Sunday, 1873, led a mob of three hundred white militia into Colfax. In the battle that ensued, over a hundred blacks were killed. After Reconstruction, Nash founded the White League, was elected parish president, and appointed deputy sheriff. His family purchased some of the plantations from the now bankrupt or vanquished Republicans in the area. He finally died in 1922 and was buried in Natchitoches in a ceremony befitting a general.

The Louisiana press of this time was extremely partisan. Albert Leonard, the owner and editor of the *Shreveport Times,* the largest newspaper in north Louisiana, was a general in the White Militia. James Cosgrove, the editor of the ultra-right-wing *Natchitoches Vindicator,* was arrested in the Twitchell murders, but never convicted. He was later appointed brigadier general of the Fifth Military District of Louisiana and elected to the state legislature.

Both the Coushatta and Colfax incidents garnered extensive national headlines, but in each case, no one was ever convicted. These are only a sampling of the events and characters from this area during Reconstruction. It would take a book or two to list all the murders and crimes. The battles of Liberty Place and Cabildo, the riot at the Mechanics Institute, and the Shady Grove and Opelousas massacres are a few more well publicized tragedies. Many more, nameless to history, occurred in the decades after the war. In almost all cases, the perpetrators went unpunished and remain largely unknown to this day.

In 1951, at the site of the Colfax Massacre, the State of Louisiana erected a historical marker. It still remains in place today. It reads: *On this site occurred*

*the Colfax Riot in which three white men and 150 Negroes
were slain. This event on April 13, 1873, marked the end
of carpetbag misrule in the South.*

In fact, it was not until the second half of the
twentieth century that the mysterious societies that
promoted or participated in most of the heinous
crimes, terrorizing African Americans and exterminating Northern interests, were disbanded or
brought to justice.